Linda Corbett lives in Surrey with ... and three permanently hungry g... being an author, Linda is a member and former Treasurer of Shine Surrey – a volunteer-led charity that supports individuals and families living with spina bifida and hydrocephalus. For many years she also wrote a regular column for Link, a disability magazine, illustrating the humorous aspects of life with a complex disability and she is a passionate advocate of disability representation in fiction. *What Would Jane Austen Do?* is her second published novel.

twitter.com/lcorbettauthor

facebook.com/lindacorbettauthor

instagram.com/lindacorbettauthor

WHAT WOULD JANE
AUSTEN DO?

LINDA CORBETT

One More Chapter
a division of HarperCollins*Publishers*
1 London Bridge Street
London SE1 9GF

www.harpercollins.co.uk

HarperCollins*Publishers*
Macken House, 39/40 Mayor Street Upper,
Dublin 1, D01 C9W8, Ireland

This paperback edition 2023
First published in Great Britain in ebook format
by HarperCollins*Publishers* 2023

3

A catalogue record of this book is available from the British Library

ISBN: 978-0-00-855458-3

Printed and bound in the UK using 100% Renewable Electricity
by CPI Group (UK) Ltd

This book is produced from independently certified FSC™ paper
to ensure responsible forest management.

For more information visit: www.harpercollins.co.uk/green

For my sister Diana, who always believed I could be a writer.

Chapter One

There is a stubbornness about me that never can bear to be frightened at the will of others. My courage always rises at every attempt to intimidate me.

Elizabeth Bennet, *Pride and Prejudice*

It was a truth universally acknowledged that being on your own on 14th February entitled one to feel miserable, but being dumped by your employer on Valentine's Day demonstrated a staggering level of mean-spiritedness … and came with an additional financial problem.

Maddy stared at the email on her phone for what felt like the millionth time.

We are sorry to advise…

This was clearly a business definition of the word

sorry that wasn't even distantly related to regret or apology. Why did they feel her column was no longer required for the magazine? Did she even have any right to object?

We wish you every success in the future…

So what future were they referring to? The one where she signed on for Jobseeker's Allowance? Or the one where she couldn't afford to rent in even the scruffiest part of London and was forced to go back to living with Mum and Dad? Not to mention letting down her best friend who would have to find another flatmate, otherwise she would also be in the same pecuniary position.

Once word got around, any requests for blog interviews or podcasts like the one she was supposed to be doing this evening, would quickly dry up. No one wanted an ex-agony aunt. A few tears escaped and splashed onto the screen, and she wiped them away angrily.

Maddy wouldn't even have minded quite so much if she'd hated her job, but she enjoyed being the love and relationship correspondent for *UpClose* magazine, and especially loved her weekly column, *Dear Jane*. 'Jane' received plenty of requests every week, and many of the emails and letters actually thanked her for the advice. Now she was effectively jobless with one month's pay in lieu of notice and the barest minimum redundancy payment. A sick, empty feeling lodged in her stomach as she turned back to her dressing table.

Her flatmate's voice was, therefore, a welcome intrusion. 'Can I come in, Madds? I've brought you something.'

'Is it a winning lottery ticket by any chance?'

'Nope, but maybe the next best thing,' Alice said as she pushed the door open and put a glass of chilled white wine next to the eyeshadow compact. 'Here, have a huge swig of this.'

Maddy took an appreciative sip before returning to her makeup, which now needed a bit of repair.

'So, you're still going ahead with the podcast interview thingy?'

Maddy paused with the powder brush in her hand and looked at her flatmate, Alice, in the mirror. 'That's the plan.'

'I just thought that … you know … you might not feel like—'

'—chatting about romance and relationships in fiction when I've been sacked on Valentine's Day?' Maddy finished for her. 'There's definitely an irony there somewhere.'

'Still, at least you get to meet that swoon-worthy crime writer,' replied Alice, hugging herself. 'Can you sit together so you can gaze at his gorgeous bod?'

'Nice try. However, in the first place it's not that sort of interview, I just happen to be the next guest on the panel. Secondly, I agree the shop window is extremely well presented, but from what I've heard the customer service needs a bit of improvement.'

'You'll definitely need to channel your inner Jane Austen this evening then.'

Maddy lifted her chin, squared her shoulders and addressed the mirror in a condescending voice.

'He is tolerable, I suppose, but not handsome enough to tempt me.'

Alice laughed at that, and—despite the misery of the day—Maddy found herself smiling.

Maddy took a hurried swig of her wine and then rummaged in her drawer for her waterproof mascara. 'To be honest, I'm expecting the questions to be variations on the usual themes, including the all-too-predictable question of whether Jane Austen is actually still relatable in the twenty-first century,' she added, widening her eyes as she carefully stroked the mascara brush along her pale lashes. 'Well, I suppose it's paid work at least,' she said with a forced cheeriness.

If she was being completely honest, she also didn't fancy spending the evening sitting on her own in the flat while the rest of the population was off doing romantic things with loved-up partners. Even though Alice didn't have a regular boyfriend, she had been invited to make up a foursome at a local Italian restaurant and probably wouldn't be back until late.

Alice gave her a sympathetic smile and a brief hug. 'It's probably a bit late, but I can phone in sick for you, if you like?'

Maddy patted her hand. Even at school Alice had been a loyal friend, and had once smacked a boy over the head with her geography book after he'd called Maddy a carrot top. Rather than being upset, seven-year-old

Maddy had been more amused that the attempted insult wasn't even remotely original.

'Thanks, Alice. Kind of you to offer but it's fine, and anyway, I need the work now.'

She checked the time as she slipped her watch bracelet over her hand. The interview was being recorded live so she aimed to get to the studio in plenty of time to read through her notes. She was not about to let Ms Austen down through lack of preparation.

'Do I look okay?' Radio interviews always felt strange. She knew listeners could only hear her, not see her, but she didn't want to feel underdressed. Especially not in the company of bestselling author, Cameron Massey. Being a redhead, choosing the right colours was important; she opted for her favourite dark turquoise top, and teamed it with her Jane Austen scarf for luck.

'You look lovely. Now go and charm that gorgeous bloke!' Alice shooed her out the front door.

They had chosen the flat largely on price, plus the proximity of buses and Clapham Common underground station. It hadn't been the cheapest place on the rental market, but with both of them sharing the costs, it was just about affordable, as long as they staggered the bills a bit. Now, as Maddy walked in the direction of the bus stop, she experienced an unpleasant stirring of panic.

It had been a bright sunny day with a light breeze, the sort of day where you could snatch a few minutes in the sunshine without feeling like you might catch hypothermia. However, clear skies meant the temperature plummeted after sunset and Maddy tugged her coat around her as she sat on the bus and pondered her job prospects. Being able to pay the rent came significantly higher up the necessities list than liking what she did, but moving back home was definitely last resort—she had worked hard to be financially independent and she loved living in London. In any case, her relationship with her mother improved with distance. However, in between those two options there must be plenty of possibilities if only she could find them.

Just think of goodbye as hello in a different language; that was one of her mum's favourite expressions. She had a whole armoury of sayings that were—at least in the early years —intended to either encourage Maddy to try something new or to cushion her from disappointment. In later years, there was usually a helping of boyfriend advice in there too, most of it in the large economy size. Mrs Carolyn Shaw had firm ideas on the suitability of the opposite sex, although Maddy had often wondered if things might have been different if she'd had siblings and her mother had been able to spread her maternal advice over a wider audience. Today, as Maddy pushed open the doors to the small studio where the interview was being recorded, she hoped her mum might accidentally be right for once.

A girl in black leggings and a purple floral tunic top who looked like she'd just left school – a definite sign of getting old according to her mother – escorted her through the small reception area into an equally small visitors' waiting area. 'The other guest is already here,' she murmured as they reached the door. 'I'll be back as soon as we're ready for you.'

The walls of the waiting room were painted in a restful pale green colour. Light grey sofa-type seating occupied a large part of one side of the room, with a couple of individual chairs added in vibrant—verging on clashing—colours. In the corner, a spindly spider plant trailed down the side of a tall cupboard in a token nod to office greenery.

A dark-haired man with carefully contrived scruffy stubble and a tan that shouted winter holiday was tapping his phone in an agitated manner and glanced up as she entered the room. She took in the lightly patterned open-necked shirt, tailored navy blazer and smart shiny shoes, and was grateful she hadn't just rocked up in casual gear.

'I'm guessing you might be Madeleine Shaw?'

'My friends call me Maddy,' she replied with a smile and an outstretched hand. 'And you must be Cameron Massey.' After the merest of hesitations, he shook her hand, made an attempt at a polite smile that was so brief it could have been a facial twitch, and then gestured at his phone. 'Sorry, just got to finish this.'

Maddy tried to ignore what she already knew about Cameron Massey and his reputation for snarky interviews; after all, even her heroine, Jane Austen, would give her characters the benefit of the doubt at the start, and Jane had always been her personal go-to adviser on relationships ever since she'd read *Pride and Prejudice* for GCSE English. While her classmates were grumbling about being told to read what they considered to be some ancient creaky old story, Maddy had fallen in love with the older Bennet sisters while wishing she had one, sympathised with Mary, and cringed at their overbearing mother, and no boyfriend—teenage or later—had ever measured up against the fictional Mr Darcy.

Alice was right though about Cameron Massey; he was certainly good-looking, even if his – admittedly sexy – eyes were currently saying, *can you leave me in peace?* rather than, *well, hello there!* She busied herself studying the notes she had made on her phone, which unhelpfully decided that now was a good time to launch into a jaunty ring-tone. Cameron looked up at the disturbance.

'Sorry, it's my dad ringing,' said Maddy as she swiftly cancelled the call and put her phone on silent. 'He usually rings for a chat on Thursdays as that fits better round his busy social life; except for last week when he rang on Sunday, but that was because the cat had gone missing overnight,' she explained, even though she felt pretty sure that Cameron Massey wasn't the slightest bit interested in her family's telecommunications habits nor the where-abouts of her dad's cat.

She gave Cameron a look that was meant to say, *parents, eh?*

'Such a British thing, isn't it?' he observed wryly. 'Apologising for something that's outside of your control.'

Maddy wasn't sure whether he was attempting to be humorous or sarcastic, but was spared the need to reply by the reappearance of the same girl who had shown her in. 'We're ready for you now,' she announced to Cameron in a sing-song voice, then looked over to Maddy. 'I'll come back shortly and then we'll get you set up as well.'

Maddy sat back down again and sent a quick message back to her dad:

Sorry, work thing. Will call later.

While she waited to be summoned, she spent a bit more time looking over her notes. It was less revision and more distraction really; letting her brain go into free-form thoughts invariably led back to the email from her employer. *Former employer*, she silently corrected herself.

A few minutes later the girl returned and Maddy was shown into the studio where the presenter Angie Turner was already talking to Cameron Massey, presumably about one or several of his books. As soon as she was miked up, she gave the producer the thumbs up sign and started paying attention to the discussion in progress.

'...so given that several of your previous books have topped the bestseller lists, and both *The Dangerous Woman* and *The Cornish Key Cutter* were awarded the coveted crime writers' Silver Spanner, you must have been disappointed that your latest book didn't do quite as well. Why do you think that is?'

Although they were on different sides of a glass screen, Maddy saw a distinct look of annoyance flash across Cameron's face.

'Clearly, authors hope every book will sell well, but I suspect you'd be better off directing that question to the book-buying public, who may or may not have purchased it.'

'Point taken. So, what's next for Detective Inspector Jason Friend? Are you able to give us any hints as to what he might face in the next book?'

He did one of those twitchy smiley things. 'Not at the moment. You'll all have to wait a bit longer.'

'O-kay. Sorry folks, looks like the secrets box is staying locked for now. So Cameron, as it's Valentine's Day, perhaps I can ask what your view is of romance in crime novels, and have you ever considered giving DI Jason Friend a love interest?'

'Look, readers of my novels enjoy the challenge of solving a puzzle alongside the detective. They don't need to be distracted by some lightweight romance subplot.'

Maddy couldn't believe her ears and just about managed not to shout across the studio as she mouthed the word 'What?!'

'So you're not a fan of the genre then?'

'Not personally. It's hardly much of a challenge to write a story where you know the ending, is it?'

Without waiting to be introduced, Maddy leaned in to the microphone in front of her. 'I think if anything, writing a romance makes it more of a challenge. And while it guarantees the reader the emotionally satisfying happy ever after, it's the journey the couple go on that makes the book interesting.' She flashed a smile at Cameron. 'I think many books would benefit from including a bit of a romance.'

'An interesting opinion from agony aunt Maddy Shaw.

Cameron, is that something you agree with?' Angie asked. 'Have you ever added a touch of romance to your plots?'

'I don't shy away from sex in my novels, if that's what you mean.'

'But sex doesn't automatically mean there's romance, does it?' Maddy replied.

'And have you actually read any of my books?'

'Yes, I've just finished reading *The Diamond Case*.' Maddy believed in research but tactfully refrained from adding that the story felt very soulless. The brief sexual encounter between the detective constable and the jeweller's wife was more functional than passionate and she had suspected long before the end of the novel that the jeweller's wife had an ulterior motive.

'And?'

'It was interesting,' she replied diplomatically. 'But it didn't give the characters time to develop any meaningful romance.'

'But that's precisely what turns people off. My readers want to see things happen, not just follow two people swanning around the countryside for two hundred pages when you already know they'll get together eventually. It's all the same stuff—it's too predictable.'

'Rubbish! Giving someone the assurance of a happy ending doesn't necessarily make it "predictable".' She made speech marks with her fingers. 'And Cameron may be aware'—she flashed him an apologetic smile—'that some people who reviewed *The Diamond Case* used precisely the same adjective.' Cameron glared at her as though she'd just made that up; in fact, she'd seen several reviews along the same lines. 'In any case you can argue lots of things are predictable. For example, if you went on holiday to Greece, everyone goes to the same airport, gets on the same plane for a few hours, they mostly stay somewhere in or around the same city for a week, go back to the airport, get on another plane, arrive home tired and minus a chunk of money. But everyone's holidays and their reasons for going are widely different.

'You wouldn't say to a plane load of people they are all doing the same stuff,' she added, borrowing Cameron's earlier phrase. 'When you open that book you go on an individual journey with the characters, whether it's a romantic one, a daring escape, a voyage to the stars. And what's wrong with a satisfying ending? Even you would have to agree that most crimes in novels are solved at the end. It certainly was in the book I read.'

'That's because,' Cameron said with a smug expression, 'the point of a crime novel is usually to find out whodunnit.'

'But you would agree that in real life, police statistics show that only a proportion of crimes are ever solved? While the methods of detection might be based on reality, there's a huge degree of artistic licence in the resolution.'

'So, is this the crime readers' version of the Happily Ever After?' Angie asked, looking at both of them.

'Absolutely,' replied Maddy.

'Of course it isn't. A crime or mystery is resolved. It doesn't have to have a happily ever after as long as readers find out who did it or why. Romance readers on the other hand just want a bit of frivolous escapism. It's wish fulfilment with—'

'Sorry, but that's ridiculous!' interrupted Maddy, almost vibrating with indignation. 'Just because romance books can be set in any period of history doesn't make it escapism. Whether it's set in the past, present or future, characters can struggle with all sorts of problems. I've read romance books that deal with family breakups, bereavement, domestic abuse, racism—good luck trying to describe that as cosy escapism—but it is real life for many people. These books are no less important just because they can engender a feeling of community and have a romantic relationship at their heart.'

She glared at him through the screen but he seemed to be oblivious to her reaction. If anything, there was almost a hint of a smirk around his mouth as though he was enjoying himself.

'So do you think in some minds there is a stereotyped view of people who read romance novels?' asked Angie.

Maddy nodded. 'It is certainly true that more women than men read romantic fiction, but the idea of the typical romance reader being some bored housewife secretly reading her escapist romance while her husband is out at work is totally out of place in the modern world.'

Cameron held his hands up in a gesture of surrender. 'I wouldn't presume to—'

'And furthermore,' Maddy continued, 'that completely ignores those romances read by and written by men; listeners might be interested to know that a significant proportion of audiobooks in the erotic fiction genre are downloaded by men.'

Ha! That caught him off guard. Maddy enjoyed the brief look of surprise that flashed across Cameron's face. She wasn't normally this combative but after the day she'd had there was an excess of pent-up frustration waiting for an opportunity to escape. In any case, from what she'd seen so far, Cameron seemed to enjoy a bit of verbal sparring.

'Now that is interesting,' said Angie. 'Cameron, have you ever been tempted to download a racy romance?'

Cameron refused to be drawn in and simply stared at her. It was such a shame he was so testy, Maddy thought, as she mentally redressed him in a white shirt and breeches. Yes, that look definitely suited him better.

Angie looked at Maddy. 'So, do you think that romance books are viewed by some people as inferior because they deal with feelings and relationships?'

'Absolutely. Which is ridiculous as they frequently top the bestseller lists.'

'Although that depends what benchmark you're using,' added Cameron. 'In terms of numbers, they certainly sell well, but how many romances have won the major literary prizes?'

'Oh, not that old chestnut!' said Maddy waving her arm in an exasperated gesture. 'We all know the answer to that one! So how come in nearly every list of best-loved books, the classics like *Jane Eyre* and *Pride and Prejudice* are near or at the top?'

For a brief second their eyes met, both challenging

each other. Cameron laughed. 'You don't think people have these titles on their bookcase purely to show off? Look at me, I'm educated; I read the classics!'

Maddy felt a rush of heat to her face, but before she could respond with something suitably witty, Angie jumped in again.

'So while we're on the subject of the classics, what do you think it is about Jane Austen that has such an enduring appeal? It's over two hundred years since her books were written and yet her stories are as popular as ever, and still being turned into films, stage plays and dramas.'

'It's pure nostalgia for the past,' said Cameron. 'Her characters lived in another era and many people view it all through rose-tinted glasses. She has such a huge following that it's now almost blasphemy to say that you haven't read a Jane Austen book or don't love her characters.'

'I totally disagree. Her books are timeless in their appeal,' Maddy responded. 'People may have dressed differently in that era and they had none of the conveniences of modern life, but the situations the characters find themselves in are still relevant to today's readers. Jane Austen wasn't simply agreeing with the mores and manners of the regency period, she was poking fun at the snobbery of the class system, commenting on social injustices, and—if you know where to look— offering relationship advice that is still as pertinent today as it ever was. You only have to look around to see that there are just as many Mr Wickhams in today's world as there are Mr Tilneys.'

'And there, sadly, we have to leave it for today, but I hope you've enjoyed our lively debate.' Angie smiled at her through the glass screen. 'My thanks to our two guests, Maddy Shaw and Cameron Massey for sharing their thoughts on the world of fiction and romance, and do join us again next week.'

'You are off air now,' said a voice in her headphones a few seconds later, and Maddy tugged them off, ruffling her hair in the process. Her fellow panellist left the studio without a backward glance. Good riddance. His book was going to the local charity shop tomorrow.

———————

As she expected, Alice was still out when she returned home. It was only just gone eight thirty so she topped up the wine glass that Alice had brought in for her earlier that day, took several grateful sips and then kicked off her heels and sank onto the sofa. To avoid thinking about her current jobless situation, she let her thoughts trail back to the studio. So that was the famous Cameron Massey! You couldn't go through an airport or a bookshop without seeing his novels crammed onto the bestseller shelf and it was one of the reasons she had been eager to accept the invite from the radio station.

He looked different somehow in real life; maybe it was because he was smiling in all his publicity pictures, which made him look infinitely more attractive. He was probably ordered to. She took another mouthful of wine before calling up her dad's number. She hoped it wasn't anything longwinded or cat-related—not that she didn't like the cat. She adored Tabitha and it wasn't her fault she was saddled with the world's most unoriginal name for a tabby cat, but she craved a quiet evening and an early night.

'Hi Dad, sorry I couldn't take your call but I was doing a radio interview. Is everything okay?'

'Maddy, love, I've just had a very strange conversation with a firm of solicitors.'

A flutter of anxiety shot through her. 'You're not in any trouble, are you?'

'Quite the opposite. You're not going to believe this. Are you sitting down?'

Chapter Two

A large income is the best recipe for happiness I ever heard of.
Mary Crawford, *Mansfield Park*

'So let me get this straight,' said Maddy, trying to mentally cobble together her family tree, 'this person who's died was Grandad Shaw's brother's son, is that right?'

'Yes.'

'I don't think I ever met your cousin Nigel, did I?'

'No. No one in the family had seen him for decades.' Maddy heard her dad's wistful sigh down the phone, but it was hard to feel sad about someone dying whom she'd never met. Actually, that wasn't entirely true, as she'd cried when Whitney Houston died and obviously she'd never met her either, but cousin Nigel was hardly a revered celebrity. If anything, quite the opposite. She might not have met him but she'd certainly heard his name enough times as a cautionary tale of what might happen if she went off the rails.

According to her father, Nigel had been someone who lived life to the full and regarded rules as something of a challenge. The accepted family version of events was that Nigel had dropped out of university and thrown away an Oxbridge education in favour of a hippy commune in America. He'd been last heard from over thirty years ago, still allegedly living the sex, drugs and rock 'n' roll lifestyle in San Francisco. Maddy had always thought it sad that Grandad Shaw and his siblings had never tried to mend bridges with Nigel. She remembered her dad writing to Nigel's last known address to notify him that his father had passed away but it probably never reached him.

'But you'd met him, hadn't you?'

'Yes, as children we often saw each other at family occasions but we weren't what you'd call close. He was very clever. Loved language and poetry as I remember. After he left the UK he sent a forwarding address to his family, but I think I was the only one who ever bothered to write. I admit it was more out of curiosity than anything else, but I don't recall ever getting a reply. Somewhere in the mid-eighties it dwindled to just the occasional Christmas card and even that stopped eventually.'

Her aunts referred to Nigel as the black sheep of the Shaw family. Her paternal grandparents had refused to even mention his name. As the decades passed, the antics and whereabouts of cousin Nigel were reduced to speculation at the occasional gatherings of the Shaw clan. Even her dad would admit after a beer or two that he had probably wasted his time trying to keep in touch. Now what would the family find to gossip about over their Christmas sherries?

She dimly became aware that her father was still talking.

'…but they must have had some information as I was traced by this firm of solicitors. Anyway, turns out it's you they want to speak to.'

Maddy sat up abruptly. 'Me? Whatever for?'

'Apparently, you're a beneficiary in Nigel's will. I'll send you over the address – I made an appointment for you for three o'clock tomorrow.'

When her father had mentioned he'd made an appointment with a firm of solicitors, she had assumed in the absence of further information that he meant in London. Or somewhere local. At the very least somewhere she'd actually heard of. She'd had to check Google Maps to even work out where Haxford was: west of London and then on a few centimetres. Maps had never been her strong point.

Thankfully, there were a couple of taxis waiting outside Haxford train station. If it had been somewhere familiar, she'd have enjoyed the walk but she was worried about getting lost. Plus, the weather dial had been jammed on 'drizzle' this week, and the damp seemed to seep into her bones. She hoped that whatever the bequest was, it would at least cover her travel expenses for today. It seemed very random that some relation she'd never met had left her something in their will, but given her recent disappointing loss of employment, it was certainly well timed.

The firm of Chapman & Latimer was located at the end of a street of smart-fronted shops and small businesses, looking not dissimilar to many other English market towns. However, once inside, Maddy got the distinct feeling she had stepped through a time portal into a more genteel world. The painted panelling in the reception area could have once been an elegant morning room. Two leather sofas stood on one side of the room, and a Dutch flower painting hung on the wall. She half-expected the place to smell of beeswax or lavender like they did in books.

Without too much waiting, she was shown into another room and introduced to the senior partner Mr Chapman—a dark-suited, bald-headed, middle-aged man, who couldn't look more like a solicitor if he'd tried. After someone had brought in cups of tea and oaty biscuits on a disappointingly cheap-looking white plate, they got down to business.

'So, Miss Shaw, thank you for coming in today. I am Mr Nigel Shaw's solicitor and also the executor of his will. Have you had any recent contact with the deceased?'

Maddy shook her head. 'I've never met cousin Nigel.

The family didn't even know where he was living; all we knew was it was somewhere in the United States.'

Mr Chapman coughed politely. 'That was a considerable number of years ago. For the last twenty-eight years of his life, Nigel Shaw lived in the village of Cotlington.'

'Oh.' Maddy wasn't sure why this felt significant.

Mr Chapman picked up a black folder from his desk and pulled out several sheets of typed paper. 'So as Mr Shaw's executor, I can tell you that there are a number of bequests made to friends and charities, and there will be an amount of inheritance tax due, which will be payable from the estate.'

He picked up the papers and tapped them together on his desk. 'The Grant of Probate has been applied for but until such time as the estate is settled, I will remain responsible for the management of the estate's finances. The funeral is arranged for next week—I apologise for the short notice but it took a little longer than expected to find you.'

Until he mentioned the f-word, Maddy hadn't even thought about going to the funeral. After all, cousin Nigel was more of a distant relation—both genealogically and geographically speaking—and until the conversation with her father, she hadn't given any consideration to his whereabouts for years. However, if he'd left her some money in his will it was only decent to go along to say thank you. Not out loud of course, that would be weird.

'I'd certainly want to go to the funeral and it's very kind of him to remember me in his will. I guess, as executor, you might need my bank details or something? I'm not sure how all this works when someone leaves you money in their will.'

'There will be some legal processes to work through, but Mr Shaw hasn't actually left you a monetary bequest in his will.'

'I see,' said Maddy automatically, even though she didn't see at all.

'He has left you his house, although it does come with a small housekeeping budget.'

For several seconds Maddy wasn't aware her mouth had fallen open. She had to have misheard. Nobody would leave her a house … would they? Her heart thumped as a woosh of adrenaline shot through her body. She didn't know whether to laugh, cheer, leap in the air, or all three. This was the answer to all her financial problems. She sent up a silent thank you to her heavenly benefactor.

'I see this has come as something of a surprise to you, but hopefully a pleasant one,' said Mr Chapman, picking up a biscuit from the plate and snapping it in half.

'Yes … it's just…' Maddy struggled to find a suitable response. Yippee didn't seem appropriate in this stuffy formal office.

'I expect you'll want to go over there and visit the property before you make any fixed plans, and assuming you're planning to attend the funeral, I can arrange a viewing at the same time.'

Maddy found herself nodding. 'Yes, I'd like to see the house before it goes on the market.'

There was a distinct hesitation before the solicitor

responded. He brushed biscuit crumbs from his lips with a neatly pressed handkerchief. 'Ah. I'm afraid that won't be possible just yet.'

Maddy frowned. 'Sorry? You said he'd left a house to me. In his will. Or have I misunderstood?'

'No, that is correct, but—'

'I live in London, you see. I'm a city girl; I don't have plans to do all that escape to the country thing so it would be helpful from a financial point of view to sell the house as soon as possible. Obviously, it's very kind of cousin Nigel to leave me his house, and I don't want you to think I'm ungrateful or anything.'

The solicitor proffered a professional smile. 'Not at all. However, the will contains a codicil. It's a legally binding additional document and it states that you will only inherit the house if you agree to live there for a period of twelve months. I'm afraid the house cannot go on the market before then.'

'And if I don't want to live in…' Maddy refrained from adding the words *the back of beyond*. 'Coltringham, was it?'

'Cotlington.'

'Right. So, if I don't want to live in Cotlington, what happens to the house?'

Mr Chapman consulted his papers although Maddy suspected he already knew the answer. 'It would go to a Mrs Myra Hardcastle.'

'Do you know who she is? Is she another relation?'

'I don't believe so.'

Maddy stared at her now cold tea. She had inherited a

house, her money worries were over, probably for good, but she couldn't sell the house, only live in it. Bugger.

'How long do I have to make up my mind?'

'It would be helpful if you could let me know by the date of the funeral. I can then put the wheels in motion.'

Chapter Three

The distance is nothing when one has motive.
Elizabeth Bennet, *Pride and Prejudice*

Despite feeling like she was ten years old again, Maddy was secretly pleased that her dad had offered to drive her to the funeral service. Aside from wishing to pay his respects – the official explanation – she suspected there was also a not inconsiderable degree of nosiness involved, as after the wake she was going to get a guided tour of Nigel's house. *Her* house, she silently corrected herself.

The news of her inheritance had elicited great excitement in her immediate family and it seemed that—in some quarters at least—Nigel Shaw's status as official family black sheep was being rapidly reconsidered if not rescinded. His erstwhile tarnished reputation was being buffed up by various aunts and uncles who, over the last week, had got in contact to make the appropriate sympathetic noises even though none of them actually knew anything about Nigel's life over the last three decades. It amused Maddy enormously to see how everyone suddenly wanted to chat to her; she had often observed that popularity went hand-in-hand with an inheritance.

She hadn't mentioned the details of the codicil to anyone in the family except her dad. Mum would fuss way too much. She had told Alice though, since she would be affected by whatever decision Maddy made, and therefore had a right to know. Everyone else could wait until she had made up her mind.

She might not have seen the house in person but she had already done a bit of searching online after being given the address by the solicitor. There were no pictures of the actual house, but the street views she had looked at were those of a typical English country village. There were certainly some beautiful cottages that looked lovely for a holiday but to live there on her own? Apart from the village store and a chemist's, the nearest shop was in the next town, and she'd have to travel to Haxford for anything significant. Would she be bored in the countryside? Did takeaway places even deliver to Cotlington? Since she had first heard about this bizarre bequest, an almost endless number of questions had rattled round her brain, but the big question—the one she kept returning to and to which there appeared to be no rational answer—really puzzled her. And today she had to make a decision.

'You've been very quiet, love.'

'Sorry, Dad, just lots of things to think about. Don't you think it's odd though that cousin Nigel left the house to me instead of you?' She turned to look at her calm, dependable dad. 'Why would he do that?'

Even though Maddy hadn't inherited many physical features from her dad—her copper hair and hazel eyes very obviously came from her mother—they shared many other traits, and even as a child it was his opinion she valued and respected.

'Who knows what he was thinking? Maybe he realised I'd have to give up my job, move the family over there? Maybe he just picked a family member out of the air? Maybe he added the codicil as some sort of amusement— the family could inherit as long as they upped sticks and moved to the country for a year.' He chuckled. 'It's like the plot from some Agatha Christie novel. Without the murder obviously,' he added quickly. 'And whatever your mother says about it, it doesn't matter about the money; if you don't want to stay there, you can always come home again until you find yourself another job.'

Maddy patted his arm. 'Thanks. Let's just get today over with first.'

According to Maddy's earlier internet search, the village of Cotlington grew around the church, which was built in the eighteenth century and owed its existence to the rich patronage of the fifth Earl of Haxford. The church was constructed in a gothic style and like many buildings of that age, now needed more maintenance than it could afford. Inside the porch there was a notice-board displaying a totaliser showing how much money was required each year to keep the church going. There were also various colourful posters, including one detailing the funeral of Nigel Shaw, which announced in a fancy font:

No drab colours. Nigel hated dreary occasions!

Maddy exchanged glances with her father who, like her, was dressed in the time-honoured black attire deemed appropriate for funerals. Except this one apparently. It felt rather odd attending a family funeral while knowing next to nothing about the deceased person.

As they stepped inside, Maddy could see that everyone else had clearly noted the instructions on the poster. The little church was already filling up, and dotted around between the wooden pews were bright daubs of colour: A yellow scarf, a red coat, a purple jacket – very Michael Portillo – and any number of fancy hats. A woman who looked around the same age as her mum was handing out orders of service and greeting everyone as they wandered in.

She was wearing an elegant royal blue dress coat trimmed with silk cuffs and a navy butterfly lapel, and a matching colour hat that was part flower, part feather. Her greying hair was cut in a neat bob just below her ears, and a string of pearls rested against her collarbone.

'Welcome to St. Peter's. Good to see you, thank you for coming. Good afternoon, and welcome to St Peter's.' Maddy took the service sheet and, walking forward slowly, looked for somewhere to sit. At weddings there were unwritten rules about these things—bride's family and friends on the left, groom's on the right. She tried to recall whether the same applied to funerals. Sitting on the right might be safest.

'Are you looking for someone?'

Maddy spun round to see a pensioner in a floral dress, a bright pink hat and a green chiffon scarf beaming at her. Clearly, the locals had taken this colour themed thing to heart. Even her walking stick matched her colourful dress.

'We were just trying to see if there were any other family members here,' her father replied. 'I'm Doug, Nigel's cousin, and this is my daughter, Maddy.'

Immediately, the hum of conversation died away and several heads turned to look at them.

'Family? Well, how lovely to meet you. My name is Joyce Sedgefield.' The woman waved her walking stick in the air, almost knocking a couple of candles from their sconces as she called out over the heads of those already seated. 'Myra, this is Nigel's cousin!'

The woman in the blue hat shoved the orders of service at someone and hurried over. Joyce had called her Myra. Was this Myra Hardcastle? It wasn't exactly a commonplace name. Maddy got the distinct impression she was being looked over, and not purely because she'd turned up wearing the wrong colour outfit. Did Myra know that she might inherit a house?

'We didn't know he was in touch with any of his family.' She said it in a vaguely accusatory tone. 'Come this way. You ought to sit at the front.' She ushered them down the aisle towards the front of the church and after a hurried bit of finger pointing, the two people already sitting in the front pew scurried to the one behind. Her dad gave Maddy an amused look and murmured, 'I think we've found out who runs the village.'

The problem with sitting in the front pew was that everyone could stare at you indiscriminately while it was nigh on impossible to look at anyone without swivelling round. Maddy got the distinct impression that they had just become the main topic of conversation in the church.

As music started playing, she turned ever so slightly so she could glance behind her. Joyce was sitting directly behind them along with Myra and two other men—the former occupants of the front pew. The older man looked to be in his late fifties and had a tired, careworn expression on his face. The light grey suit was clearly his idea of colourful. In contrast, the younger man wore dark trousers and a dark orange shirt. He had a round friendly face, and a mop of dark blond hair that looked like a poorly arranged pile of straw. He gave her a quick sympathetic smile. Based on observable body language and the fact that they were chatting together, Maddy's best guess was they were Myra's husband and son.

Cousin Nigel must have been popular, going by the number of people filling up the pews. In between all the bright coloured outfits, she was relieved to spot a dark suit at the back of the church – at least they weren't the only ones who hadn't seen the poster. Maddy gasped and quickly turned back.

'Everything okay?' whispered her dad.

She must be seeing things. From a distance the man had looked like Cameron Massey, but that was just ridiculous. She hadn't slept well for the last week and she was obviously tired.

'Fine,' she whispered back. 'Just thought I saw someone I knew. I was mistaken.'

As the congregation stood up, Maddy glanced back again but the man—whoever he was—had disappeared from view.

Based on the unusual funeral dress code, Maddy had been looking forward to discovering whether the rest of the service was going to be equally unconventional, but other than a rousing rendition of 'My Way' to close the service accompanied by some enthusiastic humming along from the back of the church, it all seemed disappointingly normal.

The wake was held in the village hall, only a short stroll from the church. Built in a light buff-coloured brick with timber-framed windows, it was set back from the road behind a small area of grass that was already studded with early flowering crocuses. Maddy had to admit that it was a lovely setting—the sort of image you saw on a country postcard or attached to a box of fudge.

Inside, lots of chairs had been set out around individual tables, many already occupied. Along one wall, a number of tables had been pushed together and were covered with white damask tablecloths. They held a series of cake stands containing a selection of sandwiches and all manner of dainty cakes and scones. Maddy didn't spot the Cameron Massey lookalike in the dark suit, but she did spy Mr Chapman already holding a plate of sandwiches and balancing a cup of tea. He made his way over to where she was sitting.

'It's so good of you to organise all this,' she said after introducing her dad.

Mr Chapman waved away her appreciation. 'I can't claim any credit for this delightful buffet—that is all down to Mrs Hardcastle and her estimable army of supporters. They have even organised a few speakers, I believe.' He beamed, as though spending the afternoon listening to a group of strangers making speeches at funerals was the highlight of his week. If they ever remade *Pride & Prejudice*, here was a ready candidate for the role of the obsequious Mr Collins.

Did people even have speakers at funerals? Was that a thing? Weddings certainly had traditional speaking roles but Maddy's experience of funerals was limited to her grandad's ten years ago and this one. Before she could persuade her dad it might be a good time to make a polite escape and move on to the house tour, someone rapped the side of their teacup and called for quiet.

'Thank you all for coming today,' said Myra in a voice that reminded Maddy of her headmistress in junior school who could silence a room with her little finger. 'I know Nigel would be thrilled to see so many of you here today.'

'Although technically he probably wouldn't,' piped up a man in a blue shirt, 'because he hadn't planned on dying so suddenly.'

'Good point, Leonard,' said Joyce, nodding her head

vigorously and making the feather in her hat waft around. 'He wouldn't have wanted his funeral to be just yet. He was only seventy-four. Nigel still had plans.'

'I've written him a poem; he loved silly limericks, didn't he?'

'He did. He always had a good ear for that sort of thing—'

Myra tapped her teacup again. 'Yes, he certainly did, Joyce. Anyway, as I was saying I would just like to thank you all for coming today. Nigel was an incredible and generous man, who gave his time and money to many worthy causes in the village, including the recent new roof on the scout hut.'

'We don't need the tin buckets now!' shouted a voice from the back of the hall, which prompted a gale of laughter.

'Indeed,' Myra continued with a smile. 'And on behalf of all his friends here in Cotlington, I would like to offer our sincere condolences to his family.'

Maddy was unsure how to respond. She wasn't expected to make a speech, was she? What on earth could one say that didn't sound trite or ridiculous? Before she could make up her mind, her dad raised his teacup in a regal fashion and murmured a 'thank you' to the assembled crowd. To Maddy's intense relief, the hum of conversation resumed in the hall.

'Thanks, Dad,' she whispered. 'You're the master of understatement.'

She was dying to ask her dad what he thought of everything. He was adept at seeing through people, and had a love of the ridiculous. Personally, she felt like a fish out of water at this gathering. They were the family members and yet they were clearly the ones who knew Nigel the least. The Nigel she had grown up hearing about was selfish, disrespectful, uncaring. That didn't fit the description of someone who had just paid to re-roof the scout hut.

Having realised she had no idea how long it would be before they got back to London, Maddy ate a few of the sandwiches while she waited for Mr Chapman to escape from the group of women standing around him; it was like watching pigeons flocking round a person carrying an obviously large bag of breadcrumbs. Clearly knowledge was currency here, and there were no prizes for distributing second-hand information.

She reckoned that he'd be under siege for at least another twenty minutes and had just started on a slice of delicious cherry cake when Mr Chapman appeared at her side.

'Would it be convenient to view the house now?' he asked in a discreet voice.

'Absolutely,' Maddy confirmed. She stood up. Was there a goodbye etiquette for funerals? At weddings, it was easy as either the bride and groom departed first in a blaze of confetti and good wishes, or else you sought them out on the wedding party dancefloor. In this case, the person in whose honour the gathering was being held had already departed this earth. In order to avoid dithering further, Maddy sought out Myra Hardcastle, expressed her thanks for organising the refreshments and then followed Mr Chapman out to the car park.

They drove in convoy the short distance to the house. Either Cotlington had a 15mph speed limit, or Mr Chapman felt that the funereal pace was more appropriate to the occasion. Either way it gave Maddy a chance to take a proper look at the village. Cotlington seemed mainly comprised of quaint cottages—either brick-faced or rendered and painted in pastel shades that reminded her of seaside houses. One or two even had a thatched roof. There wasn't much traffic at all, but then the majority of the residents were probably still in the village hall finishing up the free sandwiches.

After a short distance, they turned off the main street and down another road that led out of the village. It wasn't long before the houses gave way to trees, behind which Maddy glimpsed fields. The car in front slowed even further as they approached a pair of decorative brick gateposts and turned into a curving driveway flanked on either side by rhododendrons and other evergreen shrubs. It wasn't until they pulled up outside and got out that Maddy got her first proper look at the house.

Mr Chapman smiled confidently as he approached. 'So, what do you think of Meadowside?'

Maddy gazed up at the imposing structure. This surely couldn't be all hers? It was like something out of a novel! The brownish grey stone gave the building an aged brooding look, and its quirky gabled roof lent an added air of mystery. Whether it had ever started life as a rectangular building was debatable but over the years it had clearly been added to and was crying out to be explored.

'I think it's beautiful!'

Mr Chapman gestured to the imposing porch. 'Shall we?' He fished a large keyring from his jacket pocket and unlocked the sturdy wooden front door. Inside the house it was much the same temperature as outside, minus the chill wind. Back at the flat, Alice had gas central heating that was controlled by a dial in the hall. Maddy suspected that this size of property might require something more than a couple of radiators.

The wood-panelled entrance hall had a musty air that reminded her of old bookshops and Grandad Shaw's pipe tobacco. There were various framed photographs hanging on the wall and a painting of the San Francisco Golden Gate Bridge. Doors led off the hall to various rooms including a generous-sized dining room, a cosy snug, a larger, more formal sitting room, and various small storage cupboards.

At the far end, a smaller, narrow hallway led to a kitchen with a red quarry tiled floor, which clearly last saw an overhaul in the 1980s judging by the oak cupboards and Formica worktops. In the centre of the room stood a sturdy pine table, its surface scarred by years of use. The freestanding dresser at one end held a dusty selection of patterned plates that definitely needed a visit to the dishwasher. She would have liked to inspect the contents of the cupboards but Mr Chapman clearly didn't regard the kitchen as very interesting and led them swiftly back towards the hall, where the narrow hallway continued on towards the opposite side of the house and led to yet another door.

'Allow me,' he said, opening it with a flourish which could have doubled as a small bow. Maddy tried not to giggle as she stepped inside. The smothered giggle turned into a gasp as she gazed around yet another generous-sized high-ceilinged room. Even without the commentary from Mr Chapman it was obvious this was Nigel's library.

Two sides of the room were lined with tall bookcases jammed full of fiction books, reference books and leather-bound volumes, and Maddy could have happily spent hours looking over them all. Her eyes alighted on a couple of familiar titles: *The Dangerous Woman* and *The Cornish Key Cutter*. How ironic that even in the middle of nowhere-ville she could still stumble across a reminder of that highly unromantic Valentine's Day chat with Cameron Massey. It had to be some sort of cosmic joke that his name was actually an anagram of the word romance.

A mahogany leather-topped desk stood against one wall—it was a perfect ready-made writing room, with plenty of light flooding the room from the wide French doors that looked out towards the rear of the property. In front of the windows stood a cosy-looking sofa covered by a yellow-gold throw, that would make an ideal space to curl up with a book, Maddy noted to herself.

Upstairs, there were six bedrooms, some of which had clearly not been used for many years judging by the level of dust everywhere. Some of the large items of furniture were covered in large white dust sheets and Maddy wondered what lay beneath. Nigel's bedroom was easily identifiable and still held a number of personal objects and a wardrobe of clothes. How had cousin Nigel lived alone here all those years? Perhaps some of those family rumours about him being a bit eccentric were actually true.

'There are also a couple of attic rooms,' said Mr Chapman, opening yet another door revealing a hidden staircase. 'Nothing worth looking at though.' He led the way back down to the entrance hall. 'So, do you need more time to think it over, Miss Shaw?'

'It's certainly impressive,' her dad acknowledged as he looked around. 'But an awful lot of work. Keeping up a house this size will be a challenge, Maddy. You need to think carefully about this.'

Maddy didn't want to admit that her dad was right. It was a ridiculous-sized house for one person and she'd be stuck here for a year—365 whole days—not just a long weekend. It could be cold over the winter; she knew nothing about whether the electrics or the plumbing were in good order, and the housework alone would take hours. But surely that was only looking at one side of things; after all, Elizabeth Bennet didn't get her first glance of Pemberley and think, *ooh, I bet that will involve a lot of dusting*.

Even allowing for inflated London property prices, by selling this house Maddy could probably afford to buy a small place somewhere in London and be mortgage free. Maybe even with some savings left over, so she could pick and choose where and when she wanted to work. How many people her age could do that? Chucking all that away for being separated from her friends and family for 365 days, plus a bit of domestic inconvenience was foolhardy. The sooner she started the sooner she'd be finished.

'I don't need any more time, thank you, Mr Collins— sorry, I mean Mr Chapman. How soon can I move in?'

Chapter Four

14TH MARCH

If adventures will not befall a young lady in her own village, she must seek them abroad.

Narrator, *Northanger Abbey*

'Well, that's the last of your boxes,' said her dad as he deposited another sturdy packing box in the hall. 'Do you want some help unpacking these?'

Maddy shook her head. 'Thanks, but I need to do a bit of cleaning first.'

'Your mother seems to have taken that task in hand already,' he replied with a smile. 'She's already scrubbing the kitchen worktops and I suspect the floor will be next. You know how she likes to keep busy.'

Maddy exchanged amused looks with her father. 'In that case I'll just sort out the clothes for now.'

Between them, they carried upstairs the black bags

containing the contents of Maddy's wardrobe. Job number one was to choose which bedroom she wanted. Definitely not the one Nigel had used. There was something creepy about the idea of sleeping in the bed of a deceased relative, and it wasn't as if she was short of choice. As she walked along the landing, peering into each of the rooms, she could see how this could have been a wonderful family home. It should be full of laughter, and parties, not just her rattling around. Hopefully her successor would be able to make better use of it. The décor in most of the rooms seemed to predate the 1990s, when Nigel had moved in, so either he had no money for decoration or it didn't offend him.

She finally settled on the room next to Nigel's, which had a slightly more feminine style and was painted in a pale duck-egg blue, with ivory and gold damask curtains at the window. A large mahogany wardrobe stood in one corner and her dad moved in a bedside table from another room. Once she'd run the hoover around and unpacked a few of her things, it would look quite cosy, she decided.

In truth, it hadn't taken long for Maddy to pack up everything from the flat. Mainly her clothes, books and a few boxes of personal items. Alice had agreed to hold on to the rest as it didn't take up much room, and the now empty bookcase would come in useful, she said.

It had been predictably emotional saying goodbye to her best friend. Even with the benefits of modern technology and promises to keep in touch, it was still a wrench, and the only saving grace was that the countdown had now officially started. As she made her way back downstairs, she forced a smile on her face while reminding herself that in 365 days she'd be back home again, and several hundred thousand pounds better off.

She managed to keep up appearances right up to the moment her parents' car disappeared down the gravel driveway. Although her hand was still waving, a fog of uncertainty settled over her. Was she really doing the right thing living out here all on her own? Despite her best efforts to remain cheerful, a solitary tear trickled down her cheek, and she brushed it away swiftly, even though there was no one to see it.

Her mum had left the fridge and freezer stocked with enough food for an army to withstand a lengthy siege, and Maddy made herself a supper from some cold meat and cheese. Later that evening she remembered Alice's present and as she sat up in bed wrapped up in her pastel-pink love heart blanket, she looked over it again in detail.

On their last evening together, Alice had presented her with the homemade calendar that instead of recording the days and months of the year, counted down the 365 days until Maddy was back in London. On specific days she had added a few extra details such as Maddy's birthday or Christmas Day. In other sections she had attached photos, cartoons or just funny pictures of the two of them. Maddy couldn't help but be cheered by pictures from her past. Countdown Day 28 was a big red heart for Valentine's day. Maddy hoped next year's would be significantly better than this year's. One month ago exactly she'd been stuck in a studio with Cameron Massey listening to him rubbishing her favourite books.

She fell asleep trying to work out which Jane Austen character he was most similar to.

It was the noise that woke her up first. Maddy sat up, momentarily disorientated by her surroundings. Was it morning? How many hours had she actually been asleep? She had stupidly left her rechargeable torch charging downstairs and her phone was switched off, but she peered around in the darkness. There it was again—some sort of knocking sound, not like knuckles on wood but more metallic. What felt like a soft draught of cold air brushed against her face and she shivered as the hairs on her arms stood up.

'Hello?' The sound of her own voice gave her a boost of confidence and a jolt of common sense. Old houses always creaked, didn't they? And she already knew the house was chilly. She was getting as bad as that silly girl in *Northanger Abbey* who was obsessed with haunted houses and gothic novels. She turned over and pulled the duvet over her head and willed herself back to sleep.

Chapter Five

I will be calm. I will be mistress of myself.
Elinor Dashwood, *Sense and Sensibility*

Despite a thorough examination of the upper rooms in the morning, Maddy failed to discovered the potential source of any knocking noise. However, she did discover that the carpet in the end bedroom was damp, with a corresponding circular patch on the ceiling. Brilliant. Day two and the house was already creating problems.

Over breakfast she added *Find Builder* to her list of things to do; hopefully he could sort out the heating at the same time as she was currently wearing several layers under her warmest jumper. She cheered herself up by tearing off the first page on her countdown calendar. Only 364 days to go.

Her next task this morning was to go through the file of papers Mr Chapman had left for her. With not a lot else to keep her mind occupied, she diligently read through the letters relating to the transfer of house owner-ship, noted the details of where the emergency water stop-cock was – hopefully not required within the next 364 days – and looked over a copy of the small housekeeping budget that had been provided for in the will.

Her experience of women inhabiting country houses was limited to reading – and watching televised adapta-tions of – Jane Austen books, along with reruns of Downton Abbey. So what would Jane Austen do with her day? Her ladies of leisure went for lunches, worked at their embroidery, entertained friends on the pianoforte or went for bracing walks around the countryside. The first three options were ruled out either due to lack of finances or sheer lack of ability, but she could give option four a spin.

After lunch, Maddy pulled on a warm padded jacket, rummaged in one of her bags of unpacked stuff for her green knitted hat with the pompom on it, then unlocked the kitchen door which opened onto the side of the house. Yesterday she'd been too busy inside to investigate the grounds, but now she felt the urge to explore. Along the side of the house was a neatly laid out series of garden beds which she guessed had been a kitchen garden in former years, now looking unused and tired. She followed the path round to the back of the house, where it opened onto a wide paved area bordered by stone balustrading. A couple of wide stone steps led down to a large expanse of

lawn and wide borders filled with shrubs, and small ornamental trees.

Winter hadn't quite loosened its grip but there were
signs of green shoots poking out of the ground and early
spring bulbs were already providing a splash of colour
across the garden. Maddy wondered what the grounds
would look like in the summer. There was no way she'd be
able to manage this on her own – it would be a mass of
weeds by midsummer – and she was pretty sure that the
meagre housekeeping budget would not cover the cost of
a gardener.

Looking down at her feet she decided she also needed
to invest in a sturdy pair of wellington boots. Living in a
London flat did not make those essential items, but the
grass had already dampened the tops of her trainers. The
air was fresh and invigorating though, and she breathed in
several deep lungfuls. None of that daily dose of London
pollution and car fumes. At the far side of the lawn she
followed a paved path that led her into a smaller garden
bordered by trellis and planted with roses and plants she
couldn't identify, and on through a less cultivated area
towards a waist-height wooden gate, set into a gap in the
hedge. This presumably marked the edge of the property.

She wondered how many people in years gone by had
walked round these grounds; her imagination conjured up
women in beautiful dresses carefully shading their faces
from the sun with white parasols and chatting as they
walked along.

The bolt on the gate was stiff and clearly hadn't been
used for a while, but Maddy persisted and eventually

wriggled it loose. She was now standing in a large expanse of open undulating land. It was mostly grass, with the occasional shrubby-looking thing and, in the distance to the right, a line of trees. In the opposite direction she could see the rooftops of the village. Meadowside was aptly named.

As she headed towards the trees, she wondered how she was going to manage the house and grounds. It was all very well Nigel leaving her the house, but there was barely any money for its upkeep. The villagers seemed to have beatified him already but unfortunately Saint Nigel had departed this life without making adequate financial provision for whoever would live there. The idea of owning a beautiful house in the country scored ten out of ten for theoretical appeal, but a resounding nil points for practicality. Surely the simplest thing to do would be to go back to London, inform Mr Chapman that she wasn't going to stay and let him hand the house over to Myra Hardcastle.

Maddy stopped suddenly. Was this actually Nigel's intention? To dress up his will to look like he was doing his duty by the family? He probably realised that without allowing her to immediately sell the property he had bequeathed to her, it would be hard for Maddy to live here. Why would he do that? Was he really some sort of selfish, free-wheeling, free-living individual who lived by his own rules and off the adoration of the village?

Maddy wondered if she was allowing her imagination a bit too much licence. After all, it wasn't as if she even knew cousin Nigel. None of her family did. All she knew about him was from the rumours and embellished tales passed from one member of the family to the next. Even her dad had to admit he couldn't exactly remember the last time he'd seen Nigel, and yet here he was, large as life, enjoying himself playing lord of the manor. Well, good for him, but despite yesterday's show of bravado she wasn't sure she wanted to do this for another 364 days. She stamped her damp feet to keep them warm as she marched across the open ground. The sky today was uniformly grey, with a few darker swirls of cloud dotted here and there. She hoped that wasn't a portent of rain.

A distant bark attracted her attention. She'd always been slightly wary of big dogs after getting a nip from an over enthusiastic Alsatian as a child, and she quickly scanned the area to see if she could see anything. However, the hound that galloped into view could not have looked less threatening if it had been wearing a pantomime horse outfit.

It was white, black and tan, and around the height of a low coffee table. As it got closer, Maddy could see a tail wagging enthusiastically and big brown ears flapped up and down comically as it lolloped towards her. She instinctively put her hands out but the dog came to a stop a metre in front of her and looked up expectantly. If it were anatomically possible, she would swear the dog was smiling at her. He had a long, pointed muzzle, mostly white, but with tan patches around large soulful eyes.

Maddy approached slowly, holding out her hand for him to sniff. 'Hello, boy! Are you friendly?'

As if in response, the dog trotted up to her and licked

her hand, which answered that question. But to whom did he belong? Presumably someone in the village, but even after turning in a complete circle, she couldn't see another person. The dog didn't seem in any hurry to rush off and she knelt down on the damp grass to give him a fuss. He had a lovely soft coat, and his ears were like warm velvet. He seemed to enjoy all the attention and his tail wagged nonstop.

Several minutes elapsed and there was still no sign of anyone. Maddy noticed he was wearing a collar with a name tag.

'Let's see who you are then, shall we?'

She turned over the silver disk to see the name BUSTER and a mobile telephone number.

'Have you run off, Buster?'

At the sound of his name, the dog gave a polite woof. That appeared to answer that question at any rate. The other more urgent question of where his owner was remained unknown. Was he in the next field? Maddy felt uncomfortable just walking away and leaving the – possibly lost – dog, but if she took him home with her, someone might think she was stealing him.

'Let's see who you belong to then, shall we?'

She pulled out her phone and rang the number. After several rings a male voice answered.

'Good morning. I found this number on Buster's collar—I didn't know if you were out walking or whether he'd escaped. I can't see anyone, but I thought I ought to ring, just in case.'

'Oh not again! I thought he was in the garden—he

must have found a way to escape. That dog should have been called Houdini.'

Buster had found a stick and was gambolling around in circles with it making Maddy laugh.

'Aw, he's gorgeous! I think I'm in love with him already.'

'I'll come straight over if you don't mind waiting? Whereabouts are you?'

'I'm just on the edge of Cotlington.' Maddy looked around for a suitable landmark. 'I don't know the name of the field, but—'

'Don't worry, I know the village. Throw me a road name.'

'Springfield Lane—as you drive away from the village it's on the left-hand side. I've only just moved to the village so I'm not sure of the exact distance but—'

'That's okay. I know that road.'

'There's a house at the end of the lane called Meadowside. I'm in the fields behind the house.'

'Right. I'm on my way. Thanks for the call.'

'No problem, I'm—'

The phone had already cut off, but then he was obviously in a hurry. He sounded like a caring, albeit slightly harassed, pet owner. In fact his telephone voice was altogether sexy, even though they were only talking about a lost dog. Admittedly he sounded a little agitated but then Mr Darcy wasn't exactly Mr Genial at the outset. Maybe her mother was right about meeting a nice country gent, even though most of her ideas were half a century out of date.

Maddy pointed her finger. 'You, Buster, are causing everyone a lot of trouble this afternoon. Come here.'

Buster seemed remarkably unconcerned by his apparent disgrace and looking hopeful, dropped the stick at Maddy's feet.

'Oh no, I'm not throwing that stick so you can run off again.' Maddy curled her fingers around his collar and sat down on the grass. 'You know I'm going to get a wet bum because of you, don't you?'

Buster turned and licked her face. 'And now you're just trying to curry favour,' said Maddy wagging her finger in mock admonishment.

She leaned in to his warm body and they sat together as they waited. All she could hear was the occasional distant sound of a car, the tweeting of some unidentified bird and the panting of her companion. It would be nice to have a dog for company. She had enough space here and it would be fun, but then what would she do with it when the year was up? A dog wasn't just for a year and wasn't really suited to life in a flatshare.

'You wouldn't like living in a flat, would you, Buster?' She untwined her fingers from his collar and let them trail along his coat. 'You are a very handsome boy, aren't you? Although when my mother mentioned the possibility of meeting a handsome stranger, I don't think she meant the canine variety.' To pass the time, Maddy pulled her phone from her jacket pocket and took a selfie with Buster with a backdrop of open sky and green fields. It made it look like they were in the middle of nowhere, and Maddy had a sudden pang of longing for suburban streets, coffee vendors and bustling, brightly lit shops. She sent the picture to Alice with the caption, *Playdate with a handsome stranger*, and added a few smiley emojis.

Buster picked up the stick and dropped it on her lap. 'Okay then,' Maddy said, getting to her feet. 'Just one more go.' She lobbed the stick in the air watching Buster tear after it. It must be wonderful to feel so easily pleased by the simple act of having someone throw a stick for you. Instead of returning though, Buster let out a single bark and raced off in the opposite direction.

'Buster! Come back here!' Maddy yelled, but her erstwhile charge was now running full pelt towards a dark-haired man in a navy weatherproof jacket. Was this the person she'd spoken to on the phone? Surely not, because from this distance he looked for all the world like…

'Excuse me, do you mind not throwing sticks for my dog?' he shouted.

Maddy found herself staring at the familiar figure striding towards her. What the hell was *he* doing here? And how come even in casual gear he managed to look like a model from a clothing catalogue, whereas she had windswept hair and a grass-stained bottom?

Buster didn't seem worried about any sartorial considerations and having abandoned his stick, was happily jumping up and wiping muddy paws all over his trousers.

As the man, now very obviously identifiable as Cameron Massey, closed the last few metres between them, his startled expression said he clearly recognised her too.

'You?' he said, coming to an abrupt halt.

Not quite the greeting she'd been expecting. Maddy politely held out her hand. 'What a surprise. Are you—'

'Don't you know sticks can cause serious injuries to a dog's mouth or throat?'

Maddy withdrew her unshaken hand. 'Erm no, I didn't. Sorry.'

Hang on, why on earth was she doing that automatic apologising thing? And hadn't he skipped over the grateful thank-you-for-finding-my-dog bit? Just looking at that irritated expression was like pressing an instant rewind button and she was straight back in that recording studio again.

'Because if I had,' she continued, her voice louder now and ripe with indignation, 'I would obviously *not* have thrown the stick for him, would I? I may be lacking in veterinary facts but I'm not stupid. And in any case Buster found it lying on the ground in the first place.'

'So it's the dog's fault, is it?'

'It's nobody's fault,' replied Maddy tartly.

Cameron squatted down and with his fingers, carefully checked over the inside of Buster's mouth. He clearly didn't find any fragments or splinters, and he gave the dog a fuss before tugging a lead from the pocket of his jacket and clipping it onto Buster's collar.

'Right. Well, I'll get Buster back home before he picks up anything else he's not supposed to.'

Maddy watched him turn and walk back in the direction from which he'd come. She raised her chin slightly and smiled politely as she called out, 'Thank you. You're welcome, it was no trouble at all.'

At least the dog was no longer lost or her responsibility. Ms Austen had been right about the bracing country walk though, and Maddy headed back to the house with a purposeful stride.

What she needed was a plan to make the house habitable and then she could look at getting herself some work. She didn't need to be in London—these days huge numbers of journalists worked remotely. Why should she cave in and crawl back to London?

'You have a pair of hands and a brain, Madeleine Shaw, so get busy and use them!' she said out loud.

As soon as she'd made herself a warming cup of coffee, she sat down at the kitchen table and started making a list. Apart from her bedroom, the other upstairs rooms were not a priority. However, if she was going to live here for any length of time the ground floor needed to be tidy and habitable. Her mother had already given the kitchen a good scrub but it was clear from the other rooms that there would be plenty to keep her occupied.

She started with the sitting room at the front of the house. The centrepiece of the room was a dark oak fireplace, although clearly the fire hadn't been lit recently and the grate was full of ash. Yellow floral curtains hung either side of the large bay window, and the room was filled with an eclectic mix of furniture styles. The sofas, upholstered in a dark orange, reminded Maddy of the poster in the church: No drab colours. There was definitely a seventies feel to this room, she decided, as she flicked the duster round.

Keeping active didn't stop her thoughts from trailing

back to her earlier encounter. How strange to run into Cameron Massey of all people; he was still clearly demonstrating how he'd earned his reputation for being argumentative. If anything, he'd rubbed even more people up the wrong way since that interview, as after rubbishing Jane Austen and the entire romance genre on air, he'd incurred the wrath of several romance writers who had taken to social media to express their feelings. He must spend as long having pointless arguments on social media as he did writing his books.

Slightly more worryingly, he'd also mentioned getting Buster home so clearly he lived round here. She hoped for both their sakes that they could manage to avoid bumping into each other too often over the next twelve months.

Chapter Six

Seldom, very seldom, does complete truth belong to any human disclosure; seldom can it happen that something is not a little disguised or a little mistaken.

Narrator, *Emma*

'Hello! The front door was unlocked, but I'm not a burglar!' The shout reverberated through the hall, and if it was possible to tell from just eleven words, the voice sounded friendly.

Maddy welcomed the break from housework and dropping her duster, she hurried in the direction of the sound. Day three of Operation Meadowside Needs Urgent Cleaning had moved on to the dining room, which could have come straight from the pages of a Victorian novel. While the sitting room had contained books, magazines and other personal items, this room was more formal with its chunky mahogany furniture, heavy curtains, and large court cupboard covered in ornate carvings. It was also not much used if the layers of dust were anything to go by.

A young woman—Maddy guessed in her twenties—stood in the middle of the hall in a pink, stripey, long-sleeved T-shirt and denim dungarees, with a broad, welcoming smile, and looking like an over-enthusiastic children's TV presenter. Her white-blond hair sported pink highlights and was held back off her face by a fuch-sia-pink hairband.

'Wow, looks like you're already settling in,' she said, looking around at the unopened boxes still littering the entrance hall that suggested the complete opposite. 'My name's Sally by the way.' She giggled. 'That sounds like I've got a weird surname. It's Sally Cartwright. I live in the village and thought I'd pop along and say hello, welcome'—she grinned and gave Maddy a quick wave in case she was in any doubt about who the welcome was for —'and I've brought along a few supplies.' She held out a large basket with a proper wicker handle that wouldn't have looked out of place in a Fortnum & Mason's promotion, containing a bottle of wine and other items. 'I hope it's all still in one piece—I had to clip the basket to the back of my bicycle.'

'It's lovely to meet you. I'm Maddy, but then you probably already know that. Do you want to stay for a coffee? You'll be rescuing me from more cleaning so I hope the answer's yes.'

She led the way to the kitchen where she unpacked

the contents of the basket at the wooden table. Along with the bottle of wine there was a box of eggs, a small seeded loaf of bread, a coffee cake, a packet of chocolate biscuits, a box of Maltesers, and a few items of fruit. Just looking over the gifts gave Maddy a warm fuzzy feeling inside.

'This is so kind of you, I don't know what to say.'

'Well, it's a good excuse to pop over and visit your new neighbour, isn't it? Oh, and I nearly forgot.' Sally reached into the canvas bag hanging over her shoulder and produced a slightly bent A5 booklet. 'Your very own copy of *Cotlington Chat*. It's a sort of cross between a newsletter, an information board and a chat forum. Anybody can send anything in for publication and it keeps you informed of what goes on in the village.'

Maddy put aside the pamphlet for later reading. She has assumed—clearly erroneously—that very little went on in this sleepy village, and certainly nothing that required a several-page brochure.

Sally sat herself at the table while Maddy made them both coffees. 'Sorry, it's instant,' Maddy apologised. 'We used to have one of the Nespresso machines in the flat but it belonged to my friend so I had to leave it behind.'

'I'm happy with anything,' replied Sally cheerfully. 'Shall I open the biscuits?' Without waiting for a response, she opened the packet lying on the table and offered one to Maddy. It reminded Maddy of those sitcoms where hospital visitors brought grapes and then ate them themselves.

'So tell me all about Nigel's family! I bet you were

thrilled to hear you'd be living here! Nigel must have been very fond of you,' she added in only a slightly less enthusiastic voice.

On the basis that the answer to statement two was 'not really', and to statement three was 'don't have a clue', Maddy started with the easy answer. 'Well, the rest of the Shaw family is pretty ordinary really. My dad is—was—Nigel's cousin. Mum and Dad live in Kent, but there are aunts and uncles dotted around the south and east of England.'

'They must be so proud of what Nigel achieved.'

'Well…'

'I guess they'll all be rushing over to visit now.'

That, Maddy definitely agreed on, although not for the same reasons. A change of focus was required. 'So, as you cycled over I'm guessing you're a local; do you live in Springfield Lane?'

'No, but if you follow the road back towards the village, you get to a row of cottages off on the left, painted in pretty colours. I live there.'

'And let me guess, yours is the pink one?'

Sally pulled up a lock of hair and laughed. 'Good guess.'

'I think they're charming. They've got real character.'

'Oh yes,' replied Sally, her eyes sparkling. 'I love my little cottage but sadly I only rent it. My jobs are a bit intermittent so Mum and Dad help out sometimes with the rent which I feel a bit guilty about, but it's better than trying to find a room to let. People round here seem to like their privacy too much to have paying lodgers.'

'Well, you can always stay here if you change your mind,' said Maddy. 'I seem to have enough space for any number of lodgers and it'd be fun to have company. I used to flatshare with my best friend when I lived in London.' She didn't add that the money would come in handy too.

Sally wrinkled her nose. 'London is too noisy for me. But I'll put the word out and if anyone's looking to rent somewhere I'll send them in your direction.' She looked around her. 'This is a gorgeous house. One day I'd like to have a place of my own although it won't be as grand as this one. Mind you, I don't know what I'd do with all these rooms.'

'Me neither. Goodness knows what cousin Nigel did rattling around here all by himself year after year.'

'Oh, he was always busy. Either organising the literary festival or planning the next one.'

Nigel Shaw organised a literary festival? That would certainly be a surprise to the family! Maddy couldn't wait to update her dad on this snippet of news, and made a mental note to Google the event.

'It's held every year at the end of the summer,' Sally continued. 'The date for this year's is 3rd September—I hope that's okay for you? The date was fixed before...' She pursed her lips, clearly trying to find a diplomatic way of stating the obvious.

'Before he died?'

'Exactly. So we wanted to make sure the date didn't clash with any plans you had.'

Maddy shook her head wondering why her attendance was important. Maybe they just wanted her to feel welcome and part of the village. 'No plans at all, other than to try and fix a leaky roof and keep the house standing for the next 362 days.'

'What's the number of days got to do with anything?'

'Oh, it's … erm…' Maddy inwardly cursed her own carelessness, 'just a figure of speech, you know?'

'Right,' Sally continued after a slightly awkward pause. 'I'll tell Myra you're okay with the date for the festival; she'll be so thrilled. Well, we all will actually. We didn't know whether that was your sort of thing.'

'It sounds fun. It will be something to look forward to.'

'Oh it is. The next committee meeting is on 6th April so I'll tell Myra to send round a copy of the last minutes. Leonard always does them very promptly and he's ever so good—probably because he used to be a teacher. Then you'll be up to speed at the next meeting.'

Maddy struggled to keep up with Sally's logic. 'Next meeting? Sorry, I'm not with you here. Why do I need to know about the meeting?'

The look of excitement on Sally's face vanished and her facial barometer eventually settled on something between confused and apologetic. 'Oh. They didn't tell you?'

'Tell me what?'

'You're the new chair of the Cotlington Literary Festival Committee.'

How on earth had she been landed with organising a literary festival in less than six months? Was there an opt-out clause? Perhaps she could just say no? Sally clearly thought it was the highlight of the social calendar. Maddy needed to find out more about this thing before agreeing to anything, and it was as she washed up the coffee cups that she remembered about the pamphlet Sally had brought round, which might contain some helpful information.

At first glance, the March edition of *Cotlington Chat* appeared to have a gravestone on the cover, although according to the note on the inside, the cover was a pen and ink drawing of the original village mile-marker situated at the bottom of Springfield Lane, and had been drawn by a local artist.

The first couple of pages were dedicated to a write-up of cousin Nigel's funeral. Yet again, Maddy was stunned that he had made such an impression on the village, and it flew in the face of everything she had heard from her own family. Her eyes scanned the glowing comments:

A great loss to the village…
A hugely popular man who shared his wealth with his neighbours
…a wonderful service with representatives from his family in attendance…

That made her and her dad sound like some sort of London ambassadors on a UN peacekeeping mission.

Underneath the main article were various individual quotes from the local population:

Thanks for the new roof, Nigel!
1st Cotlington Scouts
I've been saying that stretch of road was dangerous for
years. Gone but never forgotten,
Maud Hartnell,
Secretary, Haxford & District Road Safety Committee

There was also a limerick written by Leonard, who appeared to be secretary of the Literary Festival:

There once was a man named Shaw
Who reached aged seventy-four
He had one last hurrah
Then (accidentally) crashed his car
Now's he's off to the great evermore

Good grief, was this really what passed for literary entertainment out here? Maddy was not at all sure she wanted to be saddled with this job. It was certainly a long way from the glossy UpClose magazine that she used to write for, which had a circulation of around 140,000.

After she was back in London, she might write a humorous look back on her year in the country, although the jury was out on whether the Cotlington Literary Festival would feature on her CV.

On page four there was a full-page article about this year's literary festival:

The Cotlington Literary Festival 2022

As longstanding residents will know, this is our annual cele-bration of all things literary in the village, and 3rd September is the planned date of this year's fabulous festival. Following the tragic death of festival founder, Nigel Shaw, the committee are in talks with the new owner of Meadowside, but hope that the festival will take place as usual in its glorious grounds.

What? Maddy almost leapt out of her seat. So not only was she expected to chair the committee but she was also the hostess! On the housekeeping budget she had, the catering alone would be a nightmare. And who organised the speakers? This had all the hallmarks of a disaster. And why hadn't Mr Chapman informed her of this obligation? The article continued in its fulsome praise:

Nigel loved the annual festival and you can be assured that your committee will do everything possible to ensure that his legacy continues here in Cotlington, and are working hard on your behalf.

She had mistakenly assumed that Sally's visit was a neighbourly welcome but now she wondered whether she had been the bearer of a Trojan basket. Maddy scanned down the page to see who had written this glowing paeon. Myra Hardcastle—of course it was. Well, if she was so keen to keep the festival running maybe she'd prefer to run it herself.

Chapter Seven

*I wish, as well as everybody else, to be perfectly happy; but, like
everybody else, it must be in my own way.*
Edward Ferrars, *Sense & Sensibility*

I t had been a few days since Sally's visit and Maddy
was still undecided about what to say to Myra. Given
that she had to live in the village, she didn't particularly
want to antagonise anyone, but she needed to be clear
about how she felt. And decisive. So was this a great
opportunity or a poisoned chalice?

For someone who used to give advice as part of their
day job, she was finding it curiously difficult to make up
her mind. What she really needed was impartial advice –
and preferably also assistance – from someone in the
literary world, and this morning she decided to contact

her old friend and colleague Briony, in order to pick her brains.

In the aftermath of her rather sudden departure from the world of employment, Maddy had had little time to think about her former job after being sucked into the whirlwind of her inheritance and subsequent packing-up operation, but she had emailed a couple of friends to update them on what had been happening. It was only Briony who had bothered to reply to congratulate her. Maybe the others were suffering from a bout of food poisoning after eating sour grapes.

Maddy always did her best thinking outdoors, so she pulled on her warmest jacket, scooped her hair into a ponytail and headed out through the garden gate, this time turning left in the direction of the village. The ground sloped downwards in a gentle gradient so she had an unimpeded view of the village. From here it looked like a model village surrounded by acres of fields, with darker green lines of trees marking field boundaries. Maddy tucked her phone in her pocket and plugged in her earbuds so she could chat while she walked.

She supposed at some point she should delete the contact details for her colleagues, but Briony was both friend and colleague and now hopefully adviser.

'Hi, Briony!' Maddy almost shouted down the phone. 'How you are? How is everything?'

'Maddy?'

'Yes! It's lovely to hear your voice!'

'Hello, stranger. What are you up to?'

'Mostly cleaning this week. I only moved in a week

ago—the place is amazing but it's too big and too quiet. Except at night when the house creaks for England.' She didn't mention the strange knocking noises in case Briony thought she was mad. 'How is work? What is everyone up to?'

For a few minutes the business of catching up occupied them both, but as the conversation paused, Maddy decided to come to the point. 'Actually, Briony, I was hoping to enlist your help. You're not going to believe this but I've inherited the position of chair of the local literary festival!'

'You've certainly got stuck into country life quickly.'

'I didn't exactly volunteer. And now I don't know if I can get out of it. I haven't the first idea of how to plan an entire festival and I was hoping you might be able to sound out a few people for me. Daanesh used to organise events, didn't he? And I'm sure Carrie has given speeches at this sort of thing.'

'Yes, she did, although—'

'It'd be great to go along to the first meeting with some suggestions and positive input. Remember how Kara always used to say "don't bring me problems, bring me a solution"?' Maddy chuckled at the recollection. 'I'm still channelling her advice so any offers of speakers gratefully received. And of course I've got bags of room to put people up.' She made a mental note to start sorting out a proper guest room.

'I can't promise anything, Maddy. Things have changed a bit in the last few weeks.'

'I know, I know. But I appreciate you trying to help. You're a star.'

'Don't thank me yet—just give me a call in a few days.'

Listening to Briony's happy chatter was a poignant reminder of the camaraderie and feeling of busy usefulness Maddy was missing right now. Just because this was cousin Nigel's passion project didn't mean it had to be hers too. Instead of playing at literary hostess, she ought to look at getting some work, assuming there was no clause in Nigel's will that prevented it, and tonight she would start jotting down some ideas for articles. She could really do with the income as the housekeeping budget had clearly been worked out based on 1970s prices.

As she headed back to her chilly house, she decided she had acquired a lot more sympathy for the poorer relations in Jane Austen's novels, particularly Fanny Price who got plucked from the slums of Portsmouth to live with her rich relations, but still didn't have any income of her own. When this experiment was over, Maddy would certainly never grumble about lack of pay rises again.

In times of stress, her flatmate, Alice, would slink back to bed with a cup of tea and a good book, but Maddy preferred to keep busy. As her heroine Jane Austen would say:

One man's ways may be as good as another's, but we all like our own best.

In her initial exploration of the house she hadn't bothered about the attic. If it was anything like her parents' loft it'd be a crowded dingy space containing boxes of Christmas decorations, with barely enough height to stand up in. This afternoon, with not a lot else to do, she decided to explore.

In the bright afternoon sunshine the attic stairs looked less like part of the set of a gothic novel and more like a secret staircase from her children's storybooks. Armed with a water bottle, some biscuits, a face mask and some rudimentary cleaning equipment, Maddy paused at the top of the stairs where a small landing led to rooms on both the left and right.

Choosing the left hand side first, she tentatively pushed open the door to reveal a space around twenty foot square, piled up with all manner of old furniture and bric-a-brac including a random collection of chairs, side tables, lamps of varying heights and some children's toys including a very elegant rocking horse.

The elderly rug had long given up the pretence of having any pattern and the room had possibly last seen a dustpan and brush during the regency period. There was an equally dusty dormer window that looked out over the back lawn. That was probably where the literary festival was held. As a flutter of panic rippled through her, she reminded herself that she did not volunteer for the job. On one of the chairs there was an open cardboard box containing some candles in glass jars and a box of matches. They at least would be useful and Maddy deposited the box at the top of the stairs before venturing over to the other side of the attic space.

This room was of similar size with a similarly thread-bare rug. The steep pitch of the roof meant there were no issues over headroom, and in another universe where she'd just won the lottery, this would make a lovely bedroom. Two dormer windows afforded fabulous views over the gardens giving the room an airier feel, provided you didn't mind a side order of dust with each lungful of oxygen. However, unlike the junk shop across the landing, this room looked more organised. On the wall opposite the windows was a long row of utility shelving filled with dozens of boxes of all colours and shapes. Stacked up on the floor were bigger packing boxes and in front of the window was a long wooden table on which sat a colourful letter rack, a selection of stationery and various ancient bottles of coloured inks.

The modern-looking office chair, upholstered in a cushioned faux leather material and sitting in front of the desk, seemed incongruous in this cardboard dumping ground. She sat down tentatively. It was actually very comfortable although as she quickly discovered, the lever operating the reclining function was broken so the first time she leaned back she found herself almost flat on her back.

Having managed to wrestle open the windows, the first hour was spent cleaning them and sweeping the floor. She then examined the contents of some of the boxes. Many were filled with brochures, postcards, small knick-knacks, printed sheet music, old faded photographs, even an award for something. There were various boxes with KEEP written on the side that suggested there had been some effort at decluttering, although the evidence pointed more towards cousin Nigel never actually having thrown anything away. Having found an empty, sturdy-looking box, she wrote RECYCLE on the side and then began to fill it up with things that were obviously rubbish.

Maddy had always enjoyed putting things in order; as a child she'd never needed to be told to tidy her bedroom, and her cuddly toys had sat in descending order of size on top of her chest of drawers. At school, she had quickly been appointed tidy monitor, and in the office her filing skills had been legendary, as was her obsession with stationery.

One box was filled with old newspapers and she put that to one side for future perusal. The next box she looked at was intriguingly labelled 'F books'. Fancy books? Free books? Family books? This box was only half full and seemed to consist of various dog-eared volumes, mostly paperbacks. She pulled the first one out entitled *New Age American Poetry*. Clearly nothing family-related then. She examined the first few dusty pages and was scandalised to see that someone had scrawled things in the margins; at university a few of her friends had done that in textbooks and they'd laughed at her for being so shocked. To Maddy, books were something to treasure and look after, not write all over. This lot looked like they had lived a hard life. It wasn't even like the notes were intended as an aide memoire either. She flicked forward a couple of pages and found parts of poems had been circled. She inwardly cringed at the blatant vandalism as she flicked through a few more tattered pages.

The warning bells are ringing clear had been scribbled down one side of the page. A few pages further on she found, *The danger signs are getting near*. It was like odd phrases had been scribbled down at random intervals. Didn't Nigel own any notebooks for heaven's sake?

The next volume was another poetry anthology. While there weren't any scribbled notes, the pages were creased and torn and half the front cover was missing. Inside the flyleaf, someone, presumably Nigel, had scrawled the word, *Chuck*. Sadly, that was probably the best thing to do with this one.

Tucked down the side of the box in among all the scruffy reading material was an envelope that might once have been white but was now yellowed with age. There was nothing written on the front but inside she found an old newspaper cutting.

The headline was:

Verdict of Accidental Death for Bar Room Brawl

Maddy took the article over to the window to study it in more detail. The print had that aged, slightly fuzzy look about it, and there was an accompanying black and white image of what looked like a group of people standing outside an official building with stone pillars flanking the entrance. A courthouse? Town hall? In the background were various people, and someone had ringed a face in the crowd with a blue biro. Who were these people? And why had Nigel kept this all these years?

Giving herself a break from sorting, Maddy sat down

at the desk to read the article to see if there were any more clues.

The death of Mason Garcia, age 32, at the Hope Diner in Lemon Hill on Tuesday July 29th has been ruled as accidental by the Medical Examiner's office. Witnesses reported seeing Mason attempting to break up the fight at the diner. He got caught up in the scuffle then fell hitting his head against the bar, sustaining fatal injuries. Alcohol and drugs are not thought to have been a factor in the cause of death.

Mason Garcia, originally from Carson City, worked as administrator for the city council and also as occasional roadie for a local rock group.

Carson City? Medical examiner? This was clearly from an American newspaper and probably just another bit of random rubbish that her cousin had accumulated over the years. It was odd that one figure had been ringed though—was that someone Nigel knew? Her journalist antennae twitched. The obvious answer was that this was something he'd read about while he'd been living in America, but how, or why, or even if, he was connected, was a total mystery. She dropped the cutting back in the box where she'd found it.

Chapter Eight

Surprises are foolish things. The pleasure is not enhanced, and the inconvenience is often considerable.
George Knightley, *Emma*

One of the less obvious disadvantages to living in a house the size of Meadowside was that the door knocker was wholly inadequate unless a) the occupant was within close proximity to the front door or b) the knocker was rapped with force against the plate.

Maddy had already observed that Sally preferred the self-entry and yoo-hoo arrangement. In contrast, the military tattoo being performed on the door plate that reverberated through to the kitchen meant whoever was at the front door this evening almost certainly was not Sally Cartwright. Did Jehovah's witnesses bother with remote country houses? Or maybe they were door-to-door salespeople? If so, they'd be out of luck unless they were from Poundland.

There was no safety chain on the solid oak door—clearly Nigel wasn't bothered about personal security—and it suddenly occurred to Maddy that this could be anyone. In films, women grabbed a poker for self-defence but all she could see in the hallway was an umbrella with a carved wooden handle in the shape of a duck's head. She grabbed it and cautiously opened the front door a couple of inches.

'Oh, Myra!'

'Good evening, Maddy. Were you just off out somewhere?'

Maddy followed Myra's gaze to the object in her hand. 'Er … no … I…' She opened the door fully and gestured politely. 'Come in.'

Myra stepped over the threshold, and wiped her shoes on the doormat. Maddy wondered whether she was going somewhere nice afterwards, or whether she always wore her pearl necklace when visiting neighbours. 'I'll get straight to the point as you're probably busy. I heard from Sally that you were looking for a lodger.'

'Well, I—'

'And a neighbour of a friend of my nephew was looking for somewhere temporary. They're very quiet. You won't even know they're here.'

'Right,' said Maddy uncertainly.

'You don't mind animals, do you?'

'No, on the contrary I—'

'I thought not. You look the practical type. Well, that's

all very satisfactory. I hope you don't mind, I took the liberty of bringing Luke along so that you can meet him and agree a moving in date.' Myra turned and gestured impatiently. 'Don't dawdle around on the doorstep, come inside, she won't bite you.'

Maddy hadn't noticed anyone standing behind Myra but now, as she stood aside, she almost choked in surprise.

'Maddy, this is Luke Hamilton; he's an author who needs space, peace and quiet. Luke, this is Maddy Shaw who owns a large house and has peace and quiet in abundance.'

'Luke? I think you mean Cameron Massey,' said Maddy, still struggling to work out how he was connected to Myra while simultaneously trying to think of a reason to refuse the offer. Looking at Myra in her pleated skirt and smart sweater, she felt rather self-conscious wearing her old but cosy fleece-lined leggings and her *Pride and Prejudice* sweatshirt that had become rather shapeless after too many washes, but then up until a few minutes ago she hadn't planned on inviting anyone in.

'It's an easy mistake,' he replied in a rather condescending voice. 'Cameron Massey is a pen name.'

'And maybe Maddy might succeed where we have previously failed, and persuade you to talk at our literary festival.'

That seemed rather a vain hope given their previous encounters weren't what one would describe as particularly amicable, but before Maddy could respond, they were interrupted by Myra's phone.

Myra raised her forefinger. 'Excuse me, I need to take

this call.' She took a few steps away and turned as she held the phone to her ear. 'Hello, how are you?'

'You didn't tell me you lived at Meadowside,' muttered Luke crossly, his eyebrows furrowed in disapproval.

'Well, you didn't exactly give me a chance to say anything; you just started yelling about sticks,' Maddy replied in the same urgent whisper.

'That's because I didn't want another four-hundred-pound vet bill.'

'So maybe you need to improve your dog security.'

Myra covered the phone for an instant. 'Everything okay?'

Maddy and Luke both replied in unison, with an attempt at a polite smile.

'Yes, thanks.'

'Absolutely.'

Maddy waited until Myra had put the phone back to her ear before asking the obvious question: 'So why are you looking for somewhere to stay if you live round here? What's wrong with your own house?'

'While that is not really any of your business, I have builders in at the moment. It's very disruptive; I can't write and Buster hates the noise.'

'Poor Buster.'

Luke threw her a pointed look. 'So are you looking for a lodger or not? Myra seemed to think you could do with the money.' Before Maddy could respond he continued, 'I'm looking at paying up to five hundred a month but I'd stretch to five fifty if I can work in the library.'

Five hundred and fifty pounds a month! She could do a lot with that. Get the roof fixed for one thing. And get someone in to overhaul the central heating. It would be nice to be able to walk around indoors without wearing two pairs of socks and her padded jacket. If he was holed up in the library every day she wouldn't really see much of him anyway, and having a dog around the house might be fun.

Myra's voice wafted over. '…yes, yes, okay, I'll pick you up from the station. I'll be there in thirty minutes.' She jammed her phone back in her bag and turned back to her lodger-in-waiting with an enquiring look. 'All settled?'

'I don't think Ms Shaw actually wants—'

'Yes, thanks,' Maddy said brightly. 'We've agreed on five hundred and fifty a month to include the library. And I'll throw in some doggy daycare too.'

'Excellent. I have to dash; my son's returned from holiday and missed the coach, so I'm picking him up from the station.'

Maddy waited for Myra to walk ahead before she murmured to Luke, 'If it makes you feel better, I'm doing this for Buster and not because of your charming wit and manners.'

Luke spun around. 'What are you on about? I don't have any charming wit and manners.'

'Precisely.'

Chapter Nine

1ST APRIL

I have no idea of being so easily persuaded. When I have made up my mind, I have made it.
Louisa Musgrove, *Persuasion*

Over the course of the following two days, Luke moved across his computer equipment, books and notebooks, various writing essentials, Buster's dog bed, food and toys, and a selection of clothes. After inspecting the meagre contents of Maddy's kitchen cupboards he also retrieved his coffee machine and several packets of Hobnobs, which he maintained were essential items.

Clearly being a bestselling author wasn't as money-making as Maddy had assumed, judging by the state of the scruffy-looking Vauxhall Astra that was now parked outside. Just to be on the safe side, she had re-read all the legal papers Mr Chapman had left with her and nowhere did it mention anything about taking in lodgers with pets. Today was the 1st April—the official moving-in day—and she'd received April's payment in advance which made the whole arrangement far more agreeable from her point of view. She had already decided that having Buster around would be fun although she hoped he wouldn't be too unsettled by the change of scenery.

Like her, Luke had avoided choosing Nigel's old bedroom, and instead opted for one of the bedrooms at the other end of the landing. Although smaller, it had clearly been designed as a guest room and had a small ceramic wash basin and shaving mirror in the corner of the room.

'Right then, Buster, now you've sniffed round the entire house, who's up for a nice walk this morning?'

Luke looked at her warily. 'Are you sure about this?'

Maddy drew herself upright and pulled her shoulders back. 'Absolutely. I enjoy a good walk and as I said, I'm happy to keep Buster entertained.' She didn't add that it also helped fill up her rather empty day. 'Go and write your book and we'll see you later, won't we, Buster?'

They had barely taken two steps outside before she heard a strange, low-level rumbling noise, and it was several seconds before she realised the sound was emanating from Buster. 'What is it, boy? What's the matter?'

As they crossed the terrace, she spotted what Buster had clearly already heard: a man in a khaki gilet and a black beanie hat was digging a hole in the flowerbed at the far side of the lawn. With an alarming burst of energy, Buster raced forward, straining at the lead, and Maddy struggled to hold on to him as he bolted across the lawn. She hadn't even completed one morning of doggy daycare and now her charge was possibly seconds away from trying to rip someone to shreds. And what was this person doing in her garden anyway? She tried to dig the heels of her trainers into the grass but the ground was damp and had little purchase. Her shoulder strained as she was dragged across the lawn like an inexperienced water-skier, ploughing a furrow as she went.

'Stop! Buster, wait!'

Suddenly there was a bump, an awkward fall followed by a jolt of pain and then the lead slipped out of her hands. Despite the shock of the fall and the indignity of pitching headfirst onto the wet grass, her first thought was one of relief that Luke wasn't around to witness it.

After a manic charge across the lawn followed by judicious sniffing, Buster was clearly now content that the man was no threat to Meadowside's security, and lay panting on the grass. 'You silly dog!' Maddy shouted tearfully. 'What did you do that for!' Buster's ears drooped and his tail stopped mid-wag.

'You've got a good guard dog there. Thought I'd have to leg it.'

'He's not mine, he belongs to the lodger. And he's in disgrace.'

The man's face was a picture of apology. 'Sorry to give you a fright, I've been away for a week so I'm trying to catch up.' He held out a work-roughened hand and helped her up. 'I'm Jem. Nice to see you again.'

Maddy attempted to brush the mud and grass stains from her clothes. The flood of adrenaline had left her feeling shaky, but even so her rescuer, whose straw-coloured hair poked out in random clumps from under his beanie, looked familiar.

'You sat behind us at the funeral, didn't you? Are you Myra's son?'

Jem nodded. 'Yes. Can't afford my own place so I'm still living with the parents.' He upturned the bucket he was filling with weeds and brushed the top with his hand. 'Here, park yourself on this for a minute.'

Maddy smiled thinly and gently lowered her bottom. The bucket was hard and unyielding but it gave her a minute to catch her breath. Her hand was grazed from her fall and her trainers were a greener shade of white.

'Look, I'm sorry if this sounds blunt, but why are you here?'

Jem's eyebrows furrowed together. 'I don't follow you. I do the gardens here. Have done for years. Three times a week—Monday, Wednesday and Friday. One of my best jobs. Didn't Mum mention it?'

'Right. No. Well, the thing is…' Maddy scrabbled around to find a polite way of saying what she needed to. 'The thing is, I can't afford a gardener. There's only a small housekeeping budget you see, most of which is likely to go on utility bills. Much as I'd like the gardens to look pretty, I'm sorry but I don't have enough money to pay you, or anyone else.'

Jem chuckled. 'Ah, I get where you're coming from now. That's all taken care of. Mum says Nigel left money in his will to pay for the gardening for as long as you're here.'

Yet again Maddy felt wrong-footed, and she was beginning to feel that Mr Chapman's notes contained some serious omissions.

'Oh, I nearly forgot.' Jem pulled off soil-stained leather gardening gloves and upzipped a pocket in his gilet, from which he tugged a folded and slightly crumpled piece of A4 paper. 'Mum asked me to give you the agenda for the next meeting of the literary committee. Sally said you were okay with all the arrangements.'

That was a major understatement. She tucked the piece of paper into the pocket of her jeans. She would read that away from nosey villagers.

'So how is your first day of doggy day care going?' asked Luke as he wandered into the kitchen to make himself a cup of coffee later that afternoon.

Maddy gave Luke her best confident smile. He might not be overly enamoured with his choice of landlady but Maddy could see how attached he was to Buster. 'It was great, wasn't it, Buster?' She certainly wasn't going to mention the bruised hip and muscle sprain in her shoulder. 'We've done a great walk, explored a bit of the field behind the house, and the final score of the chase-the-ball challenge was Buster sixteen, Maddy nil. How is your writing day going?'

'Fine.'

Maddy waited two seconds in case there was any other information forthcoming. 'A win-win solution then.'

Luke's eyebrows gave an ironic twitch. 'You like finding solutions to things, don't you?'

'What's wrong with that?'

'Must be your agony aunt genes.'

'I'm not an agony aunt anymore.' Why had she just blurted that out? Of all the people to confess to, she had to pick the county's most unsympathetic person to reveal what was still a very painful admission.

His eyebrows rose a millimetre. 'So Jane Austen finally reached her sell-by date?'

'No,' replied Maddy taking a defensive tone. 'If you must know, *I* did. I got sacked via email on the day of that interview.'

Luke didn't reply instantly, nor did he break eye contact. It was unnerving but Maddy wasn't in the mood to back down now. 'I'm really sorry to hear that. You enjoyed your work.'

'And how would you know?' demanded Maddy.

'Because you were so passionate about it. Too many people have lukewarm opinions on things and just say what they think other people want them to say. You stuck to your guns, despite coming under fire. I admire that quality.'

For some strange reason, despite the rather back-handed compliment, Maddy felt a tiny flicker of appreciation and couldn't help but smile. Maybe there were other facets to her argumentative lodger as yet undiscovered.

Now they were having a conversation rather than a debate, Maddy was curious to find out more about her lodger. 'You said you had builders at your house—so what are they building?'

'Once the destruction is completed, it's going to be an extension, plus some internal re-modelling of the original house but there's been endless problems already.'

'Oh dear,' said Maddy sympathetically.

'And it's very noisy. It felt like they were pulling the existing house down around my ears—the clatter and commotion was non-stop. After a few days, Buster started whining from the minute they showed up in the morning. Then it progressed to attempted escapology, as you discovered a couple of weeks ago.'

'I think he's turned pro,' Maddy said, giving Buster a fond glance.

For a few moments the conversation lulled. It was a slightly uncomfortable pause since the lodger/landlady relationship was not at the point yet where there might otherwise have been a companionable silence. Maddy decided now would be a good opportunity to elicit his opinion on something.

'Changing the subject, can I ask what you know about the Cotlington Literary Festival?'

Luke's gaze slid sideways in a distinctly shifty manner. 'Some local get-together for amateur wannabe writers.'

'Would you ever consider taking part?'

Luke almost choked on a mouthful of coffee. 'Hell, no!'

'There's no need to look so scandalised. Anyone would think I'd just asked if you'd like to take part in a public orgy. You know, they'd probably really appreciate the help of a world-class author.'

'It seemed to run perfectly well without my involvement, thank you. Although as the house is now under new ownership'—he gestured at Maddy—'we've probably seen the last of it, thank goodness.'

'Oh come on, it can't be that bad! I think you're being a bit harsh.'

'I don't believe in fudging it, and it's not as if it's my responsibility, is it?'

'But if it were, what would you do?'

'Well, for a start I'd line up a high-profile keynote speaker. Someone who will attract paying punters as well as other authors. Then cut the deadwood. Advertise on social media. Obtain sponsorship.' He gave her a penetrating stare that generated a response somewhere between a flutter of excitement and shiver of anticipation. 'Why are you so interested in all this anyway?'

Clearly Luke was not an avid reader of *Cotlington Chat*, for which Maddy heaved a private sigh of relief. However, she ought to own up, oughtn't she? At some point it would become patently obvious that she was not only hosting it but supposedly running it.

'Well, I—'

Her planned confession was halted by a strident ringtone. She had never been so pleased to hear a phone interruption, and was even more delighted that it was his. Luke pulled his phone from his pocket and looked at the screen.

'Builders again,' he muttered.

'Hello,' he barked into the phone. 'What now? Can't it wait until tomorrow?… Yes… No, I don't…. What the hell d'you mean, you've found bodies?'

Chapter Ten

I could easily forgive his pride, if he had not mortified mine
Elizabeth Bennet, *Pride and Prejudice*

'Surely you're not that gullible?' said Maddy, trying hard to smother a snort of laughter.

In the short time she'd been acquainted with Luke Hamilton and his alter ego Cameron Massey, she had quickly found out that he detested being teased, but this had to be a prank. She had a sudden mental image of a group of muscled workmen, sitting round a concrete mixer, mugs of tea in hand, having a good chortle at their employer's expense.

A small snigger escaped her lips. 'Just look at the date on your phone.'

After years of working in various offices, Maddy had

seen dozens of April fool's jokes—some better than others. Years ago, she'd worked as an office junior in the city where the culture of long hours meant that the kitchen area often doubled as a breakfast bar. One day a new toaster appeared with a laminated card on which was printed the words *Voice Activated*, together with a series of numbers indicating the degrees of toastiness. Those sitting near the kitchen were entertained for the entire morning by people shouting numbers at the toaster, then swearing at the chargrilled offering that popped out, having failed to notice that the toasting dial was already set to maximum.

'I thought April fool's jokes were meant to expire at midday.'

Maddy shrugged. 'Maybe they didn't twig that bit.'

Luke put his empty coffee cup in the sink. 'I'd better go. I won't be impressed if this is a joke.'

'You won't be impressed if it isn't, either.'

After Luke had left, Maddy removed today's page from the countdown calendar, now hanging up on a nail in the kitchen. It was a picture of her and Alice laughing and pointing at Maddy's burned banana cake disaster. Only 347 leaky roof days to go.

It was over an hour later before Luke returned. As soon as he heard his master's footsteps, Buster barged past Maddy and bounded into the hall with the energy of a squirrel on steroids, and threw himself at Luke.

'Hello, boy!' After a fast and furious bout of tail wagging, Buster promptly rolled over onto his back, waving his paws in the air.

Maddy laughed as Luke crouched down to scratch his tummy. 'I think everyone needs a Buster in their life.' She looked enquiringly at Luke as he continued fussing Buster.

'Come on then, what was the joke? Was it the remains of someone's dinner or did they go the whole hog and acquire a medical skeleton?'

Luke stood up and his mouth tightened. 'Neither. They've unearthed actual human remains.'

Maddy's smile froze. 'What? You mean like … someone's died in your garden?'

'Yes, although clearly not recently. The builders have had to cease work until it's been investigated. Now they're calling in a team of archaeologists to dig up the rest of the garden. The person was buried with a silver artefact—'

'Really!'

'—and there's more than a possibility that there could be more burials. It's an utter nightmare; the whole timetable has been set back weeks, possibly months.'

'Oh.'

'Indeed. Even you might have a tough time finding a solution to that lot.'

Maddy agreed. She had no intention of getting involved in Luke's building difficulties, having plenty of her own matters to worry about. The fact that the next meeting of the Cotlington Literary Festival Committee was imminent had sharpened her focus somewhat, and she fully intended to raise the subject with Luke again.

Over the course of the following week, both Maddy and Luke established mutually compatible morning routines. Although Maddy had first turn in the bathroom, they were nearly always down for breakfast at the same time. Maddy usually just made do with some toast but Luke preferred to create his own muesli and already had half a dozen boxes in the cupboard containing all sorts of nuts, seeds and dried fruits. Once breakfast was over, Maddy took Buster out for his first walk of the day, and Luke did stuff on his phone before heading off to write in the library.

Maddy had quickly noticed that unlike their Valentine's Day interview where Luke had been wearing what she thought of as photoshoot attire, at Meadowside he seemed to prefer jeans and a sweater, which made him appear more approachable. This morning she was about to put that to the test.

'Luke, before you head off to the library, I need to confess something.'

'Oh, this will be interesting!' Luke put down his phone into which he had been busily tapping messages. 'Let me guess, you've never actually read any Jane Austen books.'

'What? That's scandalous; of course I have!'

Almost instantly, Maddy castigated herself for rising to the bait. She was already aware that he enjoyed provoking a reaction from her. She resolved to keep her face completely neutral.

'Okay then…' Luke made a pretence of trying to

think hard. 'You once did a runner in a restaurant to avoid paying the bill.'

'No!'

Luke shook his head. 'It's just too easy with you. Go on then, what's the big surprise?'

'It's not a confession of past wrongdoings, it's just that…' She took a deep breath before continuing. 'When I asked you about the literary festival, I had a reason for needing your opinion.'

'And that is?'

Maddy readjusted the scrunchie in her hair as she decided how to phrase this. 'You know how I inherited the house? Well, I seem to have also inherited the position of chair of the literary festival.'

Whatever reaction Maddy might have expected, it was not one of raucous laughter.

'And you think *I'm* gullible! I hope you turned the offer down.'

'Um…'

Luke's mouth twitched. 'You didn't, did you?' He shook his head. 'Good luck with that one. From what I've heard it's absolutely dreadful.'

'Yesterday you said you didn't know anything about it,' said Maddy in an accusing tone.

'I don't, not really. It's just hearsay, but it doesn't get any write-ups online. Or mentions in any magazines. Still, it's your funeral.'

'But we could make it into something a lot better! Like you said before, get the right speakers, a bit of publicity.'

'And who's "we"?'

Maddy smiled persuasively. 'I was hoping that I might be able to enlist your assistance while you're here. After all, having the bestselling Cameron Massey as keynote speaker would be a huge coup. To be honest, I can't understand why they haven't roped you in before.'

'I like to have a bit of privacy. Hence the pen name. Is that bossy Myra woman paying you or something?'

'No. But think of the legions of adoring fans who would flock to Cotlington to see you. Oh, and you could read an excerpt from your new novel!' she added as her imagination got to work. 'What do you say?'

'No.'

'Please?'

'Still no.'

'Is that it?'

'Why would I want to make an appearance at the world's worst literary event?'

'Don't you think that's a bit of an over-reaction? After all Phineas T Barnum once said there's no such thing as bad publicity.'

'He also said there's a sucker born every minute.'

Maddy sighed. 'Well, it was worth a try.' She wagged a finger at Luke. 'And I haven't given up yet either.'

If she was going to be roped into this event, she would do her best to assist. And Luke wasn't the only person with contacts; she was, until recently, a full-time professional magazine writer, she reminded herself. She had some experience of attending project meetings at work and was on last year's Christmas party committee, even though that only met three times and one of those bore a marked resemblance to a pub crawl.

Despite the personal pep talk, she was still rather apprehensive about chairing a committee, and later on she needed to do some more homework on previous years' events in advance of tomorrow's meeting. The idea of turning up to her very first meeting with a bestselling author on the speaker's list would have done her self-confidence the world of good, but there was no harm in also trying other avenues.

For this morning's walk, she took Buster along the road that led out of the village for a bit of variety. There appeared to be plenty of places that required investigation, so taking advantage of the leisurely pace, she called Briony's number again.

'Hello! Guess who?' she sang down the phone as she strolled along. 'So did you have a chance to ask around in the office? I was hoping that I might persuade one or two of you down to sleepy Cotlington. Carrie was always great at giving talks, wasn't she?'

'You-know-who is lurking this morning.' Briony replied in a hushed voice. 'Give me five minutes and I'll call you back.'

Their boss was well known for patrolling the office first thing in the morning. He had only taken over as editor-in-chief seven months previously and in Maddy's opinion, his personal skills needed some serious work. He would make Cameron Massey on a bad day seem like Florence Nightingale. If anything, in the last month she'd worked there he'd got worse, and staff had taken to going in to the office as little as possible. As PA to the boss, Briony was everyone's preferred choice of contact.

'Hi there, sorry about that—I've disappeared to the loos so apologies for the echo.'

'No problem, you're doing me a favour and I'm really grateful that you've asked around.'

'There haven't been any takers, sorry.'

'Really? I thought Carrie would leap at the chance. I don't have vast funds for speakers but I'm sure I can work something out.'

'It's not that.' There was something in her voice that sounded a note of caution. 'Look, this is difficult for me to say because you're my friend, but I think you ought to know.'

Maddy's hand trembled as she gripped the phone. 'Know what?'

'You-know-who overheard me talking to Carrie and a few of the others. I didn't realise he was listening. Anyway, he made it clear that he didn't want them helping you.'

'What!'

'I know. I didn't understand it either so I did a bit of snooping around on the quiet. It wasn't until I spoke to one of the editors that I found out the real reason, and I checked it out for myself. You probably don't remember, but at the beginning of February, the Dear Jane column had a letter from Puzzled of Putney. She had written in saying she'd met this gorgeous, rich man who flirted endlessly, pestered her into going out with him, then months later when she finally agreed to move in with him he seemed to lose interest, and had been flirting with one of her friends instead. You replied to say that he sounded like he enjoyed the chase but maybe wasn't looking for a long-term relationship. You advised that he was a Henry Crawford type who should be treated with caution and that she needed to talk to him rather than be strung along.

'Yes, I remember.' Maddy was always careful on how she worded her responses, but in the end it was up to the writer to decide what to do. They were a magazine after all, not the Citizens Advice Bureau.

'Well, it turns out she got fed up of being strung along and ended the relationship.'

'That's nice of her to write in. I'm glad I was able to help.' Maddy's Dear Jane column often received thank yous from people. Knowing that she had in some small way been able to help people deal with a difficult relationship was one of the many things she had loved about the job.

'Erm… she didn't.' Briony made a strange gulping sound. 'Write in, I mean. Turns out Puzzled of Putney was You-know-who's girlfriend. And he was the one who got dumped.'

'Oh no!' Maddy stood rooted to the spot as a spasm of panic swept through her. 'I'd never have replied if I'd known who it was—I honestly didn't have a clue!' Even though her boss was a prat and a grumpy one to boot, she would never have deliberately humiliated him in his own magazine. How the hell was she to know who Puzzled of Putney was?

'We all know that. But when he heard me asking people about being able to help you out... Well, you can imagine how that went down.'

Maddy could picture it all too well. And something that had bothered her for the last month and half suddenly made perfect sense. 'That's why I got the sack, wasn't it?'

'I just want you to know that I had nothing to do with that,' Briony said, her voice resonant with emotion. 'He must have known that I would have told you if I'd found out. Honestly Maddy, if I could afford to work somewhere else right now I really would.'

'It's not your fault; please don't chuck in your job on my account.'

Bloody, bloody man. Talking to Briony had dragged all the stress and upset to the surface again. The email she'd received back in February was just a smoke screen, with its pointless platitudes and best wishes. She hadn't been sacked because the column was out-of-date and no longer relevant. Ms Austen had been used as an excuse to get rid of her because she had unintentionally dented someone's ego. Well, now he had proved just how horrible and calculating he was, Puzzled of Putney was well shot of him.

Maddy extracted a broken custard cream from the pocket of her coat for her bored charge who was clearly wondering why the walk had turned into a stand. 'Come on, Buster, let's go home.'

She marched back to the house. Why were men so difficult? She'd been banking on her friends to help her and now her only option was the person who could do the job standing on his head with both eyes shut but had declined to help for some pointless nefarious reason of his own. Why couldn't he just say a few words? Surely he'd want to promote his own book? Heaven knows that after the disappointing reaction to his last book, his agent must be desperate for a bit of positive publicity.

Maddy tugged her wellingtons off—a welcome purchase now she had some money in the bank—and chucked them in the corner of the kitchen. Without taking off her jacket she walked through to the hall.

The door to the library was closed and being a solid wood door, completely muffled the sound of activity, which meant that Luke was not disturbed by her comings and goings. He rarely appeared before late afternoon, but today she would invite him to join her for lunch and re-open negotiations. After all, even writers needed refuelling, despite the copious supply of Hobnobs.

Should she knock? Maybe that was a bit formal. He wasn't her boss and this was her house. Carefully, she opened the door and poked her head round. Maddy's nose wrinkled at the stuffiness of the unaired room, which mingled with the faint smell of coffee. Luke's computer sat open on the desk with two lines typed in the middle of the screen, but the chair was vacant. Perhaps he'd gone out? It wasn't as if he was her prisoner. She walked over to the French doors and then almost fell over in shock.

What the hell? Sprawled out on the sofa under the throw was the body of her presumed absent lodger. The throw partially covered his face but there was enough of him visible to confirm this wasn't some random squatter.

'Luke?'

An arm reached up and pulled the throw from his face.

'Are you ill? Do you need a doctor?'

'No to both questions,' he mumbled. Luke sat up slowly, pushing aside the throw and rubbing his face with his hands.

'In that case, I think you could do with some fresh air.' Maddy shoved open the doors and inhaled deeply, enjoying the cool draught that wafted in. Already there was a scent of spring flowers, mingled with that fresh country air smell that you never got in London.

'Are you checking up on me? I'm not nicking the books if that's what you're worried about.'

Maddy whirled round. 'I would hardly have let you stay if I thought you were going to pinch anything, would I? I actually came to ask if you wanted to join me for lunch. I thought you might want a break from writing. Although, it looks like you were otherwise engaged.'

Maddy waited for the pithy comeback. The snarky retort telling her to mind her own business. Technically it was none of her business what Luke did during the day but—today at least—it was obviously not writing.

Luke's rubbed his hands through his hair making him look like he'd accidentally stuck his finger in an electric socket. 'Thanks,' he mumbled. 'Lunch would be nice.'

It wasn't a particularly exciting adjective but she'd take nice. And you couldn't go too far wrong with a few sandwiches.

In the end, as she had company, she decided to make a bit of an effort and walked to the village store to buy some crisps, scotch eggs and a bag of salad to go with her sandwich plans. A rummage in one of the dining room cupboards produced a red chequered tablecloth which, after a thorough shaking out outside, she placed over the kitchen table, giving it a slightly creased French bistro look. She was pushing the boat out with a tablecloth, but ironing it was a step too far.

Luke was clearly in need of caffeine but in addition to the coffee cups she added a jug of water as it looked attractive. And a couple of pretty etched glasses. Candles would look good but that might suggest romantic overtones, which was not the intended idea. She'd forgotten about buying serviettes so folded kitchen paper would have to suffice.

It gave her something to do anyway, and she took a picture to send to Alice, followed by a quick message to update her on what she'd found out this morning.

Buster was overjoyed to see Luke appear at lunchtime. Although Luke's instructions for Buster had included a no snacks rule, Maddy wasn't so sure Buster had signed up to the agreement, and after several days of Maddy sharing bits of her lunch with her canine companion, said companion was now staring at her with a hungry expression on his face and making intermittent whining noises that clearly said, 'Feed me, I'm starving.'

Maddy surreptitiously pulled a strip of ham from her sandwich and dropped it casually at the side of her chair. Buster caught it before it even hit the floor.

'I did see that, in case you were wondering,' said Luke, with an amused twitch of his lips. 'He's hard to say no to, isn't he?'

'That we can definitely agree on,' said Maddy. 'How long have you had him?'

'Just over three years now. He's a rescue dog so we're not sure exactly how old he is. He's great with people but doesn't like noise. Especially if made by diggers and jack-hammers. It's good of you to have him here. A lot of places don't allow dogs.'

'I'm delighted to have his company. I'm used to noise so I'm still getting used to living somewhere so quiet.'

'Quieter during the day maybe,' replied Luke.

Maddy helped herself to a scotch egg. 'Oh, do you mean all the creaks and knocking? It's an old house. It's over a hundred years old—that's probably just contraction and expansion noises,' she said in an attempt to sound reassuring.

Maddy studied his face. Despite the healthy tan, he had a tired look about him, but there was definitely something about his eyes that hinted at anxiety. 'So has the house been keeping you awake at night? Is that why I found you asleep this morning?'

Luke threw her a challenging look. 'And is this part of the rental agreement?'

'What do you mean?'

'Being subjected to endless questions about what I'm doing.'

'Believe it or not, I was actually trying to sound concerned. You are a hard person to help, you know.'

'Have you ever considered, Dear Jane, that I don't want your help?'

It was probably the use of the words "Dear Jane" that did it. It hadn't been said in a particularly nasty way, but a surge of self-pity crashed over her nonetheless. She enjoyed helping people solve problems—it made her feel useful. It was what she was good at. What she used to be good at. And then maybe, just maybe, the hurt of knowing she was sacked for reasons that had nothing to do with her abilities and everything to do with a personal grudge, might not hurt as much as it did right now.

She looked down as she reached for a piece of kitchen paper and dabbed at the tear rapidly forming in the corner of her eye before it escaped down her face. She wouldn't cry in front of this arrogant man. It had been a mistake to invite him to lunch with her, but in truth she found it companionable having someone to share the house with, and knowing that when she locked up at night there was someone else around.

Buster edged closer to her chair and put his head on her lap giving her a soft whine as if to say *I'm here if you need me*. She pinched her lips and stroked his soft head as her vision blurred with more tears. Buster sat calmly and snugly, all the while making gentle, plaintive noises, and clearly doing his doggy best to be a comfort to his new friend.

Maddy heard a chair scrape against the tiled floor and receding footsteps. Clearly her concern was not required. A half-eaten ham sandwich sat on Luke's abandoned plate, and she offered it to Buster who wolfed it down.

'Thanks for sticking around, boy.' The no snacks rule could take a hike.

Chapter Eleven

There will be little rubs and disappointments everywhere, and we are all apt to expect too much; but then, if one scheme of happiness fails, human nature turns to another; if the first calculation is wrong, we make a second better: we find comfort somewhere.

Mrs Grant, *Mansfield Park*

Maddy was running hot water for washing up when Luke returned. She didn't bother turning round —he had already made his position perfectly clear.

'Oh, I see. My sandwich went in the bin, did it?'

'No actually, it went in the dog. But from your perspective, it probably amounts to the same thing. I assumed by your absence that you'd finished your lunch.'

Luke flapped a piece of paper. 'I went back to print this off to show you.'

Maddy wheeled round. 'What is it? Your terms and conditions?'

'It's an email from my editor. It might explain a few things. I'm not good at all the personal stuff; I know that's your thing and I threw your offer of help back in your face. It's unforgivably rude and I'm sorry.'

Maddy took the proffered paper but continued to stare at the floor.

'I'll have you know,' said Luke in a gentler voice, 'that I don't apologise to just anyone.'

Well, at least that was honest. Maddy gradually raised her eyes until they met his. For several seconds, they stared at each other as though they had met for the first time, and had not already had bruising clashes of opinion. Alice was right, he was gorgeous, even down to his tousle-haired stubbly look. His dark eyes fixed hers with a piercing stare. With a few character modifications he could easily be the brooding hero of the romantic novels she loved—too much to hope that he was a Darcy in disguise though.

He gestured towards the table and she sat down to read the email. It was concise and to the point. Reviews of book seven had been critical. As in derogatory, not literary. The scheduled publication date for book eight had already been put back due to disagreements over plot suggestions, and there was a thinly disguised order not to become embroiled in rows on social or other media. They would like another Detective Inspector Jason Friend novel but not with the proposed storyline. Please advise progress ASAP.

'Oh dear.' Maddy wondered whether the Valentine's debate they'd had just over seven weeks ago came under the heading of "rows on other media". 'So, when do you have to reply?'

'When I've got something to report. And right now I don't.'

Maddy pursed her lips. Clearly there was more to this than just these bland sentences, but despite Luke's apology, she wasn't sure how to respond.

Have you ever considered, Dear Jane, that I don't want your help?

The words echoed in her head. They might have been said partly in jest, but they served as a cutting reminder that she had been declared officially redundant, and not just by her employer. She was enjoying having Buster here even though Luke scored below average on the Maddy Shaw lodger rating. However, his presence in the house didn't require her to sort out his problems. She had got that message loud and clear and in any case, she had enough of her own to be getting on with.

She handed back the piece of paper. 'Sorry to hear that. I'm sure Cameron Massey has got everything in hand.'

'As a matter of fact, he hasn't. He is thoroughly pissed off with writing stories about DI Friend and wants to kill him off, but everyone wants more of the same. Then when he writes more of the same, it's labelled boring and repetitive.' Luke sighed and banged his hand against the table making Buster twitch nervously. 'Do you mind if I make myself another sandwich? I'm really hungry.'

Maddy gestured to the bread bag sitting on the counter. 'Be my guest. I'm going to head off upstairs to look through some of Nigel's boxes in the attic. There are some programmes from previous years' festivals that looked interesting. I use that term in the loosest possible sense.'

It was past five o'clock by the time Maddy decided she'd done enough poking about in boxes and needed to stretch her legs. It had been an interesting afternoon though, and while she didn't find any further information to explain what that American newspaper cutting was about or what the F box was meant to signify, she'd had a nostalgic trip down memory lane when she'd come across a letter from her dad, dated Christmas 1986, which had enclosed a photograph of her as a baby. Despite an extensive search, there'd been no other correspondence from the family that she could see, but she was touched that Nigel had kept this letter all these years.

She tried to picture a younger Nigel Shaw arriving back in the UK, moving into this amazing house. How had he afforded that? Why hadn't he contacted the family? What had they said to cause a lifetime of separation? She sighed. All those wasted years. Both her grandparents had passed away years ago but she wished she'd asked them about Nigel.

Maddy had also come across some of Nigel's notes in a folder from last year's literary festival. As she headed back down the attic stairs, she hoped she might pull together a few ideas of her own to bring to next week's committee meeting.

She emerged on the upstairs landing to find Buster sitting waiting for her with what looked like an envelope tied to his collar.

'Hello, boy!'

A tail thumped the floor in anticipation of treats.

'Are you the tailed messenger today? Is that for me?' Maddy knelt down and untied the envelope attached to his collar. Inside was a single sheet of folded A5 paper, clearly torn rather clumsily from a notebook.

Dear Jane,
> *I hear you are rather good at helping people with problems, and I know you speak from experience and honesty so would value your opinion on something. Luke Hamilton might not need any help but I do. Can I buy you dinner tonight?*
> *Best,*
> *Cameron Massey*

Buster's expression reminded her of the films where hotel bell boys waited hopefully for tips after carrying an entire cage of luggage up to someone's room. She patted him on the back.

'Come on then, you can deliver the reply and collect your payment from Luke.'

Buster followed her into her bedroom and while Maddy hunted out pen and paper, Buster had a good sniff around at everything, especially Maddy's shoes.

What should she write? She was still cross with him, although the prospect of dinner that she didn't have to cook for herself was appealing. After three uninteresting microwave meals on the trot, something that bore more resemblance to haute cuisine than simply hot cuisine would be a much-welcomed change.

> *Dear Cameron,*
> *You haven't mentioned what your problem is but I'm happy to*
> *help if I can. Dinner would be most welcome, thank you.*
> *Best,*

Maddy paused. As he'd written to Jane she ought to reply in kind. Jane's advice was normally on relationships but maybe it was time for her to branch out a bit.

> *Jane*
> *P.S. The messenger would like a chicken-flavoured tip please!*

She switched notes, putting hers in the envelope and re-fastening it to Buster's collar. 'Go find Luke!' She pointed towards the stairs. Buster didn't move. Maybe that wasn't a name he was familiar with. Maddy tried again. 'Go find Daddy!'

Buster jumped up and trotted off downstairs and Maddy headed back to her bedroom. Job number one was to find something to wear for her meal out. As she got changed, she couldn't help but smile at the idea of the somewhat abrasive Cameron Massey calling himself "daddy".

The restaurant was only a fifteen-minute drive from Cotlington, and Maddy was excited at the thought of going out—properly out—and not just across the fields or into the village. She had assumed – erroneously as it turned out – that they'd be going in the scruffy Vauxhall Astra that had been parked out the front for the last week. Instead Luke had driven it back to his house, reappearing twenty minutes later at the wheel of a sleek silver-grey Jaguar that was so shiny it almost sparkled. Maddy stared at it. Correction: it did sparkle.

The inside was just as impressive as the outside and Maddy felt like a celebrity just stepping into it; the cream leather interior was spotless and still had a hint of a new car smell. Based on the trail of evidence Buster left behind him in the house by way of hair, paw prints and randomly deposited toys, she had expected to see muddy paw marks everywhere, but it was immaculate.

'Have you lost something?' Luke asked as he navigated the early evening traffic heading into Haxford. 'You seem to be looking around.'

'Just casting admiring glances,' she replied with a smile. 'And wondering how on earth you manage to prevent Buster from leaving pawprints everywhere.'

'Ah. Well, the trick there is not to let him anywhere near this car. You may think it very flash having two cars, but I'm sure you can appreciate this one isn't very practical for everyday purposes when you have a dog. I left the Astra back at the house and I can assure you that Buster has trampled everywhere inside that car, despite the throw over the back seats.'

Maddy chuckled. 'It seems perfectly reasonable to me for Buster to have his own transportation; and I don't judge people by how many cars they have.'

'Just as well—I definitely wouldn't take anyone out in the Bustermobile.'

'So should I feel suitably honoured going in the posh car?'

'Totally. But don't forget it's only because Cameron Massey needs some advice from Ms Austen. Think of it as two professionals having a business discussion.'

He could think of it any way he liked. She was having dinner with a rather gorgeous man who owned a swanky car. Beat that, Lizzy Bennet!

The menu prices at Le Caprice were equally swanky but as they studied the menu, Luke assured her he was paying. Maddy wondered whether his half-joking sugges-tion of it being a business meeting was so that he could claim it as a tax-deductible expense, but who cared what he did—this was a treat and she was determined to enjoy it. Her titchy housekeeping budget certainly didn't run to meals at this sort of establishment and it could be many months before she got another opportunity to go anywhere. Her parents had promised to come and visit but being taken out by your mum and dad, lovely as that was, was hardly in the same league as this!

Il Caprice was situated in what was called Haxford's Old Town. Parking was pot luck round here, Luke had explained, but they had found somewhere not too far from the restaurant, and enjoyed a leisurely stroll across the river bridge, and through the quaint pedestrian area. The only parts of Haxford Maddy had seen were in the area around the railway station. This part was altogether more to her taste, especially the Edwardian stone façade of Pennewicks Clothing Emporium that stood proudly at the end of Queen Street.

After the waiter had taken food orders and brought over their drinks, Maddy lifted up her glass and took a sip.

'Cheers,' she said as she carefully clinked her glass against his. Luke reciprocated. If this was payment for advice, he was welcome to ask anytime.

As if by mutual consent, they kept the conversation light while they waited for food to arrive. Maddy talked about her shock at inheriting the house, and the problem with heating it, not to mention the leaky roof. Luke regaled her with the story of his house renovation that was rapidly turning into a three-volume saga.

'So how is the dig coming along?' Maddy asked. 'Any idea when they'll be finished?'

Luke held up his hands in a gesture of surrender. 'No idea. I don't pretend to understand the red tape and processes involved but when I popped over to collect the car, the place looked like a bomb site and they've now dug up over half the garden.'

'Well, Buster is welcome to stay for as long as he likes; he's great company.'

'Oh I see. So what happens to his owner?'

Maddy pressed her finger against her cheek and pretended to think for a few seconds. 'Well… Yeah, okay, he can stay too.' She smiled. Even if he didn't want to help her with the festival it livened up the day having company, and her agony aunt antennae, even though no longer in daily use, told her that he was troubled about something.

'Trout in a wild garlic sauce for madame, and for you sir, steak béarnaise. The waiter placed the dishes in front of them and for several minutes the business of eating took centre stage.

After a few more sips of wine, Maddy felt sufficiently emboldened to ask what she'd been curious to know since reading the note round Buster's collar. She put down her knife and fork for a second. Luke clearly felt more comfortable discussing difficult issues using his alter ego so she followed suit. 'So Mr Massey, what can I help you with?'

Luke's shoulders tensed, and his mouth twitched as though someone was pulling an invisible string.

'I'm not sure you can, to be honest. But I wanted to take you out for dinner anyway. Just to say thank you for having me and Buster to stay. I know it was foisted upon you.'

His words blossomed inside her like small flower buds opening in time lapse photography, until her mouth parted in a broad smile, and little tingles of happiness skittered around inside.

'But I can at least try,' Maddy said, still smiling. 'If there's something you want to get off your chest?'

'The only thing I want to get off right now is this relentless merry-go-round.'

'Are you referring to the house building project, or your bestselling novels that have sold hundreds of thousands of copies across the globe?'

'The latter.' He threw her a challenging look. 'Go on then, say it. There are millions of struggling writers who would happily give their right arm to be in my situation.'

'So, is just that you don't want to write another DI Friend novel? Or have you got fed up of writing altogether?'

Luke took a large mouthful of his wine, rolling it around his mouth in an appreciative manner before swallowing. 'Right now, I don't know. My agent is chomping at the bit to get the next manuscript over to my editor but I've just lost the plot.'

'Metaphorically or literally?'

Luke grimaced. 'Both.' There was a long pause and Maddy waited, letting him decide how to proceed. 'The short answer is I don't want to write it. DI Friend has had his day and I want to move on. I've sat down every day this week at the computer and written nothing. Everyone thinks I'm beavering away on the next book and I'm holding them at bay for now, and done a few interviews and stuff, but now all everyone wants is the trailer for the next book.' He threw up his hands theatrically. 'For God's sake! Leave. Me. Alone!'

'So you want to write a book.'

'Yes.'

'But not the one your publisher wants.'

'Correct.'

'Can you just write one anyway? Something different?'

Luke shrugged. 'Like what? Come on then, what would Ms Austen do?'

'That's easy—she'd write a romance. Which would of course be witty and wonderful.' Maddy sighed. 'I really wish I could write a book. I'll be honest, crime isn't my thing but I can still appreciate the time that you have to spend working out all the plot details.'

'Romances are a lot easier. You don't have all that complicated stuff.'

'Excuse me? What d'you mean it doesn't have complicated stuff?' demanded Maddy a little too loudly, as diners at the next table looked round. Luke had that smug self-satisfied look on his face, but this time she wasn't going to rise to the bait, and she certainly didn't want to ruin a lovely night out with a pointless argument. 'We've already had this discussion once—on air to boot—so we're not having it again here. In any case, if romances are that easy to write, why don't you do one?'

'I'm a crime writer.'

'That's a feeble excuse,' Maddy shot back. 'Don't forget, you've already told me how simple they are to write. If I remember correctly, your exact words were: *it's just two people swanning around the countryside for two hundred pages.*'

Luke had the good grace to grimace at that.

'You also mentioned the word predictable if I recall correctly. So go on, if you think it's that's easy, try writing one.'

'Oh no, I'm not getting drawn into that!'

'Why not? Surely that should be dead easy for a writer of your calibre?'

Maddy rummaged in her bag and pulled out a pen. Then she picked up the card advertising the restaurant, which had been propped up against the salt cellar, and scribbled quickly on the back before ceremoniously placing it in front of him. 'I, Madeleine Shaw, hereby challenge Cameron Massey to write a romance by the end of this year.'

Luke laughed. 'I wouldn't hold your breath on that one.'

When they left the restaurant an hour later, Maddy picked up the card that had been abandoned on the table and as they walked back to the car, she surreptitiously slipped it into Luke's jacket pocket.

Chapter Twelve

Society has claims on us all...
Mary Bennet, *Pride and Prejudice*

According to the agenda Maddy had been given, the Cotlington Literary Festival Committee met in the village hall at 7:30pm. She had planned to walk down but Luke had offered her a lift and she had gratefully accepted, particularly as it was in the Jag. She smiled to herself as they pulled up outside; anyone watching would definitely have something to gossip about now.

'Are you sure I can't persuade you to come along?'

'No chance. I'd rather eat my own toenails.'

'Whatever floats your boat. Enjoy your bushtucker trials.'

'Enjoy your evening with the mad locals.'

The cool evening air ruffled her hair as she stepped

out of the warm car interior, and Maddy shivered. Luke hadn't said anything about getting a ride back but she could hardly expect him to be her personal chauffeur. He did own the most fabulous car though! It was straight out of a luxury living magazine, and Maddy wondered what Alice would say if she could see this, and whether she dared take a sneaky photo.

The last and only time Maddy had been inside the village hall was after cousin Nigel's funeral when it had been decked out with bunting, and tables were laden with cakes and vintage tea cups. Today the inside was bereft of decoration, and the grey utility tables, devoid of their white tablecloths, were lined up at the side of the room with the exception of the two pushed together in the centre of the room. The tubular chairs were stacked in the corner in wobbly piles, as though someone had been setting up a game of chair Jenga.

Jem was busy lifting down chairs and Myra was sorting through a file of papers on the table. Both looked up as Maddy entered.

Jem greeted her with a big smile. 'Hi, Maddy. Nice to see you again.' Unlike his gardening attire which made him look more like a beanie-hatted Worzel Gummidge, today he was dressed in casual trousers and a grey and navy argyle knitted jumper, but his hair still stuck out around his ears. Maddy had also come casual, in comfy trousers and her Pemberley sweatshirt. Clearly, Myra regarded meetings as a more formal affair if her tailored skirt, cream blouse and matching earrings and necklace were anything to go by.

'Punctual,' Myra nodded approvingly. 'Grab a seat.' Maddy sat down obediently, the smile slipping off her face. Should she offer to help? She had the distinct impression Myra was the sort of person who liked things done her way. Working for the magazine, she'd dealt with plenty of difficult people in her time, but this wasn't work; it was a group of volunteers.

Maddy only had her creased copy of the agenda to fiddle with but she found a pen in her bag so that she could make notes as necessary, and tried to remember who else other than Sally was supposed to be coming. As if on cue, the door banged open and Sally breezed in, her pink highlighted hair flying around like escaping candyfloss, followed by a pensioner sporting a smart pair of trousers and a navy blazer.

Jem looked up, and his lips parted in a huge grin.

'Hello, hello, everyone,' Sally called, waving a Tupperware pot in the air as though she was trying to attract seagulls. 'I made some biscuits in case we all needed substance.'

'Sustenance,' corrected Myra.

Jem hurried over. 'Cor, I love your baking. What sort of biscuits are they?'

'Lemon and ginger.' Sally turned to grab the sleeve of the man next to her. 'Maddy, this is Leonard—you might have seen him at the funeral? He lives a few doors down from me. Leonard, this is Maddy. She lives at Meadowside and is organising the festival this year. Hooray!'

Sally's reserves of enthusiasm seemed limitless. Maddy forced a smile on her face as her confidence sank to new depths. How on earth was she supposed to organise this? They had barely finished the introductions when Joyce arrived, shoving the door open with her stick which seemed to be part mobility aid, part battering ram.

Myra glanced up at the clock on the wall.

'I saw that, Myra Hardcastle. I'm not late, you haven't started yet.'

'That's because we were waiting for you!' replied Myra.

Joyce seemed unconcerned by Myra's reprimand and sat down next to Maddy. 'I think it's lovely that you want to carry on Nigel's vision for the village,' she said, giving Maddy's arm a squeeze. 'It would have been awful to see the house sold off.'

Maddy gulped. She hadn't really given any thought to what would happen after she sold up.

'A house that size would probably be turned into luxury flats,' observed Leonard with a sorrowful expression. 'The council always wants more houses everywhere.'

'Well, now Maddy's here that's not going to happen, is it?' Joyce said firmly. 'So, how are you settling in, love? It's a wonderful place, isn't it?'

'It's…' Maddy shook her head as though she couldn't quite find the right adjective. 'It's certainly a fascinating house. Although the roof leaks in places and the place does make lots of funny noises at night.'

Sally's eyes widened. 'Ooh, d'you think it's haunted? That would be amazing. A friend of mine saw a ghost once—it was this little girl dressed in Victorian costume who ran up the stairs in her parents' house. We sat up all night once, waiting to see if she'd appear.'

'And did she?' asked Jem.

Sally shook her head.

'Nigel did see one or two strange things,' added Leonard earnestly. 'It was years ago. We were just sitting in the library, just chatting as it were, and he mentioned it in passing.'

'Don't be daft,' scoffed Myra. 'There's no such thing as ghosts.'

'You don't know that for sure,' said Sally. 'I'd love to see one for real. I think it's really interesting. D'you think you can communicate with them?'

'My mate knows that ghost hunter bloke off the telly,' Jem announced proudly. 'The one that goes to people's houses and listens for signs of activity.'

'Not Randall Jacobson?' Sally clasped her hands together. 'Wow, Jem, you never told us you knew someone famous! We must invite him to Meadowside. We could have a ghost hunting evening!' Sally enthused.

Jem nodded energetically like the Churchill dog on fast-forward, although Maddy suspected that if Sally had suggested a visit to the local dump he'd have been equally as keen. She had clocked how his whole face had lit up when Sally arrived.

'You can count me in for that,' added Joyce. 'What about you, Leonard?'

'That's a wonderful idea. I shall buy his book so I can get him to sign it. I bet he's got some interesting stories.'

Jem happily agreed to speak to his friend and fix up a

visit. Clearly, it was not deemed essential for the owner of the house to give permission for the planned ghost hunt—that was taken as given—but Maddy was happy to go along with the idea. Anything that livened up her evenings was welcome, although she would need to hide her countdown calendar first. And notify Luke of the planned village invasion.

'Can we please start the meeting now we're all assembled?' asked Myra.

Leonard cleared his throat. 'May I propose, before we get started on the agenda, that we introduce ourselves briefly to our new chairperson.' He turned to Joyce. 'We used to do that at the school whenever we had new members of staff. I think it makes people feel more welcome.'

Myra sighed, picked up her pen and pointed it at each person in turn. 'Myra, Jem, Leonard, Sally, Joyce. How's that for brevity? Can we get on now?'

Joyce raised her hand. 'Objection!' She beamed at Myra. 'Ooh, I've always wanted to say that.'

'What on earth are you objecting to, Joyce? We haven't started yet.'

'Maddy hasn't introduced herself.'

Maddy wondered whether as chair of the committee she ought to have a better grip of the proceedings, but at least introducing oneself was familiar territory from the world of work. Was it really only two months since she'd left? It seemed like a lot longer.

She looked at the faces assembled round the table. 'Thank you all for such a lovely welcome! As you all know, my dad was Nigel's cousin so that makes me his … erm…' She paused as she tried to work it out.

'First cousin once removed,' said Leonard promptly.

Maddy smiled her thanks. 'You probably also know he left the house to me in his will. As Jem and Myra are already aware, I have a—' She was about to say friend but that might be stretching it a little, although after last week's meal there had definitely been a thawing on both sides. 'Well, call him an acquaintance. He's staying temporarily as a sort of lodger so don't panic if you see a strange man around. Oh, and he has an adorable dog called Buster.'

'Yeah, I've definitely met him,' laughed Jem.

'So, before I came here, I worked for *UpClose* magazine as their love and relationship correspondent, and before that I did various other journalism type jobs. I've never organised a festival before but I'm happy to help and if you haven't already got speakers arranged, I can suggest a few names for you.' And hopefully add a bestselling author too, once the grump had worn off him.

'Oh that might not be necessary,' piped up Leonard. 'We always give last year's speakers first refusal.'

Maddy tried not to roll her eyes. She was beginning to wonder whether being chair of the Cotlington Literary Festival Committee might be an honorary title rather than an indication of who was actually in charge.

'So has anyone got any update on the speakers for this year?' Myra asked, looking around the table. 'I know Fraser Pennyfather passed away recently.'

'Patrick thingummy said he wasn't coming this year,'

ventured Joyce, as she pulled a pair of knitting needles and a ball of purple wool from a large canvas bag by her feet. 'And Lionel Critchley died after attending a poetry reading.'

Maddy put her hand to her mouth to suppress the giggle that threatened to make an ill-timed appearance.

'And Netty McIntyre doesn't like speaking in the afternoons,' Joyce continued chattily. 'She said last year people just nodded off during her talk about how the local countryside influenced her desire to become a writer.'

'That's probably because they'd drunk too much of Jem's punch,' said Myra, looking pointedly at her son who was grinning broadly.

'They were also drinking Ginny Peterson's homemade arthritis remedy, which she was selling on the day,' Leonard added.

'She was selling medicines?' Maddy asked, somewhat concerned at what else might go on at this festival and in her back garden to boot. 'Doesn't she need a licence or something?'

'Don't you worry, she calls it an elixir, but everyone knows it's gin really.'

This was clearly a not-very-well-kept secret judging by the universal outbreak of laughter around the table.

'So, action to be carried forward: finalise speakers for this year,' said Myra. 'Any contacts or suggestions, please forward details to Maddy. And Jem, can you ask your builder friend to go round and take a look at the roof please?'

'So you survived then,' said Luke as Maddy climbed into the car an hour and a half later. 'How was your first meeting?'

'Part meeting, part social club, and a discussion about what sort of knitted topper to make for the local pillar box. Apparently it has to contain a lot of purple. And we all swapped telephone numbers in case something urgent crops up.'

'So which hopefuls have they lined up to speak this year?'

'There appears to be a snag there,' Maddy said as she wrestled with the twisted seatbelt. 'They're either deceased, declined or difficult to pin down.'

'Allow me.' As Luke leaned over, his hair brushed lightly against her face causing her to shiver. It had to be a reaction to the change in temperature, because she had already decided she didn't fancy him. He deftly straightened the strap and then pushed the clasp into the buckle.

'And you'll never believe this,' Maddy continued. 'Last year someone was selling what sounds like industrial-strength gin, thinly disguised as a home remedy for arthritis.'

Luke snorted in derision. 'I suppose it might be a remedy for a lot of things if you drank enough of it. And you wonder why I don't want to get involved? You might have just answered your own question there.'

As they made the short journey back to Meadowside, Maddy was relieved and grateful for Luke's text offering to come and pick her up. It wasn't a long journey but the chance to have another trip in the Jaguar was not something she was going to pass up.

'So what have you been doing with yourself this evening?' Maddy asked as they hung up their coats on the coat stand in the hall.

'Trying to think of ways to leave the country without my agent noticing. Failing that, I'll try some of that arthritis remedy you mentioned earlier.'

'It can't be that bad, can it? Can't you just explain that you need more time to come up with a new idea for book eight?'

Luke made a low growling sort of noise which Maddy took to mean no.

'In that case I shall give it some thought. And before I forget, sometime next month we're apparently hosting a ghost hunting evening.'

Chapter Thirteen

2ND MAY

Interested people have perhaps misrepresented each to the other. It is, in short, impossible for us to conjecture the causes or circumstances which may have alienated them, without actual blame on either side.

Jane Bennet, *Pride and Prejudice*

I t might have helped lessen the surprise a bit if Maddy had ever seen the television programme *Ghostwalk*. Having only pre-conceived ideas about what a ghost hunter looked like, she'd expected either some strange, otherworldly person with pale, pinched features and sharp eyes, or an overly genial, mad professor-type character in a knitted tank top and owl spectacles.

She'd heard the motorbike roar up the driveway and rushed to the door in time to see her guest remove his helmet to reveal shoulder-length, blond hair, and had watched, impressed, as he swung a muscled leg over the chunky saddle with consummate ease.

She found herself staring at the vision standing on her doorstep, clad in a leather jacket and dark denim jeans and looking every inch the suburban Norse god next door. He flashed a smile that reminded Maddy of a toothpaste advert, and she half expected a star to twinkle on his incisors like they did in those cheesy adverts.

'Hi, I'm Randall. Great to meet you.' There was definitely a hint of an American accent there. He held out his hand in greeting and Maddy smiled as she took it; her fingers were clasped in a firm grip that sent a small tingle up her arm, and despite her private doubts about whether there was anything worth investigating, this was beginning to feel like fun.

Randall gazed around at the large hallway. 'Can I just say this is the most a-may-zing place you have here. How old is it? Who built it? How long have you been here?'

'I only know the answer to the last question I'm afraid,' Maddy laughed. 'And that is a month and a half.'

She left him eulogising to himself in the sitting room while she fetched some refreshments and made a mental note to thank Jem for making all the arrangements. He had swapped his days and was working on another job today but had been as good as his word, contacting his friend who worked as a runner for the production team. Maddy had assumed it would take many weeks or even months, but clearly Randall didn't hang around when there was a sniff of a job.

As it was, the choice of day worked out well for everyone; Luke had gone back to his house this afternoon for a meeting – or possibly an argument? – with the archaeologists, so there was no danger of interrupting him with any impromptu guided tours of the house. He'd taken Buster with him for company although he was being kept strictly on the lead. The house seemed strangely silent without her canine companion bucketing around accompanied by the sound of his favourite rubber ball bouncing on the parquet floor.

'So, tell me how this all works then,' she said pouring a beer for Randall and an elderflower cordial for herself. 'Do you have to inspect the house first? Measure up anything?'

'I'd certainly love to look around, get a feel for the place, if you know what I mean. Then we'll fix up a date and I'll come back with a cameraman and see what we find. Night filming works best for television—it's more atmospheric for viewers.'

'So you can actually film these … apparitions?' asked Maddy, trying to keep the scepticism out of her voice.

'It's unusual to actually see anything but there are other indications and signs.' He waved his hands as he spoke, like a magician conjuring spells. 'Sometimes you can hear strange sounds, or objects might move, and there is usually a marked change in temperature.' Randall shivered theatrically. 'If you have the sensitivity, you can always feel a presence.'

Maddy was fairly sure any cold presence in the house was more to do with the lacklustre efforts of the boiler in the kitchen, but remained silent. Who was she to spoil anyone's fun? She wondered if now was the right time to mention that half the village were also planning to join in. Probably not.

'And how long does the filming take?'

Randall smiled and shook his head. 'Our spiritual friends don't run to a timetable. However, we usually get more than enough footage from one visit.'

After he had finished his beer, Maddy gave him the guided tour, apologising for the state of some of the rooms. Buster had been into the dining room more times than she had since she moved in—it was far too formal for her tastes so meals tended to be eaten at the kitchen table. Randall seemed particularly interested in the kitchen, and also the upstairs room next to the attic stairs. He walked around the disused bedroom several times then stood in the middle of the floor with his eyes closed swaying slightly and breathing deeply.

'Very interesting,' he murmured. 'There's a distinctive smell in here too.'

That would be down to the fact that these rooms had been disused for thirty years, but Maddy kept a respectful silence. If Randall thought there might actually be something worth filming here, she could earn some money. Entertaining the locals and getting paid for it at the same time would be a win-win scenario in her book.

As if he had read her thoughts, he said, 'So Maddy, shall we head back downstairs and talk fees?'

Even getting back to the sitting room took ages as Randall kept pausing to point out the intricate coving or the carved balustrades. Maddy hadn't really paid too much attention to the architecture although she appreciated that it might be a good selling feature.

'My production company pay a contractual daily rate of seven hundred pounds,' Randall explained. 'We have a pretty standard contract for these things which I'll send over.' He proceeded to run through lots of details that largely went over her head. Maddy's thoughts drifted off into a daydream of having that much extra cash in the bank.

This could be the answer she was looking for. Instead of the usual homespun speakers that seemed to headline the Cotlington Literary Festival every year, she could attract a few well-known writers. Clearly not anyone of – expensive – celebrity status, but someone who had written a recently published book, and not one that was so old it could only be found in the British Library.

'…and there is of course an additional payment should we use photos in the book.'

Maddy's attention snapped back. Was this man some sort of mind-reader? 'Sorry, what book are you referring to?'

'My new book—it's still a work in progress but it's a sequel to last year's *Ghosts at Large*. You probably noticed it was mentioned prominently on the mystery channel.' He smiled as if it was blindingly obvious Maddy knew all about it.

'You've written a book?'

'Yes.'

'To accompany your television programme?'

'Got it in one.' He flashed another fluoride white

smile in her direction and she found herself smiling back. He was so easy to talk to, and seemed to positively enjoy her company. It was as if the gods of good fortune had suddenly remembered she existed. And now they were shining a spotlight on what was surely a golden opportunity.

'Randall, you may not be aware, but we have a literary festival here in Cotlington at the beginning of September. On the 3rd to be precise. Would you be interested in being a speaker? I'm sure there would be plenty of people interested in your book,' she added persuasively.

'How interesting! September is usually quite busy, although…' He pursed his lips as he pulled his phone from his jacket pocket, pushed his blond hair from his face and tapped the screen a few times.

Maddy kept her fingers crossed behind her back as she waited. It would be a real bonus to get a television personality signed up, and she had to try hard not to look smug as she imagined the reaction when she announced at the next committee meeting that she had bagged a celebrity.

Randall murmured to himself for a few seconds and then announced, 'D'you know what? I'd love to, it'll be an absolute blast! I'll speak to my publisher and ask them to send over a box of books—I presume you normally have an area where I could do a book signing?'

'Yes, of course,' replied Maddy, mentally adding this to the list of things to find out, along with where the marquee came from, who ordered the catering and whether her house was even insured for hosting this event.

'And who else will be speaking at your festival? I don't remember hearing about this last year?'

She hadn't heard about it either, but then that was probably because she was living in London and not scouting around the country for local literary festivals. And after Lionel Critchley's alleged death by poetry reading, the less said about last year's speakers the better. Maddy decided to strike an upbeat, if slightly apocryphal, note.

'I believe the committee likes to encourage and nurture local talent. There are a lot of people who just need the right opportunities to showcase their talents. However, we are also in negotiations with a very well-known crime writer, which will be a fascinating talk if he's available.'

'That sounds brilliant! Unless of course it's Cameron Massey.' Randall laughed as though he'd just said something amusing.

Maddy felt the air suddenly sucked out of her. She gave an involuntary cough as she stared back at him. There were literally hundreds and hundreds of crime writers in the country. Why did he pluck that name out of the air? Did he know Luke? Or was this just based on reputational hearsay? The questions spun round in her head like curious bees.

Many in the Twitter universe already had an opinion on Cameron Massey, if what she'd seen recently was anything to go by. There was certainly a group of diehard supporters who would still queue for a book signing even if he wrote a volume about watching paint dry, but for many he was a source of entertainment, and she'd seen several posts where Cameron had been tagged, presumably because the original poster was hoping for some sort of controversial reaction. He was clearly a marmite character, albeit one made of combustible material.

Having not yet secured Luke's co-operation with the literary festival she had no intention of disclosing his name. However, she did want to know why Randall had mentioned that name out of all the hundreds of others he could have chosen. The logical thing to do would be to simply ignore it. Let it go. It was as he was leaving that she made up her mind.

'It's been absolutely wonderful to meet you,' said Randall, taking her hand. 'You have an amazing house and I'm already looking forward to discovering its secrets.' He lifted her fingers to his lips and delicately kissed the back of her hand as though he was a modern-day chivalrous knight.

Maddy found herself blushing like some awkward teenager after her first prom date. What on earth was wrong with her?

'Randall, can I ask you something?' she said as he turned to leave.

'Of course. If it's about the speaker's charge for your little festival, fret not beautiful Maddy, I can offset it from the amount you'll receive from the production company.'

'No … er … that is…' Her face felt hot again and she instinctively covered her cheeks with her hands. Then realised how silly that probably looked and pulled them down again swiftly. 'Why did you mention Cameron Massey?' she blurted out. For someone who had been used to delicately guiding people through relationship minefields, it wasn't the most diplomatic of approaches, and she hoped it hadn't sounded rude. Randall's smile slipped for a few seconds, and his eyes darkened as if he'd just recalled something distasteful.

'Why do you ask?'

Now what she going to say? She could hardly explain that the aforementioned author actually lived here and that Randall could bump into him if he hung around for much longer. It was a happy coincidence that Luke happened to choose this afternoon to go over to inspect the house, although he'd made his highly sceptical views about the ghost hunting idea loud and clear over the last couple of days. It was for that reason that Maddy had deliberately not mentioned much about it or the name of the ghost hunter. Now she wondered what would happen if she did. Did Randall just dislike Cameron as a writer? Was he jealous of his success? Or was there some other reason?

'Well… I just erm…' She scraped around for some plausible answer. 'You've stirred my curiosity,' she managed after a few seconds. 'After all, everyone's read his books, haven't they?'

'I haven't.'

She'd only read one for research purposes, but now didn't seem an appropriate moment to mention that.

'He seems to have been quite successful,' added Maddy, wincing at her choice of adjective.

'He seems a lot of things,' replied Randall darkly, 'and he isn't. And that fiancée had a lucky escape. You don't want to—'

He pressed his hands together almost respectfully and inclined his head the tiniest of degrees. 'Sorry, I shouldn't be bothering you with this. Until we meet again.'

Part of her wanted to shout, *No, please, bother me with this! I need to know what you're talking about!* Even though another part of her didn't want to know. It was probably just gossip. Celebrity hearsay. But a mystery fiancée? What did she really know about this man who shared her house? He certainly loved his dog so he couldn't be all bad, but Randall had left her with some burning questions.

Maddy watched as Randall did up his leather jacket, pulled his helmet on and gave a last wave. As he roared off down the driveway, she decided she ought to watch a couple of episodes of *Ghostwalk* for research purposes and to familiarise herself with the concept. Although she had been kind of steamrollered into the whole ghost hunting thing, she was definitely warming up to the idea, and having now secured a celebrity speaker for the literary festival, she awarded herself a celebratory glass of wine.

She was just pouring herself a small top-up when she heard the front door open and Buster galloped across the hall and into the kitchen, ears flapping like semaphore flags in a gale force wind.

'Hello, boy!' Maddy squatted down so that she could

give him a big hug and almost got knocked backwards as several kilos of energetic canine launched itself at her and tried to lick her face. 'I know, I know,' she laughed. 'You've been away for all of three hours, not three months you daft dog.' She picked up Buster's favourite blue rubber ball and bounced it carefully into the hall, watching as Buster careered out after it.

She looked up at Luke's lean, handsome features. He hadn't shaved over the weekend and had that sexy designer stubble look that emphasised his jawline. If he'd failed as a writer, he could have had a career as a male model. *So are you a man of mystery?* she wondered. *Do you have a secret past? Or is Randall just insanely jealous of you for some reason?* Instead of any of those questions, she opted for the safer, 'Everything okay with the house?'

He threw himself down on one of the sturdy oak chairs around the kitchen table. 'Only if the definition of okay is zero progress on anything. How long does it take to dig up a couple of bodies for heaven's sake? Buster could do the job quicker.'

Maddy couldn't help but smile as she pictured the chaotic scene. 'I agree. However, I suspect that Buster might not observe the appropriate level of archaeological respect that is generally the norm in such situations.'

'And now they're talking about having to underpin the back of the house before they can continue with the extension,' complained Luke, thumping the table with a clenched fist and making her wineglass jiggle.

'Sounds like you need a drink. Wine? Beer?'

'Just a coffee.' He stood up. 'I'll make it, you're not a skivvy.'

'Sometimes I feel like one. I've inherited something that comes with barely enough money to live here and has a lifetime supply of tat to sort out in the attic. At least I might be earning something from having this ghost hunting evening. They'll be paying seven hundred quid for the privilege of poking round the house with the lights off.' She raised her glass in a celebratory gesture.

'Presumably the payment isn't dependent on results?'

Maddy stared at him, her glass still half raised in the air. That hadn't even crossed her mind. Could they wriggle out of paying if there were no spooky goings on or funny noises?

'Do you actually have a contract?'

'No, Randall said he'd pop it in the post.'

Was it her imagination or was there was a noticeable stiffening in Luke's shoulders? She hadn't meant to drop his name into the conversation so casually but maybe now would be a good time to clear the air.

'That's the ghost hunter by the way. His name is Randall Jacobson; he's done stuff on the telly and he seemed very enthusiastic about the idea of filming here.'

'I bet he did.'

The atmosphere in the usually warm kitchen was becoming decidedly chilly, but Maddy had no reason to dislike Randall. However, she didn't need to be any sort of agony aunt to figure out that Randall was hiding secrets too. In an ideal world, she needed both of them but right now, only one had signed up as speaker for the literary festival and she wasn't about to say no to anyone just because they had accidentally crossed swords with Mr Grumpy in the past. It would be better to be honest and open now, she decided.

'Just so that you know, because you've already said you don't like surprises, Randall has kindly agreed to be a speaker at the literary festival in September.'

Luke's head jerked up. 'What!'

'Apparently he's already had one book published, and is busy writing a follow-up, and everyone likes ghost stories, don't they?'

'I don't,' muttered Luke.

'Okay, everyone apart from you then.'

There was a few seconds of silence, punctuated only by the noise of Buster's ball thudding against the floor as he attempted to create his own doggy entertainment.

'Why are you even entertaining that bloody man?' Luke said, flicking his hand in an agitated manner.

'You know why! Because I am—not by choice, I might add—chair of this literary festival and I'm trying to do my bit to get a few speakers organised. I did ask you, but you made it clear where you stood, and now I've found one very willing volunteer. Hooray. End of story.'

She took a slow and deliberate intake of breath to try and dampen down the fury that was rising like molten lava inside her. How dare he object when he didn't even want to be involved!

'Did I give you an answer? I thought I said I'd consider it.'

Maddy had a rather different recollection of the conversation.

'So give me an answer now then. Do you want to be a speaker at the Cotlington Literary Festival?'

'I don't want anything to do with that fraudster.'

'That wasn't the question.' Maddy tried clenching her teeth for a few seconds to see if it helped. It didn't.

'So I'd be the keynote speaker?'

This mention of Randall had clearly pushed Luke's buttons.

'Yes, you can have top billing. Keynote speaker. Festival supremo'—Maddy waved her fingers around in the air—'whatever you like.'

'It's a deal. I'll do a talk and then some Q&A stuff if that works for you, with something about the new book?'

'Fabulous. I'm looking forward to hearing what the new book is about.'

Luke grimaced. 'So am I.'

'Well, I've been giving that some thought and have a few techniques that might help.' Maddy pointed in the direction of the open kitchen door. 'Cameron Massey, in the library, tomorrow at ten.'

'That sounds like a rubbish game of Cluedo.'

'I love board games!' Maddy protested. 'Don't knock it till you've tried.'

Chapter Fourteen

We have all a better guide in ourselves, if we would attend to it, than any other person can be.
Fanny Price, *Mansfield Park*

'This is like being back at school,' Luke grumbled as he sat down in front of the large chalkboard.

Maddy waggled a remonstrating finger. 'Don't start being a grump before we've even started. If you're very good I'll get you some stickers for your homework.'

Luke flicked an amused look in her direction.

Despite not having the faintest idea how to plot a novel, Maddy had nevertheless spent the last week or so trying to think of ways in which she could help. It had occurred to her that Luke might not know what he wanted in the next book, but it could be useful to eliminate what he didn't want, and top of that list was any repetition of previous plots. There was plenty of evidence in the online reviews of *The Diamond Case* to suggest that readers also thought it was time for a change of direction.

She had found the chalkboard languishing in the attic, which was quickly becoming a treasure trove of finds in amongst the piles of boxes and random objects from past lives. She often wondered whether some of the objects had belonged to earlier residents and Nigel had simply added his own belongings to the collection. However, unlike the popular staple of daytime television, it was definitely more *Trash in the Attic* than *Cash in the Attic*. It had taken quite a bit a manoeuvring to get the chalkboard down two sets of staircases, but she was pleased with her find.

Using a packet of coloured chalks that she'd unearthed in a box of assorted stationery items, she drew six vertical lines spaced equally across the board, followed by one horizontal line along the top.

'So, Mr Massey, what was the title of your very first book?'

'*Friend in Need*. Published 2013.'

Maddy wrote this in the first column heading. 'And what was the book about? What were the main plot points?'

'Introduction of DI Friend, who is called in to investigate the murder of a man found on a golf course, who turns out to be an old schoolfriend.'

'Anything else? Tropes? Plot devices?'

'You sound like my old English teacher.'

'Wow, thank you!'

Luke rolled his eyes theatrically. 'That wasn't supposed to be a compliment.'

'Sounded like one to me,' answered Maddy in a sing-song voice. 'So,' she tapped the blackboard with her stick of chalk, 'book two.'

'*The Jewel Thief*—2014. A body is found in a Spanish hotel room near a golf complex with a ruby clutched in his hand.'

'And is book three set on a golf course?'

'No, it's set in Sicily. But there is a golf course nearby.'

Maddy was beginning to see why these books might have not been the bestsellers that the later ones were.

Luke burst out laughing. 'The expression on your face! No, of course I didn't write three consecutive books set on a golf course.'

Luke outlined the plot details and Maddy dutifully chalked them up on the board. 'So there was a two-year gap between books two and three, is that right?'

'Change of publisher,' Luke said abruptly. 'I'm not a writing machine.'

'Right, sorry. Okay then, book four—*End of the Roadie* —that was the big breakthrough novel, yes?'

'It was. It went on bestseller lists, reviewers' choice; it won the Silver Spanner award.' Luke sighed. 'Happy days.'

'And what was it about?'

'One of the roadies with a big-name rock group tries to break up a bar room brawl between two of the band members. He falls, hits his head and dies.

Maddy paused, chalk in hand. Where had she heard

something like that before? She'd read it somewhere in a book or magazine, but there was no time to think now as Luke was still talking.

'...and there's a case of mistaken identity so it's a race against time to find the intended victim who's been embezzling funds from the band and is now on the run. Detective Inspector Friend was a lifelong fan of the group so naturally he gets involved.' Luke paused. 'Are you following all this? Perhaps I'm talking a bit too quickly for teacher,' he added with an amused look.

'I'm fine, thanks!' Maddy replied indignantly. She decided to do a bit of teasing of her own as she added, 'So no romance, then?'

'Certainly not!' Luke shot back.

Over the course of the next hour, Maddy—with assistance from her wayward pupil—gradually filled up the remainder of the seven columns with the titles of his published books and a rough outline of all the plots.

She added a large red asterisk over the column for book four, which was the one that started his career as international bestseller. The two that followed were equally as popular but book seven, *The Diamond Case*, had garnered distinctly lacklustre reviews. Last night, Maddy had sat up in bed with her phone reading through the less favourable ones and wincing at some of the harsh criticism. It must be tough, having had several award-winning books published, to now read these reviews. Or maybe he didn't. Maybe he didn't care what other people thought.

'So,' she announced, stepping back from the chalkboard, 'let's see what we've got.' She looked over all the notes that now completely covered the board. The phrase *mistaken identity* popped up several times, as did the words *jewel thief*, *blackmail* and *embezzlement*.

'Hmm, there does appear to be a few clues here.'

'Clues to what?'

'The reason why book seven wasn't quite as popular. Look'—she pointed at the words in the last column—'each of these ideas has appeared in previous novels. And you think romances are all the same!'

'So what do you suggest, o clever one?'

The longest thing Maddy had ever written was a ten-thousand-word dissertation on the impact of female novelists on English literature, as part of her degree, and that was fifteen years ago. She wasn't qualified to advise a bestselling novelist, but she hoped that seeing the premise of each book written out might help clarify his thoughts.

'Anything that doesn't involve the ideas already on the board would be a good start. Give it some time,' she added, smiling optimistically. 'Something will pop up and totally surprise you. Something you didn't expect.'

'I don't like surprises,' Luke growled.

'Not even pleasant ones?'

'There's no such thing.'

Chapter Fifteen

What is right to be done cannot be done too soon.
Mr Weston, *Emma*

Since her conversation with Luke yesterday morning where he had outlined the plots of his books, something had niggled away at the back of her mind. It had jogged a memory somewhere, and her neural pathways finally made the connections in one of those 3am clarity-of-thought moments. Maddy sat bolt upright in bed. That's what had bothered her! It was that newspaper cutting she'd found in one of the boxes of junk upstairs.

She tried to recall the details—the man had died after hitting his head in a bar fight. What was his name? Masson? Mason? And he'd been a roadie for a rock group. This was the basic set up of Cameron Massey's first big bestseller, *End of the Roadie*! Could that just be one of life's strange coincidences? But then she thought she had seen Luke at Nigel's funeral, just for that brief moment in the church. Was that a coincidence too? Maybe it was time she asked Luke a few questions, but first she needed to check her facts.

Maddy lay down again, letting the thoughts swirl around, trying to fit everything together. Luke certainly never gave any indication that his bestseller was based on a true story. Admittedly, his book had a lot more plot details, including betrayals and cheating people out of money. Maybe her imagination was getting the better of her again? After all, coincidences did occur in real life. One thing was for sure: first thing tomorrow she was going to do some investigating.

To avoid looking through the same boxes each time she had a sorting out session in the attic, Maddy had put the 'to be sorted' and 'done' ones in separate piles. It took only seconds to locate the relevant box with the large F on the side, and she retrieved the faded newspaper clipping, re-reading the article. Mason Garcia was a roadie with a rock group, who hit his head in a bar during a fight and then died, exactly as Luke had outlined the previous day.

There was a mystery here, she was sure of it, but what was the connection between an American rock band, a bestselling crime writer, and her dad's late cousin? Had Nigel simply shown Luke the cutting? Who were the people in the photograph? And who was the ringed figure? She replaced the lid on the F box, but kept hold of the envelope and newspaper cutting.

This reminded her of her early career working on the local paper when she was despatched to track down local stories; sometimes her investigation led nowhere, or there wasn't actually much of a story at the end of all her hard work, but just occasionally she unearthed a real gem of a piece, and that was why she'd loved the job.

Job number one was to look at Luke's book and see what he'd written in the acknowledgements. Maddy trotted downstairs, pausing to tuck the envelope in her handbag so she didn't lose it. She knocked tentatively on the door while wondering why she was seeking permission to go round her own house, and then cautiously peered round the door. Luke was sitting at the desk with the laptop open.

'Are you checking up on me?'

'Of course not! Personally I don't care one way or the other whether you are writing, sleeping or doing anything else in here.'

Luke raised an eyebrow and flicked her an amused look. *'Anything* else?'

'I'm not even going to answer that. I only came to look for one of your books.'

A look of surprise flashed across his features and Maddy smirked as she walked over to the tall bookcases. Figure that one out, Mr Detective!

She had spotted a couple of Cameron Massey's books on her first visit to Meadowside and she hoped that Nigel was more diligent about organising his books than he was with his paperwork. Thankfully it didn't take long to find *End of the Roadie* sitting a few books down from *The Cornish Key Cutter*, and she flicked through the back pages to find the acknowledgements. Although she didn't turn around, she was fairly sure that Luke was watching her but resisted the urge to check.

There were some grateful words about how it takes a team of people to publish a book and various thank yous to his agent—both the UK one and the US one—to his editors, the cover designers, the marketing team, his brother, Nathan, and lastly everyone who had read the book. He had a brother. Why was this such a surprise? It felt as though she'd just found out something rather secretive, which was silly really, as anyone who had actually read the book would already have this information. But there was no reference to this being based on an actual event, or any mention or thanks for Nigel Shaw.

Of course, an author wasn't legally obliged to acknowledge the source of every single idea that went into a book, but if Nigel had given him the idea, wouldn't he deserve some nod of appreciation? Luke had clearly taken what was a factual event and stuck it in his book. A book that had turned into a bestselling prizewinning book to boot. But who had come across this story first? And what was Nigel's connection to all this?

Yet again, she realised how little she knew about her erstwhile cousin or her prickly lodger. She returned the book to the shelf and turned around slowly. Was there a merest hint of disappointment that Luke had already turned back to his laptop?

'Silly, silly, silly,' she muttered to herself as she marched back down the corridor. Why would she care whether Luke was looking at her or not? She needed to put more effort into getting speakers for the literary festival, not letting her imagination run riot. She was getting as bad as Randall with his ideas of a cold presence and funny smells. If Nigel had heard about the bar room incident, then Luke could equally have done so. End of.

Chapter Sixteen

My idea of good company is the company of clever, well-informed people who have a great deal of conversation; that is what I call good company.
Anne Elliot, *Persuasion*

I t was a pleasant May evening; there was a sweet smell of blossom lingering in the air mingling with the scent of freshly cut grass, and Maddy couldn't help but smile as she sauntered down Springfield Lane. Birds cheeped and chattered in the trees, and in the distance, she heard the growling of a lawn mower. Unlike Clapham with its busy roads and wide pavements, the only vehicles that came up Springfield Lane were residents' cars or the occasional learner driver. Nettles grew in patches along the roadside and leaned in to harass pedestrians attempting to use the thin pavement.

It was a good fifteen-minute walk to the village hall but it took her through the centre of the picturesque village. Leaflets had started to appear in the local shops advertising Cotlington's participation in the Summer in Bloom competition, and Maddy looked forward to seeing what that involved. Like many Londoners, she frequented the parks during the summer months and although she missed the vibrant cosmopolitan noisiness, there were compensations to living in the country.

In around ten months, when she was back in London living in her own flat and would be financially secure, this would be an experience and adventure that she would certainly look back on. She hoped Leonard's prediction that Meadowside would be pulled down or turned into a block of flats would not come to pass.

'Hello! Maddy!'

Her musings came to an abrupt halt as she saw Joyce standing outside the chemist's and waving her stick in the air like an erratic metronome. Despite the warm weather, Joyce was dressed all in black with a black fascinator perched on her head. In case Joyce decided to make an unwise doddery dash across the road, Maddy hurried over.

'Hello, Joyce, are you on your way to the committee meeting?'

'I certainly am.' She beamed broadly. 'Wouldn't miss it for the world.'

'Really?'

Maddy was attending because she was chair of the committee, even though that seemed more of a nominal appointment, and possibly because she was more than a little worried that non-attendance might elicit a reprimanding visit from Myra Hardcastle. Maybe out in the sticks they didn't have quite the same range of entertainment options. 'So what is it that you love about the meetings?'

'Most of us have all known each other for years. Leonard is a relative newcomer—he's a retired school-teacher and only been living here for six years—but they're my friends.'

'I see. I thought maybe Myra wasn't exactly … erm…' Maddy left the sentence dangling as she wasn't quite sure how to finish it.

'Goodness me, you don't have to actually *like* your friends. Not all the time at any rate. Some of mine are extremely annoying at times.'

Maddy suppressed a snort of laughter as Joyce said, 'Myra and I go back years, and she can be a real dry stick sometimes, although it's hardly surprising given that she's married to one of the most boring people in the village. Probably in the county. Heaven knows why she married him; she used to be such a lively young woman and then just like that, she's married, and popped out a sproglet.'

Maddy tried hard to picture Myra as lively and failed.

'It's a rare sighting of her husband in the village though. No idea what he gets up to. I've only ever seen him stuck behind his newspaper. He didn't ever order them from my shop either!'

That was clearly gross misconduct of the first order in Joyce's eyes. 'What shop was that?'

As they ambled in the direction of the village hall, Maddy heard how Joyce and her husband had run the local post office-cum-newsagent's for over twenty-five years.

'Only gave up when my Ron died. I didn't have the heart to carry on after that.'

'And how long ago was that?' Maddy asked.

'Ten years, three months.'

They walked along in silence for a minute. For someone to still count the time in years and months spoke of a great loss. Maybe it was something she had never got over. When Maddy's grandad died, her gran had changed almost overnight, becoming almost a recluse in later years. Maddy remembered her mum making several unsuccessful attempts to get Gran to come and stay with them. At least Joyce had found a new outlet for her sociable talents.

The black attire made sense now. Sort of. Maddy tried to remember what she'd been wearing at the previous meeting, but before she could frame an appropriate question they had reached the village hall, and Maddy held the door open for Joyce to avoid her having to use her mobility battering ram.

Myra and Jem were already busy putting out chairs while Sally was arranging some biscuit concoctions on a plate; they were smothered in pink icing and a sprinkle of those edible silver balls that could dislodge three fillings with one mouthful.

Sally smiled cheerfully. 'Have you been to another

funeral today, Joyce? Was it better than the last one, which you said was rather dull?'

'I have. It was a beautiful service this one, lovely hymns, and I talked to some very interesting people at the wake.'

'So was it a family member who'd passed away, or a friend?' asked Maddy.

'It wasn't either. I think I'd have liked them though— Virginia Redman, her name was. They put on a good spread too, although they were a bit stingy on the cakes.'

Before Maddy could ask any more questions, Sally offered the plate around. 'Try one of these. They started off as flapjacks,' she explained catching Maddy's puzzled expression, 'but they didn't turn out quite right, so I thought some pink icing and a bit of sparkle might help. You can never have too much sparkle, can you?'

Sally's enthusiasm was infectious and Maddy found herself smiling in agreement. Jem seemed more than happy to concur, and reached for the largest one on the plate.

'Don't blame me if you spend half of next month's wages on dental treatment,' said Myra tartly.

'I'm twenty-eight, Mum,' Jem protested. 'I can eat what I like.' He took a large bite and Maddy watched anxiously. 'And I definitely like these! Sally should be on *Bake Off*.'

'Ooh I love that programme,' said Joyce, plonking herself down on the nearest chair. 'Prue Leith is wonderful, isn't she? She says what she thinks. I'm going to channel my inner Prue Leith today.'

'What's that about Prue Leith?' asked Leonard, hurrying in and earning one of Myra's pointed looks at the clock.

Maddy smiled as if it could somehow counteract Myra's frown. 'Jem thought that Sally should be on *The Great British Bake Off*, and Joyce was saying how wonderful Prue Leith is.'

'Quite wonderful,' agreed Leonard. 'She's had an amazing past. Fun fact for you: did you know that The Hollies were once her lodgers?'

As he spoke, Maddy noticed how his face became animated, and his grey eyes twinkled with excitement.

'Leonard is our resident trivia expert,' said Myra proudly. 'Always a great asset in pub quizzes, although his specialist subjects are military history, and rock and pop music from the 1960s.'

'That's my music era,' Leonard explained. 'I listened to everything and anything on the radio. I loved the pirate radio stations and drove my parents mad with non-stop rock music. They didn't think knowing about rock and pop music was very useful.'

Maddy thought it could prove highly useful. That tatty newspaper cutting was still in her handbag where she'd stuffed it for safekeeping. Even though she had little expectation of solving the riddle, she hated giving up on a story and couldn't bring herself to throw it away.

Sally leaned across the table, waving the plate of biscuits masquerading as flapjacks under Leonard's nose. He peered at the pink offerings and then declined with a polite wave of his hand and a delicate shake of his head.

Sally helped herself to one and then asked, 'So who were they then, these Hollies?'

'Who were they?' asked Leonard, his bushy eyebrows shooting up several centimetres in a scandalised expression. 'Only one of the best groups around. Fabulous harmonies too. You don't get singing like that these days.'

'You're showing your age now, you silly old duffer,' said Joyce. 'I like the modern boy bands. You have to move with the times, don't you?' She leaned over towards Maddy and said in an attempt at a conspiratorial whisper 'Do you like watching *Love Island*? You get a bit more action if you know what I mean. And talking of which,' she prodded Maddy, 'how are you getting along with that young man of yours?'

Maddy's face flushed. 'Oh no, he's definitely not my young man. We don't… I mean we're not…'

She was spared from having to make any more embarrassed rebuttals by the strident rapping of a ball point pen against Myra's glass of water on the table.

'Can we please start the meeting? Otherwise it'll be almost midnight before we finish.'

The hum of conversation faded and everyone looked at Myra, who looked directly at Maddy. It felt like some sort of challenge. Clearly Myra was accustomed to running the meetings and was now seeing if Maddy was up to the job. How on earth had Nigel coped with that woman? In the offices she'd worked in, meetings were typically something to be endured with the support of caffeine-fuelled products, not enjoyed; these participants clearly regarded the meetings as an extension of their social life. Like Joyce, she needed to channel her inner somebody, so summoning her best Emma Woodhouse, she took a slow measured breath, smiled at Myra and picked up her agenda.

'Thank you, Myra. And thank you Leonard for producing the agenda.'

'Yes, well done, Leonard,' said Sally in a loud, singsong voice.

'Well done,' echoed Jem.

In case anyone else decided to start a new Mexican wave of well dones, Maddy hurried on. 'So, agenda item one, apologies for absence. None, I take it?'

Everyone looked round as if they weren't quite sure who was present.

'Only Nigel,' said Myra. 'Gone but never forgotten.'

'Hear, hear,' added Leonard.

Maddy waited patiently in case anyone else had condolences to add. Thankfully agenda item two— minutes of meeting—got ticked off promptly with only one diversion over Leonard's use of the Oxford comma.

'So, on to speakers for the literary festival. Has anyone made any progress?' For a change, there was a ringing silence in the hall. 'Well, I have some exciting news for you all—we now have two confirmed speakers.' She paused to see if there was a gasp of surprise.

'Oh no, please don't tell me it's that dreary woman who always does a reading from her book of *Gardens I have Visited*,' said Joyce. 'I'm sure she reads the same bit every year, and she always spouts lots of Latin words that no one understands.'

'That's because plants and flowers all have Latin names for categorisation purposes,' explained Jem. 'Like a poppy is called Papaver Orientale, and—'

'Jem, your botanical knowledge is impressive,' Myra said briskly, 'but can we just continue?'

Maddy felt rather sorry for Jem, and wondered whether Mr Hardcastle was similarly henpecked. She smiled at Jem before continuing.

'Joyce, you'll be pleased to hear it's not someone doing a reading from a garden book. Our first speaker is Cotlington's very own bestselling crime writer, Cameron Massey.'

This time there was a definite collective gasp of surprise.

'Wow!'

'That's fantastic!'

Even Myra seemed impressed and stared at Maddy almost open-mouthed. 'How on earth did you pull off that feat?'

Strictly speaking the correct answer was, *I asked someone else first and being rather prejudiced against this person, his author pride took a hit.*

'Persuasion,' Maddy replied with a smile. 'He'll be doing a talk, reading from his latest novel and answering questions.' She had plenty of her own too. 'And our second speaker is none other than ghost hunter extraordinaire, Randall Jacobson, who will be talking about his book, *Ghosts at Large*.'

'Brilliant!' said Sally loudly, clapping her hands. 'I'm going to buy that. I'm dying to meet a real-life ghost hunter, and I hope we find some ghosts in your house.' She waved her palms in a conciliatory gesture. 'But not poltergeist-y things that move furniture and chuck things around. Just friendly ghosts.'

'Like Casper, you mean?' said Jem.

Sally wrinkled her nose. 'That's for children.'

Jem didn't reply but cast his eyes downward to the agenda in front of him.

Maddy was keen to steer the conversation away from ghosts and Randall, and asked whether anyone else had other speakers in mind. As no one had any other suggestions, it was agreed that Myra would follow up with any of last year's speakers who were not already in the deceased or permanently discouraged category.

It had become clear to Maddy that as far as content was concerned, cousin Nigel had been the steering force of this festival, but having taken on this role, she was determined not to let the side down, even though right now she had no idea where she was going to find another three or four speakers.

One thing she could settle this evening though was whether Leonard could shed any light on who the figures were in newspaper cutting she'd found in the attic. After the meeting formally concluded, she seized her opportunity while Jem was helping Sally stack the chairs and move the tables back against the wall.

'Leonard, before you go, can I ask a favour?'

Leonard blinked at her in surprise. In his tweed jacket and brown-framed glasses, he reminded her of a slightly alarmed owl.

'I have a picture of what I think may be musicians from a rock group but I have no idea who they are. As I hear you're the music trivia expert, I wonder if you could help identify them.'

'Well, erm, I'm not that much of an expert on modern groups I'm afraid. My era was rather a long time ago,' he added almost wistfully.

'But that's exactly what I need.' Maddy tugged the scruffy envelope from her bag, extracted the folded newspaper cutting and handed it over.

Leonard adjusted the glasses on his nose and peered at the paper. 'Goodness me, that's certainly a blast from the past!' He tapped the paper with his finger and his voice had an excitable edge to it. 'This is the old line-up of The Faultliners. They weren't as good by the end of the seventies—too many changes in the band—but this lot were brilliant.'

Maddy had vaguely heard of them, but then rock music wasn't really her thing. She wracked her brain for some connection. 'Weren't they the ones that recorded "Rock Hard Road"?'

Leonard beamed at her. 'Well done! Yes, that was their massive hit from 1972 and it's still a classic rock anthem.' He started quietly singing the opening bars, then cleared his throat as though embarrassed by the burst of impromptu karaoke. 'In the very early days they were called The Getaways or Goneaways, or something like that. That's the lead singer Chuck Hardimann, that's Rob Pinto, he was the drummer, there's lead guitarist Darius

Locke.' He sighed. 'It almost makes me feel young again. Where on earth did you find this?'

'In one of Nigel's boxes. I've been trying to sort out some of the stuff in the attic because eventually I'll—'

She stopped herself just in time. She had been about to say, 'because I'll be selling the place,' but there was no need to blurt that out now.

'And I also wondered,' she continued hastily, 'whether you knew who that was.' She pointed at the slightly blurry figure in the background ringed in biro.

Leonard shook his head. 'Sorry, no idea. I don't think he's one of the band though. He could have been one of the roadies, or just an interested bystander?'

Maddy was almost one hundred percent sure it was not a random member of the public, otherwise why would it be ringed? And what was the connection between her dad's cousin and one of the greatest rock groups of the seventies?

Chapter Seventeen

Strange things may be generally accounted for if their cause be fairly searched out.
Narrator, *Northanger Abbey*

Maddy pulled the full-length velvet curtains in the library in preparation for the evening's guests and celebrity ghost hunter, and wondered—not for the first time—why Nigel had never bothered getting them shortened. They were at least six inches longer than necessary and the surplus material pooled on the floor like a blood-coloured dust collector. It was still only 8:30pm; sunset wasn't for another half an hour, and even then, it wouldn't be properly dark until nearly nine thirty, but she wanted to be ready in good time.

When she'd first moved here back in March, she'd missed the bright London street lighting, and colourful floodlight shops and buildings where nowhere was ever properly dark. However, over the last two months she'd become used to the quiet cocoon of darkness and—since the street lighting was wholly inadequate at her end of Springfield Lane—she thought of the house as her own private little universe.

She had never been scared of the dark, even as a child, and having discovered a plentiful supply of candles around the house, she often just switched on a couple of table lamps in the evenings to better appreciate the soft ambience of flickering candlelight. Luke, on the other hand, seemed to prefer lighting that resembled Wembley Stadium in every room.

True to form, he had the main light on in the library plus two separate table lamps, and was still sitting in front of his laptop; he was working late tonight and Maddy suspected it was some form of silent protest over the ghost hunting evening.

'Are you sure you don't want to join us? You never know, it might be fun!'

'I assume you are using the word fun in its loosest possible context,' replied Luke, 'and the less I have to see of that man the better, thank you.'

Maddy still hadn't got to the bottom of why he disliked Randall so much, but Luke hadn't put up any defence other than a stony silence on the subject, despite Maddy's one attempt to delicately prise the subject open.

'And tiptoeing about in the dark is not my idea of entertainment,' Luke muttered without bothering to turn round.

Maddy smiled as a sentence from Jane Austen's novel Persuasion sprang to mind:

Would they only have gone away, and left her in the quiet posses-sion of that room…

'Well, you'll have to keep the lights down if you're staying in here.'

'Remind me why you're humouring this man?'

'Because he kindly offered to speak at the literary festival and even more importantly he's paying me to film here.' She switched off the standard lamp in the corner and the main lights. 'You've got this desk lamp and the light from your laptop. I know it's not ideal but it's only one evening. I need to finish tidying down here before everyone arrives.'

She had been running round tidying up and shoving things in cupboards nearly all day. If the inside of her house was going to be shown on telly, she didn't want it to be mistaken for one of those decluttering programmes. She hadn't asked Randall exactly where he wanted to film but hopefully it didn't involve heading up to the attic or poking around in any wardrobes. Luke's bedroom would also have to be off-limits otherwise she suspected there would be strange thumps and noises that had nothing whatsoever to do with paranormal activity.

Part of her was curious though about what they might find. There had only been one occasion when she heard something she couldn't explain, but she was aware of the powers of suggestion, and she had no intention of turning into that fictional ninny Catherine Morland, whose over-active imagination got the better of her during her stay at Northanger Abbey.

Maddy had long become accustomed to the strange bumps and noises in the house, but if it transpired that they were the result of some spirited previous occupants, well, it all added to the character of the place. She idly wondered as she went round drawing curtains in the other downstairs rooms whether selling a house that had been officially declared haunted would add or detract from its market value.

Randall and his two associates arrived at 8.45pm as previously agreed and were busily testing sound equip-ment and setting up a mobile camera as Sally's car pulled up outside. Maddy hurried to open the door.

'Hello, hello!' Sally waved as though there was an appreciative audience seated somewhere behind Maddy. 'I picked Leonard up on the way and I've brought some snacks to keep us going. Ooh, the famous Randall Jacob-son! I've seen all your programmes!' she squealed excit-edly. Sally's pink highlighted hair was being held back from her face by ghost-shaped hair clips and she was wearing a sparkly pink and white block-striped jumper that reminded Maddy of a giant slab of coconut ice.

'You didn't mention you were expecting guests,' said Randall pointedly. Maddy was tempted to reply, *wait until you see the body in the library*, but that made it sound like Luke was dead.

'Yes, umm, these are some of my friends from the village. 'Sally and Leonard—'

A car door slammed outside and fast footsteps scrunched over the gravel. 'And this is Myra, Jem and Joyce. Tell you what, I'll make everyone some tea,' said Maddy brightly, hurrying out to the kitchen.

An hour later, everything was set up, the unexpected audience were seated on folding chairs that Jem had found in the garage, and Randall was preparing to record his introduction in the hall. Unlike his previous visit where he'd turned up in a sexy jeans and leather jacket combo, for filming he was wearing a plain white shirt and black jeans. Sally gazed at him intently, watching as Randall smoothed down his blond hair and then turned to the camera.

'Today, we are deep in the Oxfordshire countryside, in a house that has a long and illustrious history.'

'Where did he get that information from?' Myra whispered to Maddy. Maddy shrugged. She'd quite like to know herself.

'Can we have quiet please!'

Myra was clearly more accustomed to being the shusher than the shushed, and glared as Randall started again.

'...and many people over the years have had experience of paranormal activity within these walls, so tonight let's see what we can find out.'

A frisson of excitement rippled through the assembled group as the lights were turned out and there was a collective and rather theatrical 'ooh' from certain quarters, reminding Maddy of childhood trips to the pantomime. She was tempted to call out 'look behind you!' but decided that Randall and co. had enough on their plate in terms of crowd control.

'Can I ask for quiet before we start filming?' announced Randall pointedly.

'Right-o,' replied Joyce, followed by a clatter as her stick fell to the floor. 'I'll change into my slippers now. Shoes make such a noise on these wood floors, don't they?'

There was a rustle of a plastic bag and Maddy put her hand over her mouth to stifle a giggle.

'Ready when you are!' called Joyce a few seconds later.

'And if you need it, Joyce, I've got my torch handy,' Leonard added giving it a quick flick on and off again by way of demonstration.

'Quiet please,' called the cameraman. 'And … action!'

As their eyes adjusted to the dark, Maddy was able to follow Randall's progress around the hall. Every so often he paused, listening for sounds, making the occasional comments to the camera. The audience watched in – mostly – rapt silence although Maddy became aware that Sally's homemade biscuits were being circulated like a collection plate in church when a Tupperware container was nudged into her hands. She hoped the camera was not picking up any munching sounds.

After filming a section in the hall, Randall and his audience moved upstairs to the bedroom at the far end of the landing. Randall stood just inside the room, and at the request of the cameraman, the eager audience stood a little way back, jostling for front-row viewing like the world's most amateur mosh pit, as Randall did his piece to camera.

Then Randall led the way back downstairs and Maddy assumed they would proceed to the kitchen—the area Randall had previously identified as 'interesting'. However, his attention was drawn in the other direction towards the library. Had she mentioned that this room was off-limits? She'd certainly meant to, but now Randall's voice became almost reverent. He gestured down the corridor.

'There's definitely something here,' he said in a theatrical whisper to the camera. 'I can see a faint glow of light from under the door so I'm going to approach slowly. You won't be able to see this at home, but I've got goose-bumps already.'

If Randall realised that any ghostly orb was simply the light from Luke's laptop and desk lamp he would think she was trying to cheat him, and Maddy could certainly wave goodbye to her location fee. What was she going to do? It was too late to worry about what Jane Austen would have done, and in any case she was fairly sure that Jane's characters had never had to prevent someone from entering a room before, and certainly not with the lights out. *Quick, Maddy, think!*

As Randall inched his way towards the door, the onlookers crowded in behind.

Randall grasped the door handle but paused for a few seconds to enable the cameraman to edge through the crowd and set up the shot. Someone's elbow jabbed

Maddy in the back, and a flurry of whispering broke out behind her.

'Oi, mind where you're going!'

'You're treading on my foot!'

'Whose arm is this?'

'Something just touched me!'

'This is a bit spooky, isn't it?'

If Randall was annoyed about the comedy version of *The Blair Witch Project* being improvised in the corridor behind him, it didn't show in his voice. Hopefully they could edit those bits out. Head still turned towards the camera, Randall whispered, 'I'm now entering the library…'

It was as he pushed open the door that Maddy realised the room was dark. In all the kerfuffle, her attention had been drawn to what was going on behind her, rather than in front. When did the light go out?

Randall walked in slowly, followed by the sound engineer who carried an EVP monitor. Maddy strained her eyes to try and pick out a silhouette, but the heavy, velvet curtains did their job too well. While the others crowded around Randall, she felt her way round the door, checking behind it. There was clearly no one hiding there. Recalling how she'd thought the room empty once before, she made her way slowly and carefully along the book-lined wall, her fingers running along the spines of the leatherbound volumes, until she reached the curtains. Had Luke escaped through the French windows?

Facing the curtained window with the warm velvet

brushing against her outstretched fingertips, she inched, crablike, across the floor.

Behind her, Randall was now speaking in hushed tones to the unseen cameraman. 'The light has gone out but I can still sense something here…'

Sally's nervous giggle punctuated the silence, and was followed by an urgent shush. As the silence descended again, Maddy continued her crablike dance.

It happened without any warning; one moment she was lifting her foot along the floor, the next it had snagged in the puddle of the curtain overflow and she fell sideways, her heart thumping, arms flailing at the curtains, straight towards the window. Except her head didn't crash into velvet-lined glass; it hit something far more solid. Something that now had hold of her. Either ghosts had become a lot more corporeal recently or she'd discovered Luke's hiding place.

'What was that noise?' whispered a female voice.

Maddy froze. She was still leaning at rather a strange angle, pressed up close against a velvet shrouded body with her head on what she assumed was a shoulder and her thigh pressed up against … well, she wasn't sure what but she was grateful for the continued darkness. Every pair of ears was straining to hear the slightest sound and she didn't dare move in case it attracted more attention.

'The door's just moved by itself!' whispered another slightly more panicked voice that sounded like Sally's.'

'Where's Maddy?' asked Joyce in a hoarse whisper.

'Sshh!'

'Can anyone else feel this? There's definitely a cold

current of air in this room,' murmured Randall. 'I can sense an unwelcome presence here…'

'That'll be you then,' murmured the body behind the curtain just loud enough for Maddy to detect. She pressed her face into the curtain to stifle the giggle. On the episode of *Ghostwalk* she'd watched, there was a palpable air of tension and mystery; but then Randall hadn't bargained on having the Cotlington Literary Festival Committee trailing his every move.

For a split second the lights flickered and someone gave a short shriek.

'Did you see that?' asked Randall excitedly. Maddy extricated herself from the curtain. What the hell just happened? She felt a cold draught slide across her shoulders and she shivered. It clearly wasn't anything to do with Luke, who she could hear breathing heavily behind her. For a second time the lights flickered madly. She caught glimpses of people standing in the room, like players on a stage being lit by a homemade and rather ineffective strobe light. Then there was an electrical fizzing noise, a bang and a scream, followed by several seconds of silence.

Then everyone forgot about whispering and started talking rapidly over each other.

'That was weird!'

'Something cold touched my neck!'

'I'm properly scared now!'

'I've never seen anything like that! Did we catch it on camera?'

Then an authoritative male voice said, 'Don't panic,

everyone, I've got a torch with me.' After several more seconds, a beam of light floodlit the room and Maddy spotted Randall shielding his eyes from the glare.

'Leonard, you don't need to wave it around, you're not sweeping the sea for capsized passengers.'

'Sorry, Myra, it's all the excitement.'

'Is everyone okay?' asked Maddy, now able to see her way across the floor without tripping over any camera cables. 'Randall, is it alright if we switch the lights on for a moment?'

'Yes, sure.'

'Jem or Sally, as you're nearest the door, could one of you switch the lights on please.'

There was a clicking sound but nothing happened.

'The ghosts may have blown the bulb,' suggested Leonard. 'Try the light in the hall.'

Using the torch in her phone, Maddy made her way out into the hall and tried the lights but they weren't working either. Nor was the lamp on the mahogany semi-circular table by the door. Or the kitchen light. It was probably safe to assume that none of the electrical fittings were working, but whether that was down to ghostly inter-ference or ancient electricals remained to be seen. In the flat, Alice had a small cupboard with the fuse box attached to the wall. Maddy had only ever touched it once when they tripped the system trying to put up too many Christmas lights, but she was pretty sure she hadn't seen anything like that here. Not that she'd ever gone looking for it; fixing an electrical outage was not on her list of anticipated activities during her tenure at Meadowside.

Jane Austen had managed quite happily in the nineteenth century without electricity and having to worry about things like fuses, but for once Maddy knew exactly what Jane's more sensible characters would do next—go and find some candles. However, she acknowledged that Lydia and Kitty Bennet would probably have preferred to keep the house in darkness so they could hide behind the curtain with a rather handsome writer who was currently in need of rescuing.

Chapter Eighteen

It is very unfair to judge of anybody's conduct, without an intimate knowledge of their situation. Nobody, who has not been in the interior of a family, can say what the difficulties of any individual of that family may be.
Emma Woodhouse, *Emma*

'They've all gone, it's safe to come out now.' Maddy pulled aside the curtain and peered round, just to check her lodger hadn't done a runner in the meantime. 'I don't know about you but I'm ready for bed.' She yawned sleepily.

'Are the lights working again then?

'Nope. Goodness knows what happened, but trying to fix it at quarter to one in the morning is not a sensible idea.'

'I guess not,' replied Luke in a slightly agitated

manner. Using her phone as a torch, Maddy had rounded up a few candles in glass holders that would throw off enough light for a quick teeth-brushing-and-dropping-into-bed operation. It would be light in around four hours anyway. If that didn't meet with Luke's approval he was welcome to go and find the fuse box himself. Knowing this house, it was probably in some obscure cupboard or —like some places she'd visited abroad—in a hut outside.

It was actually quite romantic getting ready for bed by candlelight, and she found herself smiling. Staying in this old house, with the flickering soft light and a ghost hunt for entertainment, she could almost imagine herself as the heroine of *Northanger Abbey*. Not that she was assuming anyone had murdered cousin Nigel, of course. She wasn't too sure about the ghosts either, but Randall had been delighted with the filming, and was gracious enough not to mention any interruptions from the audience. Maybe the whispering and the inadvertent shrieks had added to the atmosphere.

As Maddy curled up sleepily under the duvet, she realised she was becoming rather fond of her neighbours. Joyce was always welcoming, and Sally was impossible to dislike, with her personality dial set permanently on maximum cheeriness. Even Myra was slightly less frosty than two months ago. She decided that she would only sell the house to someone who was actually intending to live here, not just a person with their eye on how much they'd make to redevelop the land. This evening was the first time she'd had more than one or two people round and it made her realise how much potential the house had. It deserved to be full of fun and laughter, and the idea of someone pulling it down to make way for a housing development felt wrong.

Maddy was almost asleep when she heard the tapping noise. She raised her head from the pillow and listened again. There it was again: three short taps.

She sat up, instinctively pulling the duvet up to her chin. 'Hello?'

This time the tapping was louder. 'Luke? Is that you performing a percussion solo on the door? I don't think ghosts are that rhythmic.'

The door opened a few centimetres. 'Yes, it's me. Can I come in?'

'Sure.'

Over the years, this house must have seen any amount of creeping along the landing and hopping in and out of bedrooms, but Maddy had never been given any reason to suspect that Luke might want to indulge in the same activity. Not with her at any rate. He'd never given her the slightest impression that he was interested in her that way —or any way to be honest—but she'd be lying if she said she hadn't once or twice imagined what it might be like to be romantically entwined with him. Being entangled in a curtain didn't count as a romantic experience although it was rather funny. Maybe he'd found it more than that. Maybe he was the Colonel Brandon type who kept his feelings tightly buttoned up, but had harboured secret yearnings for her—his very own Marianne Dashwood.

Maddy realised she was still clutching the duvet to her neck like some terrified virgin from a Victorian novel, and smoothed it back down. Her hair probably looked like a bird's nest, so even though it was dark she did a swift bit of finger combing to try and smooth that down too. Leaning over to her bedside table, she quickly grabbed the packet of tissues, the Burt's Bees lip balm and the unicorn patterned cosy socks that came in handy when it was chilly but weren't in the least romantic, and stuffed everything under her pillow. Then she hurriedly retrieved Edward bear from under the duvet, kissed his furry nose in silent apology and hid him too.

She sensed rather than saw Luke move into the room but he stopped short of the bed. 'Sorry, I couldn't sleep.'

Not the greatest chat-up line she ever heard if she was honest, but it could be worse. 'It's probably all the excitement earlier,' she suggested.

For a few seconds Luke just stood there. 'This is a bit awkward…'

What was? Had he forgotten something? Maybe he wasn't as experienced in that department as she had assumed. *Note to self: try not to make assumptions.*

'It's a bit too dark, isn't it?'

How was she supposed to work out what that meant? Was he heading this way or was he going to stand in the middle of the room talking for the rest of the night?

'I wondered if I could sleep on your floor. Just for tonight. Until the lights are fixed. My phone has run out of charge.'

That was a definite passion-killer. The ripple of excitement swiftly ebbed away leaving a distinct aura of confusion. 'I think I'm missing something here. It's night-time. You don't need the lights fixed. They go off.'

'Not in my house, they don't.'

'Really? They stay on all night?'

'Erm … yes.'

Maddy's first thought was of how large his electricity bill must be. Her parents had always been careful about things like that, and turning lights off as she left a room had become an automatic habit. She had never been scared of the dark and actually used to find it quite exciting although she had a schoolfriend, Davina, who was terrified. On the occasions she'd been invited for sleepovers there'd been very little actual sleep as there had always been a night light left on in Davina's bedroom and Maddy had never managed anything better than a short doze.

However, Maddy had never thought of it as some-thing that affected adults, particularly males. Surely that was just unintentional prejudice on her part? Sleep was what she urgently needed right now, and she clearly wasn't going to get any until this difficulty was resolved. It wasn't as if Luke was some random burglar who had just wandered in.

'Yes, okay. If that works for you.'

She heard a sigh of relief. 'Thank you. I'll go and fetch my duvet.'

With the aid of the torch on Maddy's phone, Luke returned promptly with his duvet and pillow.

'Can I switch the phone off now?' asked Maddy.

There was a definite hesitation before Luke replied, 'Okay.'

From the way he said it, it was clear he didn't actually mean okay, but Maddy was too tired to rationalise this. She lay down again but annoyingly she wasn't feeling quite as sleepy as ten minutes ago. This was like having a sleepover without the giggling and bags of sweets—it certainly took his lodger status to a whole new level. It also aroused her professional curiosity; Maddy had always enjoyed working out what prompted people to behave the way they did, although in her professional life that had been limited to the sphere of love and relationships.

'Luke? Can I ask you something?'

'You're probably going to anyway.'

'Thanks for that. I was just going to ask if you'd always been scared of the dark, or whether there was something that triggered this?'

She heard a reluctant sigh. 'So you're a psychologist now as well as an agony aunt?'

'Just curious, I guess. You're a world-famous author who writes about all sorts of crime and dark dealings.'

'And you're a relationship adviser who sleeps with a teddy bear, so your point is?'

Had he been sneaking around in her room or something? 'Oi! How did you know about Edward?'

'Well, clearly I didn't know his name, but I saw two furry legs sticking out from under the pillow when you were waving your phone light around. I'm a writer. I observe. I decided it was either a teddy bear or you have

181

some funny night-time habit that I really don't want to know about.'

'Touché. And yes, it's a teddy,' she said extracting the slightly squashed bear and giving him an eskimo kiss. 'It was a present from my dad when I was six. Mum was in hospital for a few days and I went to stay with a relative until she came home again, so Dad gave me someone to keep me company. He's been with me ever since.'

'He sounds caring, your dad.'

'He is.' Maddy hugged Edward bear. 'I get on much better with him than I do with my mum.'

'Why's that?'

'You would understand if you'd met her. Mum is obsessed with getting on in life. I spent years hearing her tell me about the chances she never had and how I wasn't to go wasting opportunities. She was over the moon when I told her I'd decided to live here. This could be a life-changing event, she said.'

Maddy refrained from adding the coda to that speech, the gist of which was, being the owner of such a substantial property would be a useful aid to finding yourself a good husband.

'They must have been shocked when you found out about the house.'

'It's hard to know what shocked my parents more: the fact that Nigel had managed to buy this house and live here clearly comfortably off, or that he'd left it to me. In the Shaw family, Nigel was constantly used as the moral yardstick by which to measure standards of poor behaviour. Being told you were going to end up like cousin Nigel was considered somewhere between a threat and an apocalyptic warning.'

'Given that he ended up owning a place like this for thirty odd years, it doesn't sound like much of a warning, to be honest.'

Maddy rolled onto her back and stared up into the darkness. 'Not when you put it like that.'

She heard a general shuffling sound and then a few grunts and an oof. 'Are you okay down there?'

'Yeah, perfect. I'm camping on a solid oak floor with a draught coming under the door and my shoulder's aching. I think I might have to try for an upgrade and sleep in the chair.'

Maddy experienced a twinge of guilt. No one could sleep in that low-backed chair. And it wasn't as if Luke was trying to take advantage of her. Quite the opposite. And she hated feeling mean; it was a king-size bed after all.

'Okay, needs must—you can share. But it's just for one night though.'

There was a soft shuffling sound and then Luke padded round to the other side of the bed. Maddy was glad she was wearing her long nightshirt and not her baby doll pyjamas with the hearts on.

'We can do top to toe if you prefer?'

'No offence but I don't want your feet, thanks.'

She felt the mattress dip as Luke sat down and carefully arranged his legs under the duvet before lying down.

Maddy discreetly shuffled closer to the edge of the bed.

'It's very kind of you to do this. I realise it's a bit unusual.'

So was hearing Luke's voice from such close proximity. His normal speaking voice was fairly loud and often had a defensive edge to it. Now he was speaking much more softly. In other circumstances, with another man, she'd have described it as seductive.

'It's probably not what you had planned either,' she replied. 'Men aren't supposed to be scared of the dark, are they? In films, it's always the girl who screams when the lights go out.'

'If you remember, I was behind the curtain at the time so I didn't see the full effect of that.'

Maddy smiled in the dark. 'Funnily enough, I do remember.' She had been so close she could hear him breathing heavily. At the time she had assumed it was from partial curtain suffocation, but now she wondered if it was also partly from fear.

'I think it's lazy stereotyping,' Maddy continued. 'Women are seen as the weaker sex and therefore more easily scared. Is your brother frightened of the dark?'

'That's a very random question. How did you know I had a brother?'

'One of your books is dedicated to him.'

Luke made a non-committal noise. 'I've got two brothers actually. Both older.'

'Lucky you, I always wanted siblings. Preferably lots of sisters, but I'm sure brothers were nice too.'

'Not when they were younger. They used to think it was funny to torment their little brother.'

'Were you scared of the dark as a child?' she asked gently.

'As far back as I can remember I think I've always been scared of what might lurk in the shadows; even as child I had an overactive imagination. But sleeping with the light on started after my brothers became obsessed with watching horror films. My eldest brother, David, got the videos from someone at school, and my parents either didn't know or didn't worry what we were watching. My brothers dared me to watch one with them and I didn't want them telling my friends I was scared, so I did.'

'Which film was it you watched?'

'I don't remember and honestly, I don't want to. After I refused to watch any more they took every opportunity to try and scare me. They probably thought it was funny.'

'It isn't. I had a friend who was scared of the dark. One person's teasing can easily become another person's torture.'

'Very true.'

'Did you every speak to your parents about what happened?'

Luke yawned. 'No. My father wasn't the sort of person you'd describe as empathetic. Or a good listener. He was better at giving out directions.'

'My gran used to say God gave you two ears and one mouth, so you ought to talk half as much as you listen.'

'Sounds sensible. And do you always follow her advice?'

'Probably not,' admitted Maddy. 'I get a bit carried away sometimes.'

She had always longed for siblings, and had held up Jane and Elizabeth Bennet as the poster girls for sibling harmony. But what if she'd had sisters like Kitty and Lydia? They would have driven her absolutely berserk. And how would she have reacted if they had teased and tormented her like Luke's brothers did?

'Sorry, you didn't need all that stuff.'

'No worries,' replied Maddy. 'You can owe me a few favours. I've just extended the time you're speaking for at the literary festival.'

'Cheers.'

'And tomorrow you can tell me how a newspaper article from the 1970s ended up as the plot of your best-selling book, and where Nigel fits in.'

'What are you on about, you mad woman?'

'The rock group—bar room brawl—the roadie who got accidentally killed. Sound familiar?'

'Is this your idea of pillow talk? I think you might need to read a few more romance books to find out how it actually works.'

'Thanks for the advice mister I-don't-believe-in-romance.'

'Any time, Madeleine Shaw.'

She was lying with her back to her bedfellow and was fairly sure he was doing likewise. She was also fairly sure he had kept talking to cover up his fear of the dark. This felt even more weird than ten minutes ago. She'd only ever slept in this bed on the basis of sole occupancy; she didn't want to risk turning over in the night and finding she was almost on top of him.

Maddy waited until he had finished fidgeting and was lying still. She then waited several more minutes until his breathing became slower and deeper. Then she tentatively slid her hand across the cotton sheet. There was actually quite a bit of space between them which was good because— Shit! Her fingers just made contact with something soft and warm, and it wasn't Edward Bear. She whipped her hand back.

Thankfully Luke was still asleep but even so… Despite lying in the dark, she felt her face flush with embarrassment. He did smell rather sexy though; maybe he splashed something on before going to bed? Her gran used to do that with her favourite perfume, Yardley's April Violets. *In case I meet my boyfriend in my dreams*, she used to say to Maddy with a wink. Somehow Maddy doubted Luke applied the same rationale.

She closed her eyes and waited to drift off to sleep.

For the second time that night she was woken up by a strange sound. In her drowsy state between deep sleep and full consciousness, it had sounded like a soft call, like the 'oo' in 'helloo', accompanied by a muted tapping sound. The sound seemed to be drifting closer. Either there really were ghosts in this house that were being extraordinarily active this evening, which seemed highly doubtful, or she was about to have another visitation.

The short whine was the only advance warning of the canine cannon that launched itself onto the bed, trampling over her legs in the process. It clearly wasn't just her legs being squashed either.

'What the hell,' muttered Luke sleepily. 'Stupid hound.'

Buster busily sniffed the duvet and the pillows, gave Maddy a quick lick then settled down on top of the duvet between them with a self-satisfied snort. Well, that sorted out the problem of whether she might accidentally roll into Luke in the night! It was fortunate that it was not a cold night and that Maddy was now desperate to get some sleep, since her side of the duvet did not quite reach round her any more due to the doggy blockade. She tried giving it a tug but nothing happened.

She closed her eyes again and imagined she was in a luxury spa treatment room, with the warm scent of jasmine and bergamot perfuming the air, and gentle sounds of nature were lulling her to sleep under a soft feather duvet that she was absolutely not sharing with a man who wrote about murders, and a dog who took up more space than a leylandii hedge.

Chapter Nineteen

Come, come, let's have no secrets among friends.
Mrs Jennings, *Sense & Sensibility*

I t felt like she'd only been asleep for a matter of
minutes before a knocking noise slowly slipped into
her consciousness. The ghosts could do one; she'd had
enough for one night. She tried to pull the duvet over her
head but for some reason it didn't shift. Maddy made a
determined effort to ignore the noise, but if anything it
was getting louder. Maybe if she kept her eyes closed the
annoyance would go away and leave her in peace.

A faint 'Hello!' echoed from somewhere.

That was definitely a human voice. Maddy cautiously
opened her eyes and was shocked to see daylight filtering
in through the gap in the curtains. As she turned over and
realised why the duvet wasn't moving, memories from last

night came flooding back. A variety of emotions raced through her from surprise through to embarrassment. Thankfully, Luke had already vanished but Buster leapt to his feet, gave himself a shake and then jumped down with a happy woof.

Maddy rubbed the sleep from her eyes and with the benefit of full consciousness, identified the rapping noise as that of someone at her front door. She hurried over to the window and tugged up the sash to see who was making such a racket at the crack of dawn. The cool morning breeze brushed against her cheeks as she leaned out.

Her first thought on seeing Myra and Jem was that they must have left something behind last night. Couldn't they have waited until a more reasonable hour? Jem was wearing a creased T-shirt that looked like it has been through the wash too many times and had forgotten what shape it was meant to be. Maybe he'd just been dragged out of bed too. His hairstyle – or lack of it – certainly supported that theory.

'What's happened? What's the emergency?' she shouted.

'I'm sorry, did we wake you? I had no idea you slept in that late. Jem said you often took the dog out around eight o'clock.'

Maddy pulled her head back and peered over at her bedside clock. What! Half past nine? That had to be wrong, surely?

At the same moment, her bedroom door swung open to reveal Luke carrying a tray. He'd clearly been up for some time as he had shaved and dressed. 'Good morning! I've made you some tea and toast as a thank you for last night. I thought you romantic types liked breakfast in bed, but I see you're already up.'

Maddy waved her arms frantically, then put her finger to her lips and pointed at the open window.

She called down to her unannounced visitor. 'Sorry Myra, I overslept. I'll be right down.'

'Not that bossy woman!' exclaimed Luke, putting the tray down on the bed. 'What does she want now? Has she found you another lodger?'

'No idea, but you can entertain her while I find some clothes.'

'What? No way!' Luke held up his palms in a gesture of surrender. 'Once bitten, twice shy. I'm not facing that battleaxe on my own, thank you.'

'Don't be ridiculous! She's not that bad. You're telling me you write about crime and murder and you can't even manage to entertain Cotlington's version of Lady Catherine de Bourgh for ten minutes?'

'Who's Lady Catherine de burger?'

'It's too early to start winding me up,' said Maddy, jabbing her toast at him before taking a bite.

'I'm not.'

'Seriously? Okay, pretend you're Detective Inspector Friend and there's been a murder during a ghost hunt and you're off to interview a few of the suspects. Does that sound better? I know you have plans to kill off your detecting pal, but you can pretend for ten minutes, can't you?'

Luke stared at her open-mouthed.

'What now?'

'That's genius!'

'Glad to hear it. I know you think I'm stuck in the nineteenth century but we romantic types have been known to have the odd good idea, you know. Just go down and unlock the front door and make them a coffee or something. The sooner you scoot off, the quicker I can get dressed.'

Maddy quickly pulled on some clean clothes and brushed her hair, in between sips of tea and mouthfuls of toast. It was rather unexpected having Luke bring her breakfast, but then everything about yesterday night had been unexpected. She wondered what time he had slipped out of bed. She'd been so tired she hadn't noticed, but then in fairness, she'd had a snoring Buster up close and personal for most of the time. She applied a quick squirt of perfume in case there was a lingering eau de dog smell.

She was still eating the last mouthful of toast as she hurried across the hall in the direction of voices. She found Myra and Jem in the kitchen. Mugs of something hot stood on the wooden worktop and Luke was standing behind them, busying himself at the sink rearranging the drying up.

'Morning all!' said Maddy cheerfully.

'Morning,' replied Luke, as though this was the first time they'd seen each other this morning. 'Do you want a cup of tea?'

'No thanks,' Maddy replied, trying not to smirk.

'Good morning, Maddy, I'll get straight to the point,'

said Myra, as she nearly always did. 'My idiot son has a confession to make.'

This was not what Maddy had expected to hear. Glancing over Myra's shoulder at the amused expression on Luke's face, he clearly hadn't either. Jem didn't look capable of deeds requiring a confession. With his round face and gentle expression, he looked more like the sort of person who'd willingly take a day off work to rescue a pet rabbit from a well, or walk three miles to collect shopping for elderly neighbours. His mother was a totally different matter, of course.

'He admitted this morning that it was his fault the lights failed yesterday evening,' continued Myra.

Maddy laughed. 'I don't think so. I only asked him to try the switches. It's hardly his fault they didn't work.'

'I'm afraid it is.' Myra looked pointedly at her son whose face bore a rather embarrassed expression, although that might have had a lot to do with being hauled over here by his mother as though he was ten years old and had been caught stealing from the big house.

'Sorry, Maddy,' said Jem. His strong, work-roughened hands gripped the mug standing on the table in front of him. 'I guess I didn't want Randall to think there wasn't enough going on.'

Luke's shoulders stiffened at the mention of Randall's name.

'So?' Maddy prompted.

'Well, I crept out to the hall you see. The electrics are all in the cupboard under the stairs. I just gave things a bit of a jiggle… Obviously it wasn't meant to stay off permanently.'

'He only announced this over breakfast this morning,' said Myra indignantly, as though the matter should have been aired hours ago. Myra's expression was one of inquisitorial disapproval and it now turned once again to Maddy. 'Did you find enough candles? And did you both manage okay last night?'

Technically, the answer to the second question was that it was a bit overcrowded with three in the same bed but that information would not add anything helpful to the current situation.

Luke had turned and his eyes were fixed on hers, waiting for her answer. Despite all the teasing and the banter that passed between them, she had no desire to embarrass him, and certainly not in front of their neighbours.

'I was fine, thanks. What about you, Luke?'

He gave a brief nod and a flicker of a smile. 'Same.'

'While I'm here, I can take a look at the fuse box if you like,' Jem offered.

'I think,' Myra said firmly, 'we'll leave that to the professionals. Maddy needs an electrician, not an amateur ghost enthusiast. The electrics in this place are probably in need of an update anyway.'

Maddy mentally added *find an electrician* to the top of today's to-do list. 'Right. I'll erm…'

'Don't worry, it's all in hand,' announced Myra, raising hers, presumably to acknowledge the expected murmur of appreciation. 'Mr H has a nephew who's an electrician. He's only in Haxford so he'll be on his way over this afternoon.'

Maddy wasn't sure whether to be annoyed that Myra hadn't even asked her first, grateful that she knew someone in the trade or amused at the idea of this nephew – who presumably already had a busy schedule for the day – being ordered to drop everything and head over to Cotlington. Maybe he'd had a previous experience of saying no to Myra and wasn't keen to repeat it.

'The thing is…' Maddy gave an embarrassed cough and started again. 'Well, the bottom line is, Nigel didn't leave much of a housekeeping budget in his will, so while there's no mortgage payments to worry about, I don't have enough money for an expensive electrical overhaul.'

'You won't be paying for anything, Maddy. It was Jem's fault so he can foot the bill. I'll speak to Mr H about the finances later today.'

'Well … erm … thank you,' said Maddy as she picked up the Tupperware container sitting on the table and threw Jem a sympathetic glance. 'Can I offer you a biscuit, Jem? Sally seems to have left her stock here.'

'Well, that was a bit of a surprise,' said Maddy as she shut the front door twenty minutes later. 'At least with any luck we'll have functioning lights again this evening.'

'And you'll get your bed to yourself again,' added Luke. 'It was decent of you to share; I know you didn't have to. Although'—he added with a raised eyebrow—'I must admit it was a bit of a surprise being poked in the bum.'

Honestly, Maddy, what were you thinking! She was convinced he'd been asleep at that point. Why had she thought it would be a good idea to check anyway? Her face felt like it was on fire and she hurried over to the sink and fussed around rinsing out mugs and stacking the dishwasher until she was sure her cheeks had returned to a normal temperature.

'Maddy, what we talked about last night—'

Maddy waved her hand. 'It's fine. You don't need to say any more. Lots of people have things that traumatised them as children and it can have a surprisingly long-lasting effect.'

'I didn't mean that bit.'

'Oh.'

'You were waffling on about a rock group and a newspaper from the seventies?'

'Oh that! It's not urgent, I just wanted to ask what the connection was. It's clearly too similar to be a coincidence so—' She felt an insistent paw tapping her leg and turned to look at the petitioner. 'What is it, Buster? You haven't had your usual walk this morning, have you?'

At the mention of the W-word, Buster started leaping up and down as though he had an invisible extra-bouncy pogo stick, and then rushed off to find his favourite toy.

Maddy looked over at Luke. 'You've been saved by the ball. I'm not sure Buster does patience.' She slapped her thigh. 'Come on then, boy.'

'I might come with you if that's okay?' said Luke.

'Sure.' Maddy stifled her surprise. 'Not doing book stuff then?'

'I think I'd like a break from the library. I need to do some planning, and I've had the most amazing idea for a brand-new plot.'

'It doesn't involve grabbing people from behind a curtain does it?'

'No. And if we're being completely accurate, I think you hurled yourself at me.'

Maddy didn't answer and clipped on Buster's lead instead. With the passage of time, memories of falling into the body in the library might be highly entertaining but right now they were still embarrassingly fresh. If it had been anyone else, she'd have giggled over her own clumsiness but it was Luke, her lodger, and it felt almost intimate and not a little disconcerting.

Maddy liked to try and vary her morning walk with Buster, but more often than not he decided which direction he wanted to go in. Today he wanted to go down the lane towards the village and until they reached the main road, Maddy let him trot on a long lead so he could investigate all the smells and scents of the wild animals that probably passed by unobserved during the night.

It was as they paused while Buster sniffed around a tree halfway down Springfield Lane that Luke resurrected his earlier question.

'So, come on then, last night you more or less accused me of plagiarising a newspaper story. Where did you get that idea from? I genuinely don't know anything about any article in the paper.'

'But you have to admit it's a bit of a coincidence.'

'If you explain what you're on about I might be able to agree with you. Which I admit will be a wholly new experience for me.' He threw her an amused look and Maddy responded with a grin.

As they resumed the walk, Buster having satisfied his curiosity, Maddy explained as briefly as possible how she'd been searching in the boxes of stuff in the attic for information on previous year's literary festivals and had come across a newspaper cutting from the seventies about the death of a roadie.

'Leonard is apparently our resident pop trivia expert and was able to confirm the identity of most of the people in the photo, who were all part of this seventies rock band. It just seemed too much of a coincidence that the plot of your book almost exactly matched this story.'

'Is that why you were looking for my book in the library a couple of weeks ago?'

'Yes. I felt sure that there was a connection somewhere, and although it's not a crime to borrow a story, I expected some sort of acknowledgement or reference to the original incident, but there wasn't.'

'No,' agreed Luke.

For several seconds neither of them spoke. Before Maddy could frame an appropriately polite question, Luke started talking again.

'You have to understand that up until I wrote that book I still felt like a struggling writer. I'd had three books published that at the time made average sales, and I knew my parents wanted me to put more into making a career for myself rather than doing undemanding jobs so I could concentrate on my writing, so it felt like make or break for me. They had high expectations for all of us—doctors, lawyers, accountants—not wannabe novelists.'

'But they must be proud of you, surely? Not everyone who says they'd always fancied writing a book actually has the patience or effort to sit down and write one. Mine were thrilled when I got the job with *UpClose* magazine. My father bought out WHSmith's entire supply of the first December magazine I contributed to, to send to the family with their Christmas card, complete with sticky note indicating which page my article was on.' Maddy smiled at the memory.

'I'm not even sure my parents read my first couple of books,' said Luke, his voice tinged with regret. 'At least not when they first came out. My brother David is a barrister. Nathan joined the family firm. Those are what they thought of as achievements.'

'That's really sad,' said Maddy sympathetically. It was the first time she'd heard Luke talk about his relationship with his parents and she sensed that this was highly private information. Growing up as an only child had meant her parents' attention and devotion was only lavished on her, and maybe she'd taken that too much for granted. Clearly Luke's parents didn't feel the same familial pride in his achievements. No wonder he was so prickly about criticism.

'I found it helpful to meet with other writers. I had joined a writing group a year or so earlier—it's where I made Nigel's acquaintance,' Luke continued.

Maddy halted and stared at him. 'You met Nigel? As in my cousin Nigel?'

'Yes. Everyone round here knew him.'

The penny dropped. 'So I *did* see you at the funeral. I thought I was imagining things.'

'Just wanted to pay my respects, you know?'

Buster whined and tugged impatiently at the lead until the walk resumed.

'He said I was welcome to borrow any of his books— he has a fabulous library, doesn't he? We'd meet up regularly, have a drink or two, and chuck ideas around like you do. I needed an idea for book four and it felt like every idea I came up with had already been done by someone else.

'And then late one evening after several drinks over at Meadowside we were talking about Phil Lynott and his contribution to music despite his reputation as a hellraiser, and I thought that sounded like a great basis for a story. We started brainstorming ideas and Nigel mentioned something about a rock group and an accidental death after a fight in a bar. He then suggested maybe they were rowing over something. It just sounded like another of Nigel's random suggestions.

'I can't remember how it evolved from there, but the next day, once the hangover from hell had dispersed, I got scribbling. For the first time I felt like I had a great story. Around that time there had been several deaths reported in the British newspapers of rock and pop stars from the sixties and seventies, so it seemed a topical subject.'

'So you're saying it was Nigel who gave you the idea for the story?'

'Yes.'

'And you never knew it was based on a real event?'

'No, of course not! Otherwise I'd have researched it more carefully and, to be honest, may not have written it. And I know what you're going to ask next.'

'Go on then, Mr Detective, what am I going to ask?'

'You were about to frame an indignant question as to why your cousin didn't get any acknowledgement.'

'I might,' replied Maddy airily.

'I wanted my parents to think it was my idea. That I'd done this all by myself. I'm not proud of it now, and after the book did so well I felt guilty that he hadn't got the credit he deserved. Our friendship drifted apart and that was down to me. But I did not deliberately dramatize an actual event, or pinch anyone's ideas.'

'But you can see how it looks.'

'Yes. And I can see you're not wholly convinced.' Luke looked at her pointedly, his dark eyes searching hers. 'Can I ask you a question now? You don't like admitting you get things wrong sometimes, do you?'

Maddy instantly felt the challenge in his voice. Was that how he saw her? As someone who was too proud to admit to her own failings? Like her heroine Emma Wood-house, Maddy enjoyed helping people find their place in the world with their own Mr Right, but was she always right? And would she admit it if she wasn't? That was an uncomfortable question, and one to which she wasn't sure about the answer.

Verbally sparring with Luke over the rights and wrongs of literary snobbery was one thing, but this was far more intimate and personal. Like sharing a bed for the night, even though they weren't lovers—far from it!

Buster halted again and was busy sniffing around in the long grass at the side of the lane bordering the hedgerow. Spring flowers were now popping up along the verge, in between a riot of dandelions. In London, outside of people's gardens, the flowers were arranged more formally in eye-catching colour-coordinated displays in the parks, but in comparing the two, Maddy found to her surprise that she preferred the more natural arrangement. Clearly, so did Buster who was happily digging in the undergrowth of the hedgerow.

Maddy wagged her finger at him. 'If you're having fun that's fine, Buster, but dig up a cute little dormouse and you'll be in disgrace for the rest of the week.'

While they paused, Maddy stooped to pick a few of the wild flowers growing at the side of the lane. She could identify the poppies and ox-eye daisies but she had no idea about the blue or the yellow ones; she was pleased with her colourful arrangement though. She tugged out a length of ivy that was trailing through the hedge and tied up her makeshift bouquet.

Luke looked on, amused. 'Who are you planning to surprise with that? And don't say me, because I detest surprises.'

'Well, you've seen it now so it wouldn't be a surprise. However, for avoidance of disappointment, no, it's not for you. I thought I'd take them over to the church—it's not too far.'

Maddy hadn't been back to the church since the day of Nigel's funeral but as she reached the lychgate her thoughts trailed back to that day and she marvelled at how full the church had been and how fulsome the eulogy was. For years, all she had heard was Nigel's name being synonymous with disgrace and abandonment of his family. Had Nigel, like Luke, wanted something more than just a pre-ordained life plan handed down by his parents? And had she subconsciously accepted one version of her family history without considering any alternatives?

As they walked along the paved path that lead up to the church, she shortened Buster's lead and handed it over to Luke. 'Best behaviour now, Buster,' she said in a firm voice.

The gravestones between the lychgate and the church were all Victorian or early twentieth century. The ones around the side of the church were older and some of the stones had weathered too badly to even read the inscriptions. She had been informed by the solicitor, Mr Chapman, that the cremated remains of her cousin were interred in the churchyard of St Peter's, but she hadn't thought to ask where.

At the back of the church, the graveyard was more overgrown, but at the far side, a neatly mown grassy area was studded with small plaques in varying shades of white, grey and black stone. That looked more promising. Picking their way carefully between the stones, they made their way over. Sure enough, there were individual inscriptions on each one and they were clearly in some sort of date order. She found Nigel's near the far end.

In loving memory of Nigel Shaw
15.04.1947 – 31.01.2022

'Looks like you weren't the only person to have the same idea,' observed Luke.

A bunch of red and white carnations cocooned by sprays of green fern and neatly tied with a pink ribbon had been laid at the foot of the plaque. It couldn't have been the family as none of the Shaw clan lived near enough.

'I guess it's someone in the village,' replied Maddy. 'He was clearly very popular.'

She laid her homemade bunch of flowers next to the more professional looking arrangement. Where the funeral had been a colourful celebration of Nigel's life, coming here today felt more intimate and personal. She regretted not having any shared memories or personal recollections though. Maybe she could make one today.

'Hello, Nigel, I've brought you some flowers,' she said softly. 'They're from Springfield Lane so it's a little bit of home. I should have picked some from your garden, but I only thought about it halfway here. I just want to say I'm sorry the family carried a grudge for so long, but it sounds like you were happy here and I'm glad you had so many friends. And I want you to know I wish with all my heart that we'd met, even just once.'

Her eyes welled with unexpected emotion and she blinked rapidly to disperse the tears, keeping her eyes cast downward. The funeral had been more respectful than upsetting but now, having lived at Meadowside for a couple of months and encountered so many of his friends, she felt a connection to this distant relation.

'Nicely done, Ms Austen,' said Luke, placing his warm hand on her shoulder and giving it a gentle squeeze. 'Nicely done.'

Chapter Twenty

Give a loose rein to your fancy; indulge your imagination in every possible flight...
Elizabeth Bennet, *Pride and Prejudice*

'Hello, Mum, hi, Dad!' Maddy waved at her laptop screen, currently filled by the image of her parents, with a smaller one of herself in the corner.

'Hello, Maddy, how are you keeping? Are you eating properly?'

'Yes, Mum. I'm a grownup, I can look after myself!'

'Well, your hair needs a bit of a cut; it's getting rather long.'

'I'm happy with it, thanks.' Maddy peered at the image of herself on the screen and attempted to style her copper locks with her fingers. 'Anyway, how was your holiday? Did you enjoy Scotland?'

When she'd first arrived here, she had weekly catchups with her parents but for various reasons, not least her parents' extended tour of the highlands, it had been several weeks since she'd had more than a quick text message from them.

'Scotland was lovely,' replied her dad. 'Staying for two nights with Auntie Gloria was a bit of an experience as always, but she's got her children living nearby to order around.'

There was a muffled sound of amusement from the other side of the room.

'Is that the dog I can hear in the background?' asked her mother.

'No, just local interference,' Maddy replied, grinning as she flapped her hand at the source of the noise. The only consistently decent Wi-Fi signal for a FaceTime chat was in the library so this morning, with Luke's acquiescence, they were sharing the space.

'Just as well, you don't want dogs in a library.'

Maddy was tempted to ask about dogs in beds, but she knew what the answer to that one would be. Long after she realised she was going to remain an only child, she had continued to campaign for a pet, but the only thing she'd been allowed to keep was the goldfish she'd inherited from a schoolfriend who'd moved abroad with her parents and couldn't take it with her.

Her parents were always eager to hear about everything connected to the house and Maddy filled them in on how the planning for the literary festival was coming along and gave them an overview of the ghost hunt evening, excluding the bit where she fell into Luke in the dark and ended up sharing a bed with him. The opportunities for complete misinterpretation were way too plentiful.

'So you actually met *the* Randall Jacobson?' said her mother, her tone of voice one of awed amazement. 'Now he would be a great catch. Did you get much of a chance to talk to him? Will you be seeing him again?'

'Yes, he's coming back to speak at the literary festival to promote his new book.'

'Well, that clinches it. Your father and I will definitely be coming. I can't wait to tell Carol and the others at swimming club that you know Randall Jacobson.' To Maddy's horror, she started humming a snatch of Wagner's famous wedding march, 'Here Comes the Bride'.

Behind her, Luke started typing as though he was bashing out his novel on an ancient typewriter, and not a modern touch-sensitive keyboard.

'Mum! I think you're getting a teensy bit carried away.'

'Nonsense. He's a good-looking man; you've got a fabulous house. There are worse ways to start a relationship.'

'First off, if and when I do marry, the decision won't be made based on looks or income or how big someone's house is. Secondly, I accept he's good-looking and outwardly charming, but I suspect the person Randall Jacobson is most in love with is himself.'

'That's just his television persona, Maddy. You can't

afford to be too fussy, you know, otherwise you won't find anyone.'

Despite her intention not to let her mother wind her up, Maddy felt her restraint slipping. 'Right. So *you've* watched daytime TV and *I've* actually met him—which one of us is most likely to be right do you think?'

'Maddy, do you still have your lodger?' asked her dad, attempting a swift change of subject.

Maddy nodded, recognising the helping hand. 'Yes, he's working on a new book and he'll be speaking at the literary festival too.' She tried as hard as possible via a computer screen to throw her dad a grateful look, but her mother was rarely stoppable mid-flow.

'Is that the man you said was rather grumpy? That's such a shame, I looked at his photo online and he's definitely got potential.' She turned to her husband. 'You see, Doug? She's got two well-connected, rich men on her doorstep and she's only been there two and half months.'

'Give it a rest, Mum!'

'I wouldn't hang around though, Maddy. Before you know it, the year will be up and you'll be back in a very insignificant flat somewhere in London. Prices are skyrocketing right now.'

The sound of Luke's laptop lid being slammed shut was followed a few seconds later by receding footsteps. Her mother was possessed of a great imagination but zero tact. Admittedly, Maddy had used the adjective grumpy in her email communications with home, but a lot had changed recently and since the night of the ghost hunt she felt like she and Luke had reached more of a mutual understanding, even if they still totally disagreed about the merits and difficulties of writing romance. And his rent helped a lot with finances.

'On a totally different subject,' said Maddy desperate to get off the topic of her imagined love life, 'I've found a newspaper cutting in one of cousin Nigel's boxes from an American paper and I was trying to find out more about it.' She held up the article. 'It's from decades ago. It's a report of a death of someone I've never heard of but I wondered if the figure circled in the background could be Nigel.'

Close-ups of Maddy's parents faces filled the screen as they both peered at the picture.

'It's a bit fuzzy, love.'

'Hang on, let me send you a photo.'

Maddy grabbed her phone, zoomed in on the ringed figure, and then sent it to her dad.

A few seconds later, her dad was peering at his phone and nodding. 'This looks like him. He grew his hair long in his first year at university; I remember his parents complaining that he looked like a hippy. Looks like he found some friends.'

'According to Cotlington's music trivia expert, some of those people are a local group who later became The Faultliners.'

'Wow! That's a claim to fame and a half! I remember my friends and I rushing out to buy "Rock Hard Road" when it came out as a single.' Maddy's dad ran his hands through his thinning hair. 'Gosh, that must have been around fifty years ago now. Do you think that was just a fan picture?'

'No, it was part obituary, part coroner's report. An accidental death in a diner.'

'Maybe that was one of his friends? You know I've often wondered what Nigel was doing in America all those years.'

'And more to the point'—her mum leaned in causing her features to enlarge on Maddy's screen—'how did he come by enough money to buy that house? From what I heard, he went off to America almost penniless with just one suitcase. We don't know whether he made his money through drug dealing, money laundering...' She gestured theatrically. 'I mean it's all very suspect, isn't it.'

'Honestly, Mum, you've watched too many TV dramas. Anyway, I doubt we'll ever find out.'

Her dad tapped the screen with his finger. 'I bet you could, love. Don't forget we have a journalist in the family.'

'You mean the one who got sacked for trying to be helpful?'

'Being unemployed is neither a disgrace, nor a barrier to investigation. The Maddy I know loves digging out a story. Do you remember how when you were little you used to follow a paper trail of clues to find chocolate treats?'

'Yes. I was the only kid who had to work for their easter eggs!' Maddy chuckled.

'And look what you became: a smart, intelligent woman who's capable of anything. I can't speak for your mother but I for one will be delighted to inform the rest of the Shaw family that the much-maligned cousin Nigel did nothing worse than follow his own star.'

———————

'Sorry about that,' said Maddy ten minutes later as she walked into the kitchen. 'Now you can see why I get on better with my mother when we're not in the same county.'

Luke had made himself a coffee. 'She seems determined to marry you off to someone.'

'Oh, you noticed the subtle hints did you?' Maddy rolled her eyes. 'The trouble is many of her friends' children have got married in the last ten years. She's sat through endless photos of other people's wedding days, happy brides, beautiful locations. She just wants the same bragging rights, and unfortunately there's just me to brag about. And it's got worse since everyone started acquiring grandchildren. Every time she meets up with her friends at the allotment, or swimming, or knit and natter, she gets reminders of what she's missing out on. The man with the neighbouring allotment often brings along his young grandson to help out, and the knitting circle seem to make baby garments on an industrial scale.' Maddy sighed. 'I can't compete with all that.'

'And that's your fault, is it?'

'No, of course not. But since I found out about the inheritance, she's been a woman on a mission and she's desperate to identify all possible opportunities. Sorry about being lumped into the eligible marriage material category.'

Maddy wondered why yet again she was doing that stupid British thing of apologising when it was patently obvious to anyone and everyone that Luke was extremely eligible, provided you didn't expect to share the same literary tastes. Maybe that would be an acceptable compromise?

'Presumably,' Luke responded in a sardonic tone, 'she's desperate because apparently you're only staying here for twelve months. When were you going to make that announcement official? The day before you waltz off back to London?'

Maddy couldn't make out whether his expression was one of anger, disappointment or something else entirely. To delay giving him an answer, she pulled out a chair and sat down. Resting her elbows on the table, she dropped her chin into her upturned hands.

It had all seemed so clear cut at the outset. Live here for twelve months, then sell up, move back to London several hundred thousand pounds richer and pick up the threads of her old life. The bits that were still around anyway.

Did she feel the same now as she had when she first arrived here? Absolutely not. But if she stayed, what could she do besides help organise a once-a-year event? Her attempts to get freelance work had so far been unsuccessful. So how would she make ends meet? Until now, she had never even considered the possibility that she might stay on, but she had made friends here. Sally was impossible to dislike and once you go to know Leonard he was very welcoming. Maddy recalled Joyce's advice on friendship:

...you don't have to actually like your friends. Not all the time at any rate. Some of mine are extremely annoying at times...

She guessed Joyce was referring to Myra. Prickly, abrasive, occasionally blunt, and then in a complete volte-face, overly generous. Myra – or her domestic financial representative – had paid for not only the repair to the fuse box as promised, but also a complete overhaul of the electrical wiring, which thankfully wasn't as big a bill as might have been expected.

As far as her mother was concerned, the distance definitely lent, if not enchantment, certainly more tolerance. And then there was Luke.

Maddy lifted her head and met his penetrating gaze. Alice was right, he really was swoon-worthy in spite of his occasionally brash opinions. In another world, he'd be perfect for a holiday romance. 'It's true, but it might also not be true,' she said, trying to answer honestly, but instead sounding rather vague.

Luke made a huffing sound. 'So what is this? Schrodinger's inheritance?'

Maddy threw him a wry smile. 'Very funny. Look, I can't explain while you're pacing around the kitchen.' She pointed at the chair opposite.

She waited until Luke had sat down and stopped huffing. 'So—when I first heard about the house inheritance I'd just lost my job and didn't really need any more change in my life. My plan was simply to sell the house as soon as possible. Job done, thank you, cousin Nigel. Then when I met with the solicitor he informed me that under the terms of Nigel's will, I have to live here for twelve months before I can sell it.'

'That's a bit unusual, isn't it?'

'I'm not an expert on wills and probate but yeah, it was rather a surprise. So, anyway, I figured it would be rather silly to turn down a generous bequest for the sake of twelve months living somewhere else. I had no job ties, and it's not exactly a squat is it, even though half the house hasn't seen a decorator since the seventies.'

'So that covers the might-be-true part,' said Luke. 'What about the rest?'

'That's more difficult,' Maddy admitted. 'When I moved in, Nigel was just some nebulous figure from the past to whom I was distantly related. It was like everyone around here—you included—knew him better than his own family. Now I feel like I'm beginning to get to know him too, and it turns out he wasn't some profligate, dissolute layabout, he cared about the people he met. And now'—Maddy waved the newspaper cutting she'd been showing her parents—'it appears there's some connection to a very well-known rock band.'

'Ah, so this is the mysterious newspaper article we were discussing in bed the other night.'

Maddy ignored Luke's attempt to get a rise from her —she was getting wise to that now—and instead passed over the article. She watched as Luke quickly scanned it, then peered closely at the black and white photo.

'So that ringed figure is Nigel?'

'Yes, according to my dad.'

Luke nodded slowly. 'I wouldn't have recognised him but then this was taken twenty or so years before anyone here had ever met him.'

'And his hair is decidedly … erm…'

'I don't think even Monsieur Roget himself could find an adequate word in his thesaurus to describe that style.'

They both laughed and as the earlier tension between them ebbed away, Maddy realised she wasn't at all sure she wanted to leave here when the twelve months were up.

Chapter Twenty-One

1ST JUNE

If things are going untowardly one month, they are sure to mend the next.

Mr Weston, *Emma*

O ver the following week, whenever Maddy had a spare half hour, she searched on the internet for any information that might connect Nigel to The Faultliners. Annoyingly, when she typed in the search bar *Nigel Shaw* and *The Faultliners*, Google just crossed out the words Nigel Shaw, and presented her with thousands of articles on The Faultliners that all more or less said the same thing. She read them anyway, in case she was able to glean any additional details but frustratingly, despite the extensive reporting on the band, the lists of their hits, albums and tours, there was no mention of anyone even remotely fitting the description of cousin Nigel. She supposed that was only to be expected, as even if he'd been some sort of superfan, he'd hardly merit a line in a magazine.

Luke too had been fully occupied, working assiduously on his new novel. He wouldn't say whether this was a reworking of the original planned story, or whether it was something completely new, but unlike earlier weeks where Maddy suspected he spent half the day snoozing on the sofa, he now seemed totally energised, and even during dinner he had his Moleskine notebook open on the scuffed oak table and was constantly scribbling in it. Maddy tried once to have a sneaky read over his shoulder, but it was slammed shut with a 'Nose out, Ms Austen.' Fair enough; she respected his privacy despite being keen to know more about this 'genius idea' of his.

This morning there had been little time for browsing as Sally had bicycled over with not one but three items in her basket: the latest edition of *Cotlington Chat*, the agenda for the June Literary Festival Committee meeting, and a Tupperware box of biscuits.

'My friend from yum and yoga helped me make them,' Sally said proudly. Maddy peered at the star-shaped biscuits smothered in – hopefully edible – glitter.

'Definitely a masterpiece,' Maddy agreed. 'But tell me, what on earth is yum and yoga?' Her imagination was already busily trying to work out whether this was yoga for yummy mummies, or some sort of 'scoff while you squat' arrangement.

'Tuesday evenings at the church hall in the next

village. It's an hour and a quarter of yoga and then fifteen minutes of cake sampling. You don't *have* to bring cakes or biscuits, but if you do, they are supposed to be home-made. I think some people cheat though as I spotted the packaging for Waitrose sticky toffee slices in the bin the other week.'

Maddy laughed. 'It sounds intriguing. And fun.'

'My friend has all sorts of biscuit cutters so I thought I'd make some spooky ones for Randall when he comes back for the literary festival. We have a shared interest in ghostly things, which is not a bad start.' She gave Maddy a conspiratorial smile.

Maddy attempted to sound a note of caution. 'I admit he is definitely eye candy, but it's important to look beneath the surface. I interviewed various celebrities and reality stars when I was a magazine journalist, and I can tell you being a celebrity doesn't make you a better person. If you're looking for a steady relationship, I'd think about starting closer to home.'

Sally looked unconvinced by Maddy's advice. 'I tried that but the last couple of dates were a bit of a disaster. One bloke was utterly gorgeous—I met him at my friend Jenna's engagement party—but he was way too posh. Obviously that's not her fault. Anyway, we went out for a drink and he mainly talked about the economy and hedge funds and stuff.' She pursed her lips and shook her head, causing her pink highlighted hair to bob around. 'I didn't understand half of what he said. I thought a hedge fund was some sort of conservation project.'

'So what happened with the other one?' asked Maddy, her curiosity aroused.

'Oh, he was a write-off almost from the start,' admitted Sally. 'A friend persuaded me to make up a foursome and we went out for dinner. We hadn't even started eating before he got talking about how a previous girlfriend had painted a bright pink feature wall in her bedroom and how hideous it looked. I mean, I know it's totally superficial, but he was never going to like my house, was he?'

Maddy laughed. 'One day you will find your Mr Right. And in the meantime, trust in your own instincts.'

'Thanks, Maddy. You should be an agony aunt; you're a good listener.'

Sally's words were an unexpected punch in the gut. It felt like a lifetime ago now, but it unintentionally opened up a Pandora's box of memories that Maddy had tried to lock away. She still missed her Dear Jane column even though her boss had made it very clear where the magazine stood on that one.

After watching Sally pedal back down the driveway, she retrieved the agenda and the latest edition of *Cotlington Chat* and settled herself on the sofa in the snug. It was where it was easiest to picture Nigel spending cosy evenings with his literary friends, planning his festival.

She flicked through the snippets of village news.

There was a report of a shoplifting incident in the village-stores-cum-post-office, notice of a garden open to the public to raise funds for charity and a write-up of the ghost hunting evening:

Television celebrity Randall Jacobson visited Cotlington recently as part of the filming for his new series of Ghostwalk. *Spending the evening at Meadowside in Springfield Lane, he recorded several incidences of unexplained activity and we look forward to seeing the results in his upcoming new series on the Mystery Channel. Randall will also be making an appearance at the Cotlington Literary Festival where he will be signing copies of his new book,* Ghosts Abound, *the sequel to* Ghosts at Large.

In the middle, there was a full-page ad for the Cotlington Literary Festival, boasting a variety of talks, a refreshments tent and celebrity speakers.

Not for the first time, she marvelled at how Nigel had created all this, seemingly without any help. As far as she knew, he didn't have any particular journalism or literary experience but maybe he'd been involved in some university societies? Or maybe he had simply been determined.

She needed to channel that determination too, and having retrieved her laptop, spent the next half hour brainstorming more pitches for magazine articles. She then opened up Google, but by now her search engine was totally familiar with her line of enquiry and she only needed to type *Nige* before it suggested *Nigel Shaw and the Faultliners*, along with the usual three hundred thousand entries for perusal. Even looking at ten per day would take aeons of time and so far she'd only covered the first four pages. A different approach was required. Maddy scrolled down and clicked on page ten. A quick glance down the screen told her these articles weren't what she wanted:

A brief history of The Faultliners
Why The Faultliners were vastly overrated
My tribute to America's greatest band

She jumped forward a few pages. More articles on where they toured and played. She jumped forward again, and then again, each time scanning the titles. The words and headings almost became a homogenous blur until her attention lighted on a familiar name:

Rob Pinto Remembers

She knew from her earlier research that he'd been the drummer of the band and had died some years ago, so this must be a fairly old recollection. However, it was the first time she'd seen anything promising in days so she opened the document and started reading. The article itself was more recent: dated January 2020 and clearly written to commemorate thirty years since the death of the lead singer, Chuck Hardimann.

'…an inspired musician who kept faith with his friends…'
'…he was the peacemaker of the band… the rows never lasted for long.'
'…no, we didn't always agree on everything. Did we fight? Hell yes. Do I have regrets? Only one. The stupid argument over the song lyrics to "Rock Hard Road" that turned into a fight, and cost someone their life.'

'Yes!' Maddy punched the air. For the first time she had actually found something that corroborated the tatty newspaper cutting she had found. Admittedly it didn't shed any light on how or why Nigel might have known these musicians, but it was a start. Even though it had little relevance to her personally, she missed having a purpose, having a story to tease out of a jumble of facts, and now she wanted to continue.

She skimmed down the rest of the article and there, right at the bottom she uncovered another nugget.

The above recollections are taken from Rob Pinto's memoir, Taking the Hard Road, charting the early days of The Faultliners, published posthumously by Brightman Press.

Excitement bubbled up inside her, her journalist antenna quivering wildly, as she swiftly opened up another tab and typed in the book title.

'Excuse me, what do you mean, it's not available?' she demanded fifteen seconds later.

Another search on another site yielded the same result. She tried several more.

'How can it be out of print? That's utterly ludicrous! This is one of the biggest rock bands to come out of the States in the seventies, you stupid computer!'

Within a matter of seconds, Luke's head had appeared round the door. 'Do you by any chance have voice-activated software or have you lost the plot and are just having a shouting match with your laptop?'

Maddy threw him an exasperated look. 'I've finally found something tangible that refers to the early days of the band—'

'What band are you on about?'

'The Faultliners! You know, that world famous rock group? That story you said you didn't pinch?'

'I didn't, even though you don't believe me.'

'And it's not just another chronology of their hits and albums, it's the memoir of one of the band from the early days and the sodding thing is out of print!' She jabbed her finger indignantly at the screen.

'Have you tried eBay?'

'I'm not looking for a cardigan.'

'And you accuse me of being a snob! Have you even looked?'

Maddy huffed as she opened up yet another tab, typed in eBay and clicked on the dropdown categories menu.

Luke leaned over her shoulder and pointed at the screen, giving Maddy a waft of his sexy aftershave. His face was so close she could feel his breath on her neck, making it hard to concentrate on the screen. 'There, try that section, Ms Austen. Books, comics and magazines. I realise they didn't have comics in your era but—'

'Just because I enjoy regency era novels does not mean I am stuck in the nineteenth century, Mr Snooty Crime Writer. Anyway, there is such a thing as graphic novels, you know.'

Luke gave her a friendly nudge with his elbow. 'You mean comics.'

Maddy poked him back in the ribs. 'No, I mean a novel. A story.'

'With pictures.'

'So what if there are pictures? It's still a story, whatever the medium. Our stone age ancestors probably told tales around the fire of death-defying escapes from woolly mammoths, or how they went on a hunt for aurochs and then painted the scene on cave walls.'

Luke grinned. 'Well, there probably wasn't a lot else to do back then.'

Maddy seized the cushion behind her and whacked him with it. 'You just like having someone to disagree with.'

She turned back to her laptop and tapped at the keyboard for a few moments, then made an irritated noise. 'No, that book isn't on eBay either. I'll have to set up a saved search in case a copy pops up.'

'Is it that important? Why are you bothered about researching this?'

Maddy shook her head, making her hair shimmer round her shoulders. 'I honestly don't know. Maybe I just like a good story. It doesn't help that most of the original band members are dead now. Maybe I need some psychic insight from Randall Jacobson,' she joked.

'I wouldn't take advice from that man,' muttered Luke. 'He has phoney written through him like a stick of rock.'

Maddy laughed and then stopped when she saw the serious expression on Luke's face. She tugged at his arm.

'Come on then, tell me what it is about him that annoys you so much?'

'You mean apart from ridiculing my novels in one of his tacky television investigative programmes and being a generally all-round smug git? Nothing at all.'

Maddy sighed. Sometimes agony aunts needed to know when to leave well alone.

Chapter Twenty-Two

*Follies and nonsense, whims and inconsistencies, do divert me, I
own, and I laugh at them whenever I can.*
Elizabeth Bennet, *Pride and Prejudice*

O ver the last two weeks Maddy had fired off more
emails to various editors outlining ideas for articles
on a range of subjects—including the well-trodden path
of townie to country girl, a tongue-in-cheek look at the
pros and cons of sleeping with your pet, and how the
advice of a well-known nineteenth-century novelist was
still relevant to today's agony aunts—all to no avail.
Yesterday the fifth rejection had come back, which had
put a serious dampener on the day.

Luke hadn't fared any better and after yet another
setback on the building work, he had arrived back
yesterday afternoon in a decidedly grumpy mood, so

Maddy had challenged him to a game of Monopoly. It incorporated the Shaw family variations to the rules: taxes got put in a kitty to be collected by whoever lands on Free Parking; landing on the 'Go' square entitled you to either take the £200 from the bank or transport to anywhere on the board; and if you landed on a property for sale you had to buy it. The person with the most cash in hand at the end of two hours was declared the winner, with the price of victory having been negotiated at the outset. Luke hadn't even hesitated when Maddy stated her terms; it was clear from his demeanour he thought it was a dead cert that he was going to win. He hadn't.

Any hopes that Maddy might release him from his promise were dashed this morning but being a sore loser, Luke was now making it clear he was participating under sufferance.

'Remind me again why we're doing this?' Luke grumbled as he strode alongside her.

'Because', said Maddy in a patient voice as though she was explaining something to a five-year-old, 'you lost last night if you remember. The deal was if you win, I'll wash and polish your car, and if I win, you accompany me to Joyce's.'

'I didn't realise you were going to walk there.'

'You didn't ask,' laughed Maddy. 'Anyway, it's a lovely day and it's good exercise.'

Maddy swung her arms as she walked. For once she didn't have Buster tugging at the end of the lead; he'd been left at home much to his disgust, and while Jem was working on the main flower border he'd promised to keep an eye on his doggy charge.

Obviously back in regency times, the Bennet girls would have worn long, country-style dresses over neat, white petticoats for their country walks, and a bonnet adorned with flowers and ribbons, rather than faded jeans and a T-shirt with *Society of Obstinate Headstrong Girls* emblazoned all over the front, but the feeling of enjoyment was the same. The T-shirt had been a Christmas present from Alice last year so it felt like a connection to home, although her current walking companion had already found plenty to say about it.

As she sauntered down Springfield Lane, Maddy could imagine herself in a Jane Austen novel, strolling into the village to pay a neighbourly call. Going by car would not have felt remotely the same and today it was totally unnecessary. June weather was often rather variable but this afternoon a warm breeze tugged at her loose hair, and the sweet scent of freshly mown grass hung in the air like an invigorating tonic. The hedgerows either side of the road were bursting with wildflowers and long grasses, and beyond she could just make out a couple of ponies grazing peacefully in the fields. Thankfully, they were well fenced in so that whenever Buster was off the lead in the fields behind the house there was no chance of him making a nuisance of himself.

Two hundred years ago, visiting people involved handing out cards and scheduling time to make calls. Maddy could see the advantage of giving people advance notice of arrival—no need for that frantic emergency tidy-up with the odour of last night's takeaway still lingering, or fretting that guests might turn up while you're lying on the sofa in your pyjamas—but since Joyce was currently stuck at home with a broken ankle and was – according to Jem – almost begging for visitors, she'd decided to give her a pleasant surprise and also update her following last night's committee meeting. She planned to pick up some flowers on the way, this time from the village store rather than the side of the road.

Now was as good a time as any to inform Luke of the detour. 'We're just popping in here to get Joyce some flowers,' said Maddy, gesturing in front of her. They paused at the doorway and stood to one side to allow an elderly couple to exit the shop. A tall man in a navy-blue jacket nodded politely as he manoeuvred a wheelchair through the doorway. His seated companion waved her thanks. 'Lovely morning, isn't it?'

Maddy returned the smile. 'A perfect summer's day.'

She had never met them before and wondered if they were locals. Everyone round here seemed so friendly and always had time to stop and exchange a few words. Maddy couldn't help but contrast the scene to her former daily commute on the London underground: noisy, congested, and everyone in such a hurry to get somewhere. Life here seemed like a different world away.

'There's already too many people in there, I'll just wait out here,' said Luke.

'Fine. I won't be long.'

The flower section was near the front of the store where several buckets stood in a row holding multicoloured ready-wrapped bouquets. What would Joyce like? Maddy discounted the elegant but rather plain arrangements of white flowers with sprays of grey and green foliage, and the large bunches of star-gazer lilies that dropped carpet-staining orange pollen everywhere. She thought back to Nigel's funeral and Joyce's colourful outfit, and selected a mixed bouquet of butter-yellow chrysanthemums, single-stem dark pink roses, orange gerberas and something tall with delicate purple flowers that she couldn't identify.

The flowers were dripping water on her feet as she waited to pay for her purchase and as she stood in the queue she became aware of a small stone or piece of grit that was now spiking the sole of her foot. She would deal with that when she got back outside. Thankfully, the cashier had some paper to wrap around the flowers and when Maddy mentioned that they were for Joyce, she insisted on adding a pink ribbon too.

'And she asked us to send on her best wishes,' said Maddy as she stood outside the shop trying to twist her shoe off. 'Joyce clearly knows a lot of people round here.'

'Or possibly everyone knows Joyce,' replied Luke. 'Are you doing some sort of solo dance by the way?'

'Yes, it's called the I've-got-a-stone-in-my-shoe dance,' quipped Maddy. 'Oh, stupid thing,' she muttered as she squatted down, balanced the flowers across her knees and used her finger to lever off her heel so she could locate the offending piece of grit.

'Don't worry about trying to help,' she muttered

under her breath as she finally managed to prise the small stone out.

Luke grinned. 'Fine by me.'

Behind her, someone was clapping. She stood up and whirled around to see the elderly couple observing them. They weren't the only spectators either – a young woman in a shapeless grey hoodie was loitering with interest.

'What did he say?' the lady in the wheelchair asked her companion.

'He said "fine by me". Maybe that's what modern folk say these days.' He stepped forward with a broad smile and reached out to Maddy. 'Well done.'

She wondered what on earth he was talking about but out of politeness took his outstretched hand. His skin felt dry and wrinkly, but he had a firm handshake.

The man turned to Luke. 'And congratulations to you too; you're a lucky man.'

'What on earth do you mean?' Luke's hands remained firmly affixed to his side as his features rapidly formed a scowl.

In a sudden flash of clarity, Maddy burst out laughing. 'Oh goodness no, I wasn't proposing! I just had a stone in my shoe and was trying not to drop my flowers.'

'My apologies,' said the elderly man, looking rather discomfited. 'We both thought …well erm…' He cleared his throat. 'We'll leave you to enjoy your day.' With a polite nod, he turned back to his companion and hurried along the high street as fast as he could push the chair. The hooded teenager stood smirking and prodding at her phone. Maddy hoped she wasn't going to appear on

TikTok later in the day. She could see how the scene had been misinterpreted though, and it was rather amusing to think some random stranger thought she was going down on one knee to propose to a man who thought romance was a waste of effort. Elizabeth Bennet would certainly have been exceedingly diverted.

'I bet you enjoyed that, didn't you?' growled Luke.

'You have to admit it was rather funny.'

'Not in the slightest.'

'Well, if you'd offered to hold the flowers for me while I was wrestling with my shoe, it might not have looked quite so proposal-y.'

'Why on earth would anyone with any sense want to propose to someone in the middle of the street anyway? It's a bloody ridiculous idea and it encourages people to jump to the wrong conclusions.'

'Well, let them! It wasn't as if I was actually propositioning you!'

'I'm relieved to hear it,' Luke shot back. 'I'm glad you've had your fun.' He turned and marched back along the street.

'Where are you going? Hey, it was just a misunderstanding!' Maddy shouted after him. Luke continued walking. Maddy cupped her hands round her mouth as she added, 'And for avoidance of doubt, I had not known you a day before I felt that you were the last man in the world I would ever propose to, if that makes you feel any better!'

What the hell was wrong with him? It was rather an over-reaction to what was actually a harmless and amusing misunderstanding. At least Joyce might be entertained, even if Mr Grumpy was not.

Joyce lived on the outskirts of Cotlington in one of the bungalows built in the seventies as part of the village expansion. Unlike the row of terraced cottages where Sally lived, which had colourful individually painted exteriors, the row of bungalows in Heather Lane were all built in the same sandy brick colour with white window frames and topped with grey roof tiles. The main distinguishing feature of each was the small patch of garden at the front.

Joyce's front garden was a patch of grass and clover, with a small stone flower fairy in one corner and a painted gnome in a red hat and blue coat standing guard at the front door. Maddy pressed the doorbell and heard a jaunty synthesised version of 'Für Elise' playing inside. The door was opened by a woman who Maddy judged to be in her mid-sixties. She peered at Maddy from behind a pair of blue framed spectacles.

'Hello.' Maddy smiled brightly. 'I heard Joyce was unwell so I thought I'd pop over to see how she was. And to bring some flowers.'

A voice wafted along the hallway: 'Who is it, Kath?'

'It's Maddy!' Maddy called out. 'Bringing succour to the weary and all that.'

If Maddy had been asked what she thought Joyce's home was like, she'd have guessed it would be decorated in bright colours and full of knick-knacks and ornaments. To her surprise, the décor was plain, the walls painted in complementing muted colours. A couple of framed prints hung on the wall and a display cabinet in the corner held a selection of ornamental plates, a china dog, and a Lladró figurine of an angel.

On the mantelpiece there was a framed wedding photograph of a couple standing outside a church, laughing as petals of confetti fluttered around them. The attire was definitely of an earlier decade, but it was clearly a happy picture.

Joyce was sitting in a burgundy upholstered armchair with her foot up on a small, cushioned stool in a matching colour. Her face broke into a broad smile as her guest approached.

Maddy gestured to her foot. 'You look like you've been in the wars.'

'Trying to do too much as usual,' grumbled Kath.

'Maddy, this is my younger sister,' said Joyce, pointing at the grumbler. 'She thinks I overdo things. Kath would prefer it if I sat in my chair and watched telly all day, wouldn't you?'

'So how did you injure yourself?' asked Maddy. 'Did you fall over something?'

'Off something might be more accurate,' said Kath tartly, but with a caring smile.

'I was using the stepstool to look in a cupboard for the bunting I made last year for the literary festival. Nigel commented on it at the time; he thought it was ever so good.' Her voice faltered for a moment and not for the first time, Maddy realised how fond everyone had been of Nigel and how much they all missed him.

'I was reaching up to get to one of the boxes on top of the wardrobe and the next minute I was on the floor. It's a right nuisance as I'd been planning to go to a funeral later that afternoon.'

Maddy murmured the usual expressions of sympathy. She guessed that at Joyce's age it was rather inevitable that one would end up going to more funerals than weddings, but to her knowledge she'd already been to three in the last four months.

While Kath made everyone a cup of tea, Maddy filled a vase with water and arranged the flowers for Joyce.

'They're from me and Luke,' she said, positioning them on the small table to the side of Joyce's armchair, even though Luke didn't really deserve the accreditation after his earlier behaviour.

'And how is our writer in residence?' asked Joyce with a cheeky wink.

Maddy huffed out a sigh. 'You may well ask. He was planning on coming with me actually'—Joyce didn't need to know he'd lost a bet—'but he had an artistic meltdown outside the general store.' Maddy gave Joyce a quick recap of the hilarious not-a-proposal and how Luke had reacted.

'Anyone would think I'd personally insulted him the way he responded,' she said, her voice brimming with indignation. She'd had time to think as she'd walked the final two hundred metres to Joyce's house, and while it was amusing that people thought she was actually proposing, surely Luke shouldn't have been quite so offended? She was prepared to acknowledge that he was a good-looking man as well as an internationally bestselling author so he could clearly take his pick of eligible females, but it still hurt to realise that as far as he was concerned, she was totally unsuitable.

Joyce took a sip of her tea. 'Did you know he'd been engaged to someone in the past?'

'Yes, someone did mention it in passing, but I don't know any of the details.'

'Well,' said Joyce, clearly delighted to be able to share some news, 'according to my friend Daphne, it was a right row and a half when they broke up.'

Having received a few broadsides from Luke in the past, Maddy had no difficulty in imagining that.

'Well now, Daphne's daughter used to have a few cleaning jobs in the area, and one of them was for our writer in residence, and it was quite a job. He wasn't living in Cotlington in those days and his house was a total mess —and as for that kitchen! It took her ages to tidy everything away. Coffee cups everywhere, half eaten packets of biscuits—'

'So did the fiancée live there too?' Maddy asked, hoping to steer Joyce back onto the more interesting elements of the tale.

Joyce shook her head. 'Not that Daphne heard. It was him that broke it off though by all accounts. They hadn't been engaged long either. Just a matter of days. The poor girl was distraught. Not long afterwards she turned up and just stood on the doorstep and there was a real shouting match. Daphne said her daughter could hear it all over the house. Goodness knows what the neighbours thought.'

Maddy suppressed a wry smile at hearing one of her

mum's favourite expressions. So Randall was speaking the truth then about Luke's broken engagement. She had half assumed that he'd just put his own spin on some old news, but apparently not. Was this why the Cameron Massey façade was always one of a grumpy, irascible writer?

'And did Daphne say how long her daughter continued working there?'

Joyce shifted in her chair and winced as her foot moved slightly. 'I don't remember, love. Daphne passed away—it was a stroke, her daughter said—but it all seems a long time ago now,' she added wistfully. 'Of course there was a time when Reg and I knew everything that was going on in the village. Folk liked to chat when they popped into the post office. They didn't want to be rushed along like shopping on a supermarket conveyor belt. Nowadays there's hardly time for a good morning.'

Coming from her London life, Maddy had been used to rushing into and out of shops, hurrying to catch a bus or the next tube train, and couldn't recall ever stopping to talk to anyone unless she bumped into someone she knew. If anyone had started up a natter with the sales assistant there'd have been tuts, and shouts of 'get a move on!' from the people behind. She wondered how many Joyces there were in the world who were a bit lonely and just wanted a few minutes of people's time now and then.

'And now everyone seems to talk on the interweb thingy,' Joyce continued. She rummaged in the sturdy leather handbag propped against her chair and pulled out a phone. 'Can you show me how to do Twitter?'

Maddy was momentarily taken aback. It wasn't every

day that your local septuagenarian decided to launch themselves online, but surely that was just a prejudiced presumption? She smiled as she pulled out her own phone. 'I'd be delighted to be your first follower.'

It took only a few minutes to get an account set up for Joyce, and after a disappointing search through her contacts – who clearly didn't feel the need to be on Twitter – only yielded one niece, they started widening the net. It wasn't long before Joyce was following everyone in the current series of *Love Island*, the cast of *Made in Chelsea*, and Richard Osman – *very good at quizzes, that man*. She was busily searching for Prue Leith as Maddy's phone started ringing.

'Don't mind me, you answer the phone; it might be important,' Joyce said with a wave of her hand.

Maddy stood up and moved towards the door. 'Hello?'

An urgent and familiar voice barked, 'Maddy, it's Luke. Buster's gone.'

Chapter Twenty-Three

Sometimes one is guided by what they say of themselves, and very frequently by what other people say of them, without giving oneself time to deliberate and judge.
Elinor Dashwood, *Sense and Sensibility*

A jolt of alarm shot through Maddy. 'Oh no! What do you mean gone? Isn't he in the garden somewhere? I thought Jem was keeping an eye on him?'

'He was. At least he said he was. Apparently someone called Sally popped over to deliver something—'

'And he took his eye off the dog,' finished Maddy. 'Could Buster have tried to go back to your house? I know it's a building site but…'

An exasperated sound ricocheted off her ear drum. 'That was the first place I checked after finding he wasn't at Meadowside. Jem's been out to the fields behind the house. I'm going to take the car and drive around a bit. Can you keep your eyes open on the way back?'

'Of course. I'll come and give you a hand.'

'Is it bad news?' asked Joyce as Maddy tucked her phone back into her bag.

'Luke's dog's run off. He's a bit of a professional escape artist and he probably didn't like being left behind. He gets a bit anxious. The dog I mean, not Luke.' She squeezed Joyce's hand gently. 'Sorry, I'd better go and help with the search. Thanks for the tea, and I'll say goodbye to Kath on the way out. And I'm sorry you weren't able to go to the funeral this afternoon.'

'Don't fret about that. There'll be other occasions, I'm sure.'

If Maddy had had more time to think, she might have found that an odd thing to say, but her thoughts were now focused on Buster. Over the last few months, she had grown increasingly fond of the loveable rogue and she knew that despite Luke's indifferent attitude to many of his fellow humans, he was extremely attached to his dog. Since the ghost hunting evening it was clear that Buster slept with Luke every night and perhaps they provided each other with a feeling of mutual security. She didn't want to think about what might happen if Buster didn't come back. Or worse, if they discovered the unthinkable had happened.

As she marched briskly along the High Street, she kept glancing left and right, down every alleyway and round every corner, but there was no sign of him. How far could he have gone? Would he stay around the house or had he gone off looking for his master? As she reached the junction with Springfield Lane she spotted Luke's Astra heading in her direction and she waved. Luke slowed down and Maddy hurried to the passenger window. 'Do you want me to go back and cover the fields again, or is there something more useful I can do?'

Luke leaned over and opened the door. 'I was planning to drive around a bit as I can't see him in the village. Do you mind being the lookout? I prefer to watch the road when I'm driving. Sorry about the state of the car.'

Maddy jumped in, ignoring the dog hair and pawprints everywhere, and they headed out of Cotlington in the direction of Haxford, the nearest major town. For five minutes neither of them spoke. Maddy swivelled in her seat to make it easier to look down side roads and across fields. Her eyes strained as she tried to identify anything that might look like a white and tan dog with large floppy brown ears and a white waggy tail, but all she saw were fields of sheep, three ponies, a party of ramblers and something that could have been a llama.

After reaching the outskirts of Haxford, they turned back towards Cotlington via a different and more circuitous route. The vinyl seatbelt scraped uncomfortably against her neck but Maddy maintained her constant vigil. As they turned into Springfield Lane, Luke slowed down and then stopped. 'There are fewer trees at this end of the lane. We might see better from here.'

The hedgerows were still going to obstruct their view but now wasn't the time to point that out. The truth was they could be searching in completely the wrong area but neither wanted to be first to suggest going home.

Maddy got out and cupped her hands around her mouth. 'BUSTER!' she yelled at the top of her voice.

'HERE, BOY! BISCUITS!' shouted Luke, followed by every other food word in Buster's vocabulary. 'Where could he have got to?' said Luke running his hand through his hair, his voice thick with desperation. 'The hedgerows are too high here to see over.'

Maddy jumped in the air to see if it improved her line of sight.

'Try standing up there,' said Luke, pointing.

Maddy frowned. 'That's your car.'

'Yes, well spotted, Sherlock. But you'll be able to see better from up there.'

'And possibly dent the car.'

'I don't care about the stupid car.'

'But I'm an agony aunt, not an award-winning gymnast,' Maddy protested.

'Yeah, sorry. I just—' Luke shrugged. His mouth tightened and the Maddy could see the tension in his face. Who was she to deny help if it made him feel like he was doing something useful. She reached out and gently squeezed his arm. His skin was warm to the touch and she found herself reluctant to let go. 'Come on then, let's give it a try. At least I'm wearing trainers and not heels.'

Luke fully wound down the passenger window then crouched down with his hands locked together. 'I'll give you a leg up.'

Maddy stepped into Luke's hands and hauled herself

up. With Luke's help she managed to get her other foot on the edge of the open window. 'I feel like a beached whale!' she puffed.

With some more shoving and a helping hand on her bottom which felt both intrusive and sexy in equal measure, she managed to clamber onto the roof and tentatively got to her feet, keeping her arms out like an amateur trapeze artist.

From up there she had a much better view of the surrounding area and she turned a slow and careful 360 degrees, willing Buster to appear from somewhere. Both of them continued shouting and calling until they were hoarse. Luke stuck two fingers in his mouth and sent a piercing whistle across the field, to no avail.

'I'm so sorry, I can't see him anywhere,' Maddy said. 'And I'm worried about denting your roof.' She sat down carefully, letting her legs dangle over the rear of the hatchback.

Luke held out his hands. 'Slide forward and then jump. I'll catch you.'

Maddy shuffled her bottom to the edge and looked down. The last thing she wanted was a broken ankle to match Joyce's. Luke stood directly in front of her, his strong arms ready to catch her. He could often be obstinate and frequently grumpy, but she trusted his judgement, and if she was being technically accurate, he'd already caught her once before, although admittedly that was from behind a curtain.

With a deep breath, she pushed herself forward. Instead of the expected thud to the ground, she felt Luke hands under her armpits as he lifted her down gently. They were standing pressed together, her chest against his, and for a moment it was as if time had frozen and she stood in his embrace, gazing up at him. For several seconds neither of them moved and the only sounds were the twittering of birds overhead and the distant roar of a passing vehicle. Her heart thumped loudly and her body was suffused with a heat that had nothing to do with solar energy and everything to do with the man standing in front of her. Why did he have this effect on her? It wasn't as if he fancied her in the slightest. She needed to get a grip.

It was Maddy who broke the silence. 'Where shall we look now?'

Luke sighed heavily as he removed his hands from her body. 'I don't know. We've covered all the local area. What do you suggest?'

'Well, the first thing is to ring round all the vets in the area.'

A look of alarm shot across Luke's face.

'It doesn't mean anything's happened to him,' said Maddy hurriedly, 'it's just in case someone has handed him in as a lost dog. And then'—she continued—'we can make some posters for sticking to lampposts and noticeboards.'

The house seemed empty without the skitter of excitable paws on the wood floor, accompanied by the thud of his favourite rubber ball, which now sat under the dining table, a poignant reminder of its missing owner.

After making them both a cup of tea, Luke disappeared into the library to make posters while Maddy called every vet within a fifteen-mile radius of Cotlington. As she ticked the names off against her list she tried to quell the rising feeling of panic. After all, Buster had run off before, but that was because, said the little voice in her head, he didn't like the building noise at Luke's house. Why would he run off now? Was it because they had both gone out and left him all alone? Or had he just seen a brave squirrel venture into the garden?

Half an hour later, Luke reappeared with a stack of A4 posters with the heading MISSING DOG, underneath which was a photo of Buster and a description of him, plus both Maddy's and Luke's phone numbers. It was a gorgeous photo of Buster looking extremely happy with what looked like one of Luke's shoes in his mouth. Up until now Maddy had hoped Buster would appear from somewhere, barrelling in through the kitchen door leaving his usual trail of wet muddy paws, and looking inordinately pleased with himself. Now it was official: he was a lost dog.

'Oh Buster, where are you?' she said softly as a couple of tears trickled down her cheek. Up until that moment, Maddy hadn't realised just how fond of him she'd become. Somehow that mischievous canine had wormed his way into her affections and the thought that he might be lying injured somewhere at the side of the road or lost and unable to find his way home was just unbearable.

They left their posters on lampposts, bus stops, tree trunks. They posted copies through doors at random in dozens of roads. Now there was nothing to do but wait for a call.

Maddy checked her phone periodically but found only another two rejections from magazine editors which added to the air of despondency. As the evening lengthened, Luke took the car out for one last look around the village before they lost the daylight, while Maddy walked round the perimeter of the grounds, calling and shaking the tin containing his favourite doggy treats.

By ten o'clock, Luke had returned, his stooped shoulders reflecting the worry etched into his face. It was clear that neither of them wanted to admit defeat and be the first to head up to bed, nor be the one that locked up for the night, knowing that Buster was out there somewhere. Maddy fetched the bottle of Madeira that she'd discovered in Nigel's drinks cupboard, and brought it back into the cosy snug along with two small glasses. She then switched on one of the lamps in the corner of the room, and they sat side by side on the sofa, sipping at their drinks, staring at nothing in particular, like an anxious couple waiting up for their offspring to return after a night out. The lateness of the evening and the shadowy lamplight would—on another day—have seemed a very intimate setting, but Maddy was sure that Luke was consumed with the same degree of worry that she was.

'I don't know what to do if—'

Maddy reached over and placed her hand over Luke's. 'Don't let's think about that yet.'

Luke tugged his hand away. 'So when do you want to

start worrying? Midnight? 3am? Or does Ms Austen have a better suggestion?'

Maddy recognised that his sharp retort was born of acute anxiety. 'I'm not sure Jane Austen ever dealt with a lost dog,' she replied honestly. 'But she did once write "Do not give way to useless alarm; though it is right to be prepared for the worst, there is no occasion to look on it as certain."'

'Hm…'

'Careful,' warned Maddy, prodding Luke gently in the ribs. 'That sounded like you were about to approve of Jane Austen's advice.'

A thin smile flickered for an instant on his face as he turned to look at her. 'A temporary aberration, I'm sure.'

Maddy returned the smile. 'Maybe. Maybe not. You're not wholly beyond redemption, you know.'

'I'm glad you think so. Not everyone would agree with you.'

'Maybe they don't know you as well.'

Luke poured himself another drink. The creative genius apparently went hand in hand with the snarky remarks, and she'd certainly heard plenty of those, but he had also shared with her personal recollections of events that had clearly shaped his personality. Luke's comment from a few weeks ago popped into her head.

You don't like admitting you get things wrong sometimes, do you?

She didn't like admitting he was right either, but she wasn't above saying sorry, and from the moment she had received Luke's call this afternoon, she'd been increasingly burdened with feelings of guilt.

'Luke, I feel I need to apologise. I shouldn't have made you come with me to visit Joyce.' She twisted her fingers as she spoke, as though she was trying to tie them in a knot. 'Buster probably panicked being left all alone and thought he'd been abandoned. I'm so sorry.'

Luke rested his head back against the sofa. 'It's not your fault. And you know me well enough to know that if I thought it was, I'd say so. Last night was a board game, not an internationally binding peace agreement. I could have refused to come, you know.' He paused. 'Anyway, you probably think I behaved like a bit of an arse.'

'You did. Care to explain yourself?'

Luke inhaled sharply and stretched his shoulders. 'You know I don't buy all that romance stuff.'

'I think you made that clear the first time I met you. Although I suspect you like being challenged in your opinions.'

'Very perceptive of you, Ms Austen.'

'I wasn't totally crap at being an agony aunt, you know.'

Luke's silence was taken as tacit agreement to her assertion. There was more to this though: something about the events outside the general store had triggered a very visceral response from Luke. Maddy wondered how to phrase a delicate question. It had been much easier when she was writing her agony aunt column—you could spend time choosing the right way to word something and not be hampered by the fact that the person you were responding to was sitting right next to you and hadn't actually asked for your opinion in the first place.

'Was it something to do with a former relationship?' Maddy ventured tentatively. 'Joyce mentioned in passing that you had been engaged some years ago.'

Luke didn't respond. He sat motionless, staring at the empty armchair opposite. It was completely dark outside now and the windows panes were black, featureless rectangles. Maddy stood up and went to draw the curtains.

'Do you mind if we leave them open?' Luke asked. 'That way if Buster is out there somewhere he'll see the lights are on inside.'

Maddy wasn't at all sure Buster was anywhere near the house but while there was a shred of hope to hang on to, who was she to argue? She sat down again and let the silence settle around them like a delicate autumnal mist hanging in the air. She'd leave it to Luke if he wanted to talk.

Several minutes passed before Luke suddenly spoke. 'I never wanted to get engaged in the first place, you know.'

Why on earth had he then? Maddy restrained the urge to ask the most obvious question and instead asked, 'So how long had you known her?'

'We'd been seeing each other for a few years.'

Maddy was curious to know more but she didn't want to push Luke. 'I see. And … where did you meet?'

'She was the daughter of the senior director of the publishing company and had just joined the business. We met at one of those glitzy publishing parties; I was celebrating the two-book deal I'd just signed with them. I'd got used to the idea that my parents thought writing should be a hobby; it was rarely mentioned at home, like they were almost embarrassed that people knew I'd written a crime novel.'

'That's usually the response reserved for romance writers,' observed Maddy drily. 'And it's wrong. You were totally entitled to feel proud of your achievement, and I'm sure your publishers were thrilled.'

'Yes. It was quite an eye-opener meeting up with other authors who loved doing what I did. Later on, I was lucky to sign with an agent; having that wall of support was incredible. Clara was part of that amazing debut whirlwind and we went to a lot of writing festivals and events together. Then we progressed to doing a few holidays together. It was great for a while. Then she started hinting at living together.'

'That's quite a big step. How did you feel about that?' asked Maddy gently.

'Absolutely not. I stayed over at her flat in Chelsea occasionally, and she came to my place a few times but I didn't have any plans for all that cosy domestic stuff. It suited us both doing things our own way, and it had worked for the previous two and half years. Then her father had a stroke and everything changed. She wanted the sort of relationship that her parents had, and kept making comments about how happy her dad would be to see her settled with someone. The unspoken words were, *before he died*. I should have said outright that that wasn't what I wanted, but I didn't want to upset her or her dad. I knew how close they were and how worried she was about him. Breaking up seemed a very callous response.'

'So ... did something happen?'

Luke nodded. He reached for the bottle on the small table in front of them and poured himself another generous helping of the caramel-coloured liquid and knocked it back in two gulps.

'It was meant to be a shopping trip. I can't remember what for. Clara was staying over for a few days, said she had an important appointment. So, we were in Haxford —the Old Town.' As he spoke he stared at the empty glass in his hand, studiously avoiding any eye contact. 'The pedestrian area is awash with independent shops and places to eat with outside tables, and even in the winter months it wasn't uncommon to see musicians busking in the street so I paid no attention to the guitarist at first, just strumming a few chords. Then a second one appeared, and a woman in the square started singing. Clara loved that sort of impromptu schmaltz so we stood listening as various onlookers who clearly weren't shoppers joined in, accompanied by a violinist who appeared from a nearby shop. People were videoing it on their phones like they do when there's some random entertainment going on.'

Maddy nodded. 'Yes, I know the sort of thing.'

'So more and more people joined in the singing; it was clearly an organised thing, and equally clear that Clara wanted to hang around until the end. As the song finished, I started to clap politely but weirdly no one else did.'

'Do you remember the song?'

'Adele's "Make You Feel My Love".' Luke's shoulders

tensed as he spoke and he gripped the glass. 'Everyone seemed to be looking at us. Then several things happened at once. The crowd parted; a woman I didn't recognise handed Clara an armful of flowers, and the next thing I know she's down on one knee and started to propose. In the middle of the street.' He banged his glass down on the table and an unpleasant sickly feeling curdled in the pit of Maddy's stomach as she imagined the scene.

'Then the phones came out in force and there was a horrible atmosphere of expectation. I mean'—he waved his arms agitatedly—'what the fuck was I supposed to say? *"Actually, I don't think I want to marry you but thanks for organising the entertainment?"*'

'It takes a brave person to do that.'

'And of course I didn't. I couldn't,' said Luke bitterly. 'The humiliation would be all over YouTube by lunchtime.'

'So you said yes?'

Luke nodded. 'The crowd went wild. Clara was leaping up and down and threw her arms around my neck. I was grateful for that as I could hide my face, while the noisy, nosey crowd dispersed. As soon as possible I got the hell out of there.'

'So did you explain to her how you felt?'

'I didn't get the chance. We'd barely got into the car when she whipped out her phone and was screeching the news to her parents. She gabbled on about getting a ring, how clever she'd been to organise everything and how thrilled she was that I'd said yes. Like I had any choice,' he added as he refilled his glass.

Maddy realised now was not the time to suggest he dialled back on the drink. It was probably giving him Dutch courage, and she suspected there weren't many people who had heard this version of the story. She wanted to throw her arms around him and tell him this wasn't his fault. Instead, she asked, 'Did Clara not notice that you were…'—she paused to consider the right way to say this—'not quite as excited as she was?'

'Clearly not. I suggested there was no need to rush into everything, but my advice fell on stony ground. She returned to London the following day having already informed huge numbers of her friends. Over the following week I had daily updates on the engagement party that she and her mum were planning, and a text asking me to come up to London so she could show me the ring she'd seen in Burlington Arcade. I realised I needed to do something swiftly when I started receiving messages of congratulations from my publisher and a request for an interview from a country living magazine which Clara had clearly engineered. Things were escalating so quickly I had two choices: to resign myself to going along with the whole getting married thing or to call a halt to the charade.'

'And I'm guessing you chose the latter option?'

Luke nodded. His face wore a grim expression and Maddy couldn't help but feel sorry for him.

'Whichever option I chose would have awful consequences, but one would be far more permanent than the other. I didn't want to do it by text or over the phone so I arranged to come up to London a few days later, and was greeted with sheaves of paper printed from estate agent websites. Somehow in this hideous wedding whirlwind there was an inbuilt assumption that I would give up my house in the country so she could continue working in London.' He ran his hand through his hair. 'I mean, it was insane, the speed at which my life was being re-engineered to suit hers. I was greeted effusively by her parents, who had invited over several other family members to meet their new prospective son-in-law. I had to almost drag Clara out into the garden to get somewhere to talk in private. There was no easy way to say it, so I just had to get it over with.'

Maddy grimaced. 'That must have been horrible.'

'Bloody awful. Screaming, crying, shouting, recriminations. And that was before the rest of the family got started—apparently I'd thrown their goodwill back in their faces, insulted their daughter, led her to believe this was her fairytale moment—'

'That's ludicrous!'

'Oh, you wouldn't believe what they shouted at me as I grabbed my overnight bag and bolted out of the house.' Luke took another large swig of drink.

'The stinger came two days afterwards— an official letter from my editor saying regrettably my book was being pulled, with some vague excuse attached.'

'What!' Maddy stared at him open-mouthed.

'After publishing the first two novels, I'd been offered another two-book deal and had already submitted the first manuscript. It was Clara's way of taking revenge. Her daddy would do anything for his daughter.'

'But they can't just do that!'

Luke blinked slowly. 'Apparently they can when Daddy runs the company. I got loads of abusive letters from her family too. I sold up, moved to Cotlington and left all that crap behind. It was their loss in the end. I found another publisher and then *End of the Roadie* came along, and...'

'The rest was history,' Maddy finished. 'Although it can't have been easy to forget what happened.'

'The fallout from the breakup was awful. I lost friends over it. She and her coven of girlfriends made studious efforts to tell the world what a shit I was, and mud sticks. But you know what? I don't regret making that decision. Regrets are generally a waste of time, although I wish I'd kept in touch with Nigel after *Roadie* was published. It was the work of an afternoon to write the acknowledgements for that book, but the guilt of not giving Nigel the credit he deserved lasted a lot longer—even more so now I know it was based on a real story—and it caused a friendship to wither.' He sighed and looked briefly towards the window, even though there was nothing to see outside.

'So come on then, what would Jane Austen have to say about that? I'd probably be marked down forever as a complete cad of the first order, wouldn't I?'

Maddy shook her head. She knew something had prompted Luke to respond the way he had outside the village stores, but she hadn't envisioned anything on this scale. She wondered whether it was appropriate to give him a consoling hug.

'What you need to understand is that Jane Austen

wasn't some prissy do-gooder who automatically sided with her fellow sex. She understood people and trust me, two hundred years hasn't radically changed how people behave as far as relationships are concerned. Jane Austen would say that if you like someone, make it clear that you do, but don't put your feelings on public display unless you're sure they're reciprocated. Otherwise you're heading straight into Marianne Dashwood territory.'

'Who's she?'

'Another time, another place, Mr Crime Writer. Jane despised people who played games or led people on, and would always suggest that her characters should look for someone who brings out their best qualities, not their worst. There's good and bad in everyone.' She patted his arm. 'There, agony aunt advice over with.'

Their sofa vigil lapsed into a companionable silence punctuated only by the clock in the hall striking midnight. She let her head fall back on the sofa as her thoughts ran back over what Luke had just told her. The pieces of the puzzle that was Luke Hamilton certainly fitted together better now. It didn't seem to bother him that the world thought him arrogant and opinionated, but Maddy felt indignant on his behalf. She'd never had any relationship that had progressed as far as a proposal but if it did, she certainly wouldn't want it to be a public spectacle.

Was it around this time that Buster came into his life? Did he provide the support and companionship that Luke had lost elsewhere? It suddenly occurred to her that if Luke had stayed friends with Nigel, he'd have known about his death before they did that radio interview together. That would have been very strange.

'Are you asleep?' whispered Luke.

'No, just thinking,' Maddy whispered back.

'What about?'

'Oh you know, life … the way things work out … cousin Nigel.' Maddy brought her feet up on the sofa and hugged her knees. 'You're not the only one with regrets.'

'Confessions of an agony aunt—I'm all ears.'

'It's nothing riveting,' said Maddy almost apologetically. 'I just wish I'd made the effort to find out about Nigel; to make my own mind up instead of taking everyone else's opinions at face value.'

No matter how many times she tried to dismiss the feeling of guilt, or package it up as ingrained family prejudice, there was a lingering feeling of sorrow. Nigel's reputation in her family was probably on a par with Luke's reputation in Clara's family, although for widely differing reasons.

The Nigel Shaw award had started as a joke one Christmas many years ago when Maddy was a teenager. It was one of those cheap trinkets you could buy in a novelty shop—a silver-coloured plastic thing, in the shape of a shield. One of her cousins had given it to her uncle Robert as a spoof award for services to catering, after he'd been left in charge of the Sunday roast and had nodded off in his armchair having forgotten to set the timer. The piercing sound of the smoke alarm had alerted everyone to the impending culinary disaster, and it had been universally considered a 'Nigel Shaw level' dereliction of duty.

The following Christmas uncle Rob had awarded it to one of his sons for some misdemeanour, the details long since forgotten. It quickly became a Shaw family tradition, and every Christmas thereafter the current incumbent would pass on the award with an appropriately hilarious speech, enlightening the rest of the family as to the alleged gross misconduct of the recipient.

At some point the words 'Nigel Shaw trophy' had been added inexpertly with a Sharpie pen, adding a somewhat naff touch. Maddy had even won it one year for accidentally killing off her mum's indoor house plants while her parents were on holiday. In her defence, they were killed with kindness having been grossly overwatered, but she recalled proudly displaying the shield. Now she wished she had a better way of remembering her cousin.

'Is that why you're slightly obsessed with this rock group? Because you think it will shed some light on Nigel's past?'

Maddy sighed. 'It's one of the few tenuous connections to a past we know nothing about. He left the UK aged twenty in total disgrace. No money, no family support. No one hears a thing from him except a few short letters to my dad. Then twenty-five years later he turns up here, incredibly wealthy, and everyone loves him. It's sad that he never contacted his family, but he clearly wasn't a horrible person.' The juxtaposition of living in Nigel's amazing house while allowing her family to maintain their poor opinion of him suddenly felt overwhelmingly wrong.

'My dad would like to know more about what happened in America, and as I'm really just a figurehead on Myra's literary festival committee, plus no other magazine editor seems to like my ideas, I thought I'd see what I could find out. Except the only book that looks remotely useful is now out of print.' She gave a self-deprecating laugh. 'That will probably be my epitaph: Maddy Shaw, Out of Print.'

For the first time, Luke turned his head to look at her. In the lamplight his features were even more striking. His dark eyes bore into hers and Maddy's insides fluttered. 'You're being incredibly hard on yourself. You're good at what you do.'

'That's not the impression you gave back in February,' replied Maddy carefully.

'Sometimes Cameron Massey can be an idiot.'

Maddy reached over and rested the back of her hand against his warm forehead. 'Are you sure you're feeling okay?' she joked.

Luke caught her hand before she could remove it. 'Maddy…'

'Yes?' she whispered as her heart rate skipped up a notch.

'I want … that is, I want you to know…' Luke's fingers curled around her hand and it felt as though his hand was slowly melting into hers. Maddy's breath caught in her throat. 'You are a wonderful, caring person who sees the best in everyone, and you shouldn't have to go begging for scraps from magazine editors.'

Well, that was unexpected in more ways than one. But Luke was hardly going to make a romantic declaration, she told herself sternly and—if she was being truthful—somewhat wistfully. That woman Clara had a lot to answer for.

Luke made an embarrassed throat-clearing sort of noise. 'I don't mind if you want to go to bed. I'll be okay down here.'

Maddy shook her head and yawned. 'I'm fine. I'd prefer to wait … you know … just in case…' Luke's fingers were still entwined with hers and she gave his hand a gentle squeeze. 'We've shared a bed so I'm sure we can share a sofa.'

Luke shifted his position so that he could rest his head on the back of the sofa, then closed his eyes as he murmured, 'Just don't try poking me in the bum, Ms Austen.'

For a second, Maddy wondered if she was trapped somewhere. Something heavy was resting across her shoulders and she was being pressed into something warm and solid. As she opened her eyes she realised that Luke's arm was wrapped around her and she was semi-reclined across his chest—she certainly didn't intentionally fall asleep in that pose! It felt comforting though, and reminded her of being caught by Luke through the curtain.

She sat up carefully, trying not to wake him, but he made an inarticulate and rather cute sleepy noise as his eyelids fluttered open. Luke rubbed his face with his free hand and looked at the other one still hooked around Maddy, acknowledging an unspoken shift in their relationship.

It was too dark to see the hands of her watch, but the pale-streaked sky and a muted twitter of birdsong told her dawn was approaching. It was as she looked around for her phone that she heard the scratching noise from outside. Instinctively, she and Luke looked at each other.

'Did you hear something?' Maddy asked quietly.

'It could just be a squirrel.'

'Or another bit of the house falling apart.'

'Or—'

But Luke got no further as this time there was a definite yap, and they both leapt off the sofa and raced through the hall, yanking open the front door and without stopping to put on shoes, they tore round the side of the house in the direction of the sound.

'Buster!' Luke yelled. 'Is that you?'

In joyful answer, a volley of barks announced his return, and a damp, bedraggled canine threw himself at them both, jumping from one to another. Luke dropped to his knees, hugging him while Buster licked his face.

'Where have you been, you silly, silly dog? We've been worried sick.'

After several seconds of manic greetings, Maddy

grabbed hold of Buster's collar and steered him back towards the house, only letting go once they were all inside with the front door firmly shut. Maddy flicked on the light and surveyed the scene. A trail of wet footprints led across the parquet floor. Her socks were soaked with dew from the grass and they were both covered in muddy pawprints. Luke's normally tidy hair was in a state of disarray from his sofa snooze but there was a huge grin on his face that mirrored her own feelings. 'He's back!'

In two paces, Luke had closed the gap between them and swept Maddy up into a bearlike hug. A myriad of emotions swirled through her as his arms moulded her against his chest—surprise, relief, excitement and a sudden flare of desire that darted through her body.

As he relaxed his grip, Maddy half expected Luke to mutter some embarrassed apology but instead he just smiled. And then, with just the briefest of hesitation he dipped his head and pressed his warm lips against hers. For a few delicious seconds, Maddy's heart thumped wildly and every nerve ending tingled from his touch, as the rest of the world faded away. They stood gazing at each other, and Maddy willed him not to ruin the moment with an apology. For her part she would happily have it happen all over again.

Chapter Twenty-Four

1ST JULY

Her heart did whisper that he had done it for her.
Narrator, *Pride and Prejudice*

Long after they'd said a slightly awkward—almost shy —goodnight, Maddy lay on her bed, her pulse still racing as her mind replayed that kiss, the feel of Luke's warm arms around her, the closeness of his body and the way hers had responded. It was as if his lips had left an indelible imprint on hers that banished all thoughts of sleep. She instinctively reached for her phone and pulled up Alice's contact details, then texted:

You'll never guess what just happened!

She hugged her arms around herself. It had been a

264

magical and personal moment, but did Luke feel the same? Was it just relief? The release of the evening's heightened stress? Either way, Maddy realised she was happy to take it at face value. And at least he hadn't apologised. This was the real Luke Hamilton—the intelligent, intensely private man who didn't care whether people bothered to look beyond the headlines. She had seen behind the façade, and she didn't want to let that curtain come down again.

As her thoughts drifted, she must have dozed off, as by the time the strident tones of Debbie Harry singing 'Call Me' jolted her awake, it was clearly daylight. She groped for her phone lying on the duvet. 'Hi, Alice,' she answered with a sleepy smile. 'How's my best buddy?'

'Never mind all that!' said Alice in a kindly but urgent voice. 'I've got to get ready for work in a minute so what's the exciting news?'

Maddy thought about trying to play it cool and mysterious, but Alice would see straight through that. 'Okay. So you know I've got this lodger?'

'That gorgeous swoon-worthy crime writer with the off-the-scale amazing car—yes, I'm hardly likely to forget! Has something happened?'

'Sort of…'

'Ooh! What does that mean? Hurry up, Madds, I've got a bus to catch.'

As Maddy sketched over the events of the previous evening, Alice made sympathetic noises over the lost dog part of the story followed by a shriek of excitement over the kiss, which caused Maddy to grin as she pulled the phone away from her ear.

'You have to keep me updated,' demanded Alice. 'And you have to promise to introduce me when I come to visit for the literary festival!'

'Of course I will. You're my best friend and you'll get a VIP ticket. Go off to work, I'll speak to you soon, okay?'

By the time Maddy was dressed and downstairs, Luke had already finished breakfast and was flicking through his phone, a half-drunk cup of coffee in front of him on the kitchen table. He looked up and they exchanged smiles. Any worries about lingering awkwardness vanished, and they chatted about their plans for the day as Maddy dropped two slices of bread into the toaster.

Luke might not have wanted to talk about that dawn kiss, but it didn't stop Maddy thinking about it. Over the following days she found herself looking at him differently, sneaking admiring glances while a thousand what ifs murmured in the private corners of her imagination.

With no positive responses to her editorial enquiries, Maddy had devoted her spare time to tidying the attic space. She had already filled three boxes with old Christmas cards, birthday cards, theatre programmes, plus any number of brochures for all manner of events, which could all be recycled. This morning's job was to wipe the dark oak bookcase so that it could be used for the poetry books and other miscellania that she'd found in the box simply labelled F, which she had left untouched until such time as she could work out how everything fitted together. Her hair was held off her face with an animal-print headscarf and she had a face mask handy for the dusty jobs.

She paused, cloth in hand, at the sound of approaching footsteps. 'Greetings, visitors. What brings you all the way up here?'

Luke appeared in the attic doorway followed closely by Buster. 'Close your eyes and hold out your hands.'

Maddy threw him a quizzical look. 'For someone who detests surprises, you look awfully mysterious this morning.'

There was a definite twinkle in Luke's eyes as he said, 'Just humour me.'

'Okay, give me a second.' She stood up, bashed the dust off her hands on her jeans then did as she'd been asked. Something cool, flat and solid was placed in her hands. Just for an instant, Luke's fingertips brushed against hers, sparking a delicious, fizzing sensation inside her.

'You can look now.'

Maddy opened her eyes and stared in amazement at the tatty dust jacket bearing a picture of a young but recognisable Rob Pinto under the title *Taking the Hard Road*. Since setting up the saved search some weeks ago she'd found nothing and was beginning to wonder whether this mission to find out about cousin Nigel's past was all a bit of a wild goose chase to keep her journalist brain active while she rattled around in this huge house.

'Oh wow! You found a copy of his memoir! Thank you!'

Where on earth had he managed to find this? The book was out of print! It dawned on Maddy that Luke must have gone to a lot of trouble on her behalf.

Impulsively, she flung her arms around Luke's neck and kissed him on the cheek. His skin smelt warm and sexy. 'You are a genius.'

'I'll take that,' he replied with a smile.

'And clearly a very modest one,' she added cheekily.

They stood for several seconds, pressed together, looking at each other until Maddy reluctantly let go of him. 'I'm dying to know how on earth you came by this though. Not that I'm ungrateful,' she added hurriedly, 'I'm just curious.'

'You mean nosey.'

Maddy laughed. 'Yes, okay.' She pulled a face of mock alarm. 'Good grief, I've just agreed with you! Should I feel worried?'

She started flicking through the first few pages and scanned the content page. 'This looks really useful. So come on, don't keep me in suspense.'

Luke gently stroked his finger along her cheek. 'You might be queen bee in the love and romance world but I'm not without my contacts in the publishing universe you know. I asked my agent to have a word with the US editorial team who were able to track down a copy from the original publishers.'

'And they did that just for you?'

'Of course. Bu-ut…'—he drew out the word for added suspense— 'it might have helped that I was able to send my agent a detailed outline of the new book, which he's delighted with by the way, plus the first ten chapters and the promise of the whole manuscript by the end of the summer.'

Maddy clapped her hands. 'Oh brilliant! Well done. And is Detective Inspector Friend still knocking around?'

'Yes, much to my surprise. He was hoping to retire but this case intrigued him.'

'So it's another crime novel then?'

'Oh yes, but not the sort I've written in the past. I'm dipping my toe into the world of cosy crime.'

'Wow! You must be so pleased! Can I read a bit of it?'

'Yes, I am, and not until it's finished.'

Maddy put her hands on her hips and poked her tongue out. 'Spoilsport. Okay then, how's the romance novel coming along?'

'What romance novel?'

'The one you're going to write for me. You didn't think I'd forgotten did you? Ooh, big mistake!'

'Still no idea what you're on about.'

'You're bluffing,' said Maddy in a singsong voice, prodding him playfully in the chest. 'I distinctly recall someone saying, *"It's hardly much of a challenge to write a story where you know the ending, is it?"* Ring any bells yet? I think you need to prove your point of how ridiculously simple it is, and show the rest of us how it's done.'

'Don't push your luck, Ms Austen. I've got a book to

promote now, but I may have another surprise in a day or two.'

For someone who hated being on the receiving end of surprises, Luke certainly seemed to enjoy being the donor, but unsurprisingly Maddy wasn't able to wheedle any further details from him.

She decided the rest of today would be devoted to reading her new book—at least until the committee meeting this evening. Might this book shed a bit of light on her personal quest? She wasn't holding her breath but it was better than endless trawling on the internet.

She made herself a coffee and settled herself in one of the garden reclining chairs on the patio next to the sun-bleached wooden table. Maddy had found the recliners in one of the sheds and like most things in the house, they were a bit old and dilapidated. However, after a thorough cleaning and some consumer testing involving Jem throwing himself down heavily on each of them, they were pronounced safe for general use.

The French doors from the library opened up onto the patio and today they were wide open, allowing the warm breeze to waft through the house and offering a view of her rather gorgeous lodger. Luke was sitting at his laptop typing with a look of total concentration, his hair ruffled from where he'd absentmindedly run his hand through it. Maddy wondered what it would feel like if she let her hands do the same thing.

Luke suddenly looked up, a bemused expression on his face.

Maddy blushed as if he had read her thoughts. 'How's

it going?' she called out. 'What bit are you writing?' Luke mimed stabbing himself in the shoulder with the non-writing end of his biro and a large degree of theatrical embellishment. Maddy laughed. What a difference from that first time she found him sprawled on the sofa asleep, wracked with writer's block, angry with anyone or anything that disturbed his misery.

She was genuinely thrilled for him that he now had a completed book in his sights, and she couldn't wait to read it. She also planned to start reading his acclaimed novel *End of the Roadie* as soon as she'd finished reading Rob Pinto's memoir.

———

'So how's the literary investigation going?' Luke asked several hours later as they prepared dinner. Maddy's culinary skills still only extended as far as beans on toast, pasta with something or ready meals, so Luke had gradually taken charge of the kitchen with Maddy relegated to commis chef. He'd been vociferous in his dismal opinion of Maddy's eating habits and Maddy had to admit that for someone who got through most of the day on coffee and hobnobs, he was surprisingly good at cooking. Tonight's dish du jour was prawn stir fry, and she chopped up the pile of peppers and mushrooms as she updated him.

'It's really interesting. Two of the initial band members met in high school and spent years begging gigs or just offering to play for free on occasion. In later years, they could fill Madison Square Garden within two days of ticket sales, but back then, they almost had to play for free. I don't know much about 1970s rock music, but their big hits became rock classics and still get played on the radio.

'I found out why that roadie died though; apparently even after they started having hits, lots of their song lyrics still got written on backs of envelopes, serviettes, random pieces of paper, and often while they were quite intoxicated.'

As Luke dished up and they sat down to eat, Maddy continued talking about what she'd read, and how the lead singer Chuck Hardimann just wrote down snatches of lyrics or phrases he liked on whatever came to hand.

'Are you getting to the point soon?' asked Luke with an amused expression. 'Only Buster has a veterinary check-up booked for October.'

Maddy nudged him under the table with her foot. 'Rude lodger.'

Luke laughed and nudged her back. 'But accurate.'

'Anyway,' Maddy continued, throwing him her best I'm-carrying-on-regardless look, 'one of the band members, Darius Locke, came up with a great tune for what became their greatest hit, "Rock Hard Road", but no one could remember where they wrote down the lyrics.'

'Probably too stoned half the time to remember where they left their shoes,' remarked Luke, stabbing a pile of noodles with his fork.

Maddy chuckled. 'Apparently they met up in this

diner and were trying to rewrite the lyrics from memory, and it all got rather heated. Having come up with the tune, Darius was really pissed with the others and accused them of not treating it seriously enough and then a few punches flew. The roadie tried to intervene but got shoved backwards and hit his head on the bar. It was totally accidental, but sadly he died.'

'And did they ever remember the original lyrics?'

'It doesn't look like it. Rob seems to have been quite affected by the incident. He wrote in his memoir that they simply kept the revised version and then it went on to be a mega hit, but Darius Locke got all the credit for the song even though originally the lyrics had been a joint effort. I get the impression that this story of lost lyrics, bar room brawl, accidental death, just added to the rock star glamour of it all, and it was the song that propelled them from an average rock group to huge stars.'

'But there's no mention of Nigel Shaw anywhere?'

Maddy shook her head. 'Not yet, but I'm only up to chapter ten. Hopefully there may be more clues.'

'And even if there aren't,' said Luke, 'you know he was there. He's in the photo. He described the fight even though at the time I didn't realise it was an actual event. The only way he'd know about that incident was either if he was actually there, or if he knew one or more of the group.'

Maddy nodded thoughtfully. 'You're right.'

Luke smiled and quirked his eyebrow. 'Aren't I always?'

'Absolutely not!' Maddy screwed up the piece of

kitchen paper she'd been using as a serviette and chucked it at him. 'But at the risk of making your head any bigger than it already is, I'm sorry I accused you of pinching an uncredited story.'

Luke chucked it back again. 'Water under the bridge, Ms Austen.'

Chapter Twenty-Five

Silly things do cease to be silly if they are done by sensible people in an impudent way
Emma Woodhouse, *Emma*

The July meeting of the Cotlington Literary Festival Committee opened with a spontaneous round of boisterous applause led by Jem, as Sally wedged open both doors to the village hall to provide access for Leonard who followed behind, pushing Joyce in a wheelchair. Joyce waved her arms in the air as though she'd just won a paralympic athletic event, and Maddy rushed over to give her a hug.

For several minutes, there was a swirl of questions in the hall.

'So how much longer will you be laid up?'

'What did the doctor have to say?'

'Is your sister still bringing you some lunch?'

'It's a right old nuisance,' replied Joyce, although Maddy wasn't sure whether Joyce was referring to her ankle or to the visits from her sister.

'Well, it's not going to stop you from seeing us,' said Leonard resolutely, then fiddling with the collar of his shirt to cover his embarrassment.

'You're part of the team,' added Sally. 'Isn't she, Myra?'

'Yes, yes. So let's all get to work then shall we?' Myra replied briskly. Maddy wondered whether Myra had an emotional core buried beneath her prickly exterior. If so, it was well hidden.

With less than two months until the big day, there was still a lot to organise. Myra gave everyone a recap on the previous meeting and the items already ticked off the list. Myra had booked the marquee hire and Jem was being put in charge of the hospitality tent. Maddy wondered whether this would include his lethal cider concoction, and whether the woman selling industrial-strength medicinal gin was also going to pop up.

The issue of the gaps in the speaker schedule was delegated to Maddy. She suspected it had less to do with being chair and more to do with the fact that everyone else had run out of ideas and no one wanted a re-reading from *Gardens I Have Visited*. Having heard a lot about these readings, Maddy was now highly curious about said dreary volume. However, her attention snapped back into focus when she heard her name being mentioned.

'And don't forget to include your own talk.'

'What do you mean?' asked Maddy nervously. 'I thought I was arranging the talks and doing a few introductions. I'm not actually speaking.' She suspected this was another tradition that had been instigated by her now departed cousin.

'Maybe you could read some of Nigel's poetry?' suggested Joyce.

Having read a number of Nigel's poems, which filled any number of notebooks in the attic, Maddy had found his writing style rather flowery and a bit gushing for her tastes and had no intention of extending their shelf life.

'Or perhaps you could write some verses of your own?' said Sally. 'It doesn't have to be as long as Nigel's.'

The last time Maddy had written any poetry was at university and she was very sure it hadn't improved with age. However, hoping that Myra might forget about this was like changing the hands on the clock and expecting Buster to accidentally forget about dinner time.

'Sorry, what did you say?'

Myra gave her a withering look. 'I said, you and Luke between you can organise the printing of the programme as that was always Nigel's role. Is that okay with you?'

Maddy smiled sweetly. 'Yes, of course.'

'Excellent. And I will take up my usual role of catering organiser. Last year, Mrs Waite complemented me on the quality of the sandwiches.'

Maddy clamped her lips together to avoid an inappropriate remark escaping. Luke would have stomped off out of the hall by now—she could easily picture his expression of exasperated boredom.

It hadn't escaped Maddy's notice that, where in the past her go-to comparator used to be Lizzie Bennet or Emma Woodhouse or another of Jane Austen's heroines, in the last couple of weeks she had more often found herself thinking about what Luke would have done or said instead in a given situation. It was further evidence of their settled domesticity, even though it was still punctuated by the occasional exchange of friendly insults.

It was in the privacy of her own room that Maddy found herself thinking about Luke in an entirely different way, longing for a repeat of that dawn kiss that had sent sparks racing through her. Did he feel the same way? He was certainly more friendly—affectionate even—but was that all it was?

Maddy dragged her attention back to the matter in hand; Myra was still in full flow and had now moved on to book sales. 'We can set up the table for the sale of speakers' books in the rose garden like last year. Who would like to take charge of that?'

'Last year Mrs Brownlee organised it,' said Leonard.

'Oh good lord, we don't want her back again!' Myra said hurriedly. 'Leonard, can you organise this? We have two bestselling authors this year, so we don't want any mix-ups.'

Before Maddy could ask, Leonard supplied the explanation. 'Harriet Brownlee always organises the annual Haxford charities second-hand book sale, but last year lots of their books got misfiled. I was only browsing for an hour or two and I found Mike Carter's *Nine Days to*

Armageddon under the travel section, and *The Tao of Pooh* was with all the medical books.'

There was a general outburst of laughter.

'I bumped into her in the village the other day,' Leonard said as the chuckles subsided. 'She seemed very keen to talk at the festival again and wondered why she hadn't been invited to do another poetry reading.'

'Some of her poems were rather long,' Sally ventured cautiously, 'although the one about her dog was good.'

'And short,' added Joyce, winking at Maddy.

'I expect her dog appreciated it though; and at least it made sense—I didn't understand the Japanese hiking one at all. It seemed to be more about trees.' Sally's shoulders dipped. 'I don't think I understand poetry actually.'

'It wasn't about hiking; it was a haiku,' explained Leonard. 'It's a Japanese form of poetry written in three lines, usually about something in nature or a moment in time. Traditionally, the first and third lines have five syllables, the middle one has seven.'

'Huh?' Sally's nose wrinkled delicately, making her look like a puzzled pixie.

'Look, I'll give you an example.' Leonard cleared his throat and then spoke in a clear, measured voice.

'Sally's birthday gift, presented in a pink box. Hooray, she loves it!'

With a look of concentration, Sally repeated the words as she counted the syllables on her fingers. As she reached the last line her face lit up. 'Oh, I see! That's really clever! I bet you were a brilliant teacher, Leonard. No one has ever composed a poem for me before.' She beamed at the assembled group. 'I'm going to write it down before I forget it.'

A fizz of excitement shot through Maddy. 'And you two have just given me a great idea,' she said with a triumphant smile. 'Why don't we have a haiku competition?'

'A competition?' said Myra, looking as though Buster had just presented her with a dead rat. 'This is a literary festival, not open mic night at the amateur poetry karaoke club.'

Joyce jabbed her forefinger at Myra. 'Yes. And probably why the same old people come every year. And why we invite the same old people to speak every year. With the emphasis on the word *old*. Even Nigel was disappointed at the turnout last year.'

Myra's face turned a rapid shade of puce as she clutched at her necklace. 'Joyce Sedgefield! You should be ashamed of yourself talking about Nigel like that! He was not only the instigator but also the biggest supporter of this festival.'

'Yes, he was, but times change, Myra.'

'What are you suggesting?'

'Ladies!' Maddy held up her hands. 'I understand that you wish to retain certain customs and traditions.' She looked pointedly at Myra. 'But perhaps it could be good to try out new ideas from time to time. Otherwise you— we'—Maddy hurriedly corrected herself—'will just do the same thing, year in, year out. I might not have known Nigel in the same way you all did, but I know he was not averse to change. And he loved poetry. I can see that from the books he'd collected. I think he'd be really keen on this.'

'Maddy, why don't you explain your idea,' said Leonard in his encouraging-teacher voice.

Maddy gave him a grateful nod as she continued. 'We can make the competition as wide as we like, so you're not restricting entries to people attending the festival. That way it also increases publicity. We allow anyone in Cotlington to enter the competition, and they get their five minutes of fame reading out their haiku poem at the festival if they want to.'

'More ticket sales,' observed Jem.

'Shorter poems,' said Joyce, adding her agreement.

Maddy clasped her hands together. 'Exactly. And if they don't want to come, maybe Leonard could read the verses out.'

Leonard nodded eagerly. 'I'd be delighted.'

Maddy was aware that one person in the room had yet to be convinced. Being chair of a committee wasn't a popularity contest and she needed Myra's expertise and knowledge. 'What do you think, Myra? Do you think Nigel would approve of the Nigel Shaw Haiku Competition? With an appropriate prize of course, and—'

'There would need to be a trophy of some sort.'

'Great idea!' Maddy enthused. She'd been on the verge of mentioning that but she was happy to let Myra take the credit. 'Perhaps as you know his tastes, we could ask you to organise the trophy? I'll reimburse you, of course.' She looked around. 'Well then, I think that only leaves us with one decision. Leonard, could we prevail upon you to be head judge?'

Over the next few days, Maddy was kept busy with ideas for the festival programme and working out the terms and conditions of entry for the haiku competition. It was clear from the outset that Luke was disappointed not to be asked to be a judge for the competition, but Maddy was secretly relieved as she suspected that would be used to score points over Randall Jacobson.

Randall was rapidly dropping out of her good books after she'd sent a polite reminder about the payment due following the ghost hunting evening and heard nothing. While some organisations were slow with fee payments, not responding at all was impolite and distinctly unhelpful, since there would shortly be printing and other costs to settle. She had very quickly gone through the small amount of savings she had in the bank, and since April had been building up a steady debt on her credit card despite the monthly rent from Luke.

Her parents had brought her up to be independent, and to live within her means but the trouble was she wasn't living in a place of her own choosing, and it was rapidly becoming apparent that a house of this size was expensive to run. She had already shelled out for more roof repairs and gutter cleaning and that was just the essentials.

In her more fanciful moods, Maddy wandered round

the house with a notebook in her hand, noting down everything that needed doing and adding ideas. The décor needed some serious tarting up in places and the house could do with another bathroom at Luke's end of the landing. After being inspired by one of those home improvement programmes, she reckoned she could easily create one by using space from the adjoining bedrooms, although sorting out the plumbing might be another matter.

More than one of the bedroom ceilings had been damaged by past water leaks and goodness knows what else would need work if she invited a builder to take a proper look at the place. It was fun though to imagine what the place might look like if it was brought back to its former glory.

Chapter Twenty-Six

Till this moment I never knew myself
Elizabeth Bennet, *Pride and Prejudice*

I t was several days before she picked up Rob Pinto's memoir again. Maddy had almost convinced herself that this volume, like everything else she had read online, was just a rehash of information that she could find elsewhere. However, as Luke had gone to so much trouble to locate a copy for her, she felt obliged to finish it. She already reckoned she was now knowledgeable enough to appear on the TV quiz show *Mastermind*:

> *Our next contestant is Madeleine Shaw, and your specialist subject is?*
> —*The history of The Faultliners, 1968 to 1984*

This evening, Luke had offered to take Buster out for his walk and Maddy had earmarked the time for some reading combined with a lovely, long soak in the bath—something she hadn't done since her student days. Back then, during the cold winter months in her draughty shared student house, the bath was one of the few ways to warm up. There had been a limited supply of hot water though, so it was on a strictly first come, first served basis. Maddy used to set her alarm early, light lots of scented candles and enjoy reading a few chapters of her latest romance novel until the water turned tepid.

As it was well into July, keeping warm was no longer a priority, but Maddy liked the ambience of the flickering candles, which she'd placed along the cracked tiles of the windowsill. She'd added a generous dollop of her favourite Rituals bath essence and stretched out in the warm, scented water, ensuring that her book was well above the water line.

While the chapters of the book were generally intended to be in chronological order, the narrative was peppered with anecdotes that jumped around a bit in time. The bit she was currently reading covered the period in the mid-seventies after the band had become famous and could afford to tour around America in their luxury coach. It was a real eye opener into the lives of the rich and famous and although it no longer seemed useful for her quest for information, it still made for interesting reading.

1975 was set to be another busy year. More dates had been added to the West Coast leg of the tour, including three more nights in San Francisco. By this period Chuck travelled in his own motorhome with one of the more sober roadies acting as driver, and there were muttered suspicions that he wanted to distance himself from the band. Darius and Libby had no such problems slumming it with the rest of us. With our own champagne fridge, built-in music system and reclining seats, it was hardly roughing it like we did in the early days when we had Rocket.

The first transport the band ever owned was a battered old Volkswagen campervan bought from a local scrap dealer. The suspension was shot and space was cramped. It's maximum speed on the highway was forty-five miles per hour earning it the ironic nickname. Looking back, it was a miracle we actually made it to half the gigs. It regularly needed fixing up but only once were we properly stranded. It was 1970 and we were several miles out of Fresno in the middle of nowhere when we ran out of gas. We needed to get someone out here, otherwise we'd never reach Bakersfield before sundown, and no one wanted to spend the night in that van.

Our best chance of help was sending the two most respectable of our group to fetch assistance, so Libby and the English roadie headed back to Fresno. No idea how, but the combination of a smooth-talking English guy and a pretty girl did the trick, and they got us a can of gas for free.

Maddy's attention skidded to a halt. She'd been almost skim-reading but now she re-read the last two sentences.

Libby and the English roadie… Smooth-talking English guy.

How many American rock groups travelled around with anyone described as smooth-talking or English?

That surely had to be Nigel! She let out a whoop of excitement, yanked the plug with her foot and grabbed her towel. She couldn't wait to tell her dad.

'Cousin Nigel, I think I've found you!' she shouted as she flung open the bathroom door. She danced down the landing, twirling her damp towel round her head, singing, 'I've found a clu-ue, I've found a clu-ue.'

A noise behind her made her spin round and to her horror, she saw Luke peering round his bedroom door with an enormous grin on his face.

Maddy shrieked and tried to wrap the towel around her but it had got twisted round from the whirling and twirling and barely covered anything. With a squeak of panic she shot into her bedroom and slammed the door. Her heart thumped wildly as she fanned her flaming face. How was Luke back so quickly anyway? Buster rarely let anyone short-change him on his evening walk. She glanced at the clock on her bedside table—good grief, she'd obviously been reading longer than she thought!

Maddy hurriedly pulled on her bedclothes over which she wrapped her dressing gown despite it being a warm evening. Although in the privacy of her own room she had frequently entertained thoughts of her and Luke in a more intimate setting, her romantic fantasies did not run to episodes of streaking.

If she'd harboured hopes that Luke was going to

quietly ignore the fact that he'd seen her run naked down the landing, they were quickly dispelled as she entered the kitchen to be greeted with an impish grin and a wolf whistle.

'Well, if it isn't the streaker! You didn't need to get dressed for my benefit, you know.'

'Ha, ha.' Maddy grabbed the tea towel and flicked it at him playfully. 'I'll have you know I don't normally do that sort of thing.'

Luke caught the end of the tea towel and held on to it, gradually reeling her in until she was standing directly in front of him. Slowly, he leaned forward until the tip of his nose touched hers. 'You don't need to explain,' he said in a husky whisper that sent her insides into a spin. 'But if you feel the urge, next time just give me some notice, and I'll try to do the gentlemanly thing and avert my eyes.'

His breath was warm against her cheek and Maddy shivered as she lifted her eyes to his. They sparkled mischievously, and his lips pressed together as if he was trying not to laugh.

'You would, would you?'

'Scout's honour.'

'Like you did ten minutes ago?'

'Well, that was just … erm … a surprise. A very pleasant one though if I may be permitted to say so.' Maddy felt her cheeks flush in response. In such close proximity, it was like someone was sending small pulsing electrical charges through her body.

Luke took a step back, breaking the connection between them as he said, 'So come on, I'm eager to hear the reason for the unannounced streaking. Does this mean you've found something useful in that book?'

Maddy reluctantly pushed aside the feeling of disappointment, and quickly found the relevant page. They sat down at the kitchen table and she laid the book in front of him, pointing at the middle of the page. 'There. What do you think?'

Luke scanned the relevant paragraph. His face bore a neutral expression so he clearly wasn't as excited about the discovery as she was, but then he wasn't as invested in finding out the truth.

'Don't tell me,' said Maddy expecting his usual discouraging riposte. 'It could be anyone. There isn't enough information. It's all a bit vague. Blah, blah, blah.'

'Wrong on all counts, Ms Austen.' He looked up and met her gaze with an intensity that made Maddy feel quite wobbly inside. 'What I was going to say was, we need to find Libby.'

Maddy was thrilled that he said 'we' and not 'you', but enthusiastic as she was, even she was prepared to admit that searching for someone on the internet purely using their first name was beyond pointless. Nevertheless, she carried out a quick online search for *Libby*, *Faultliners* and *girlfriend* just to prove to herself the futility of the operation.

'Well, we tried,' said Maddy shutting the lid of her laptop. 'Lucky I didn't get a chance to raise Dad's hopes.'

'Before you bin the idea, let's look at what we know,' said Luke, pushing his coffee mug away from the laptop. 'Are any of the band still alive?'

'I don't think so. Chuck Hardimann died in 1990, and … hang on a minute I've just realised something,' she gushed as she tore out of the room and up the stairs as fast as she could manage.

'Hey! Where's the fire?' called Luke, following close behind as Maddy raced along the landing. 'Why are you going up to the attic in your nightwear? If you're trying to recreate a scene from some gothic novel, you'd be better off ditching the dressing gown, it ruins the effect.'

Maddy flung open the attic door, her slippered feet almost skidding over the floorboards, and hurried over to the box now residing on the bookcase she had recently cleaned.

'Look.' She held up one of the scruffy verses of poetry with scribble in the margins and opened the cover. 'I thought cousin Nigel had earmarked this to be thrown away.' She pointed at the word that had popped into her head a few seconds ago. *Chuck*. 'I don't know why it didn't occur to me before, but the logical conclusion is that this book must have belonged to Chuck Hardimann.'

Luke peered over her shoulder at the one word inscription. There was a scent of aftershave mingled with a fresh outdoors smell, and memories of that dawn kiss flooded back in a highly distracting manner. 'You're going to tell me I'm mad now, aren't you?'

Gently, Luke turned her round until she was looking at him at point blank range. 'Not at all. I thinks it's fantastic that you're so fired up with this story, and that in spite of very little information you are desperate to find out what happened to Nigel. To restore his reputation and right a wrong. It shows you care. It shows tenacity, concern, perseverance—I could go on.'

'Please do,' said Maddy feeling slightly breathless. Her face radiated heat and she marvelled at the effect he had on her, an effect that was becoming more intense with each passing day.

Luke smiled and his eyes twinkled with amusement. 'If I didn't know better, I'd say you were fishing.' He tugged at the sash of her dressing gown and it slipped open. He cupped her cheek in his hand and lowered his face to hers. 'Okay, how about—'

Whatever Luke had been about to say was replaced by a startled oof, as the thrust of Buster's paws leaping up from behind cannoned his body into hers. Maddy grabbed at his arm for balance and they tottered backwards for a second. As the back of her legs reached something solid, Maddy fell back into the upholstered office chair with Luke landing at an awkward angle on top of her and her face squashed against his chest.

A snort of giggles burst out of her.

'Maddy, are you okay? asked Luke, scrambling to right himself.

'Uh-huh,' she managed in between more giggles.

Luke helped a still amused Maddy to her feet. 'Well, it seems like it's one-all now in the catching stakes,' he said, raising an amused eyebrow.

'Best of three?' countered Maddy playfully.

They moved at the same time and as Luke's lips found hers, she melted into his warm embrace.

'In the interests of health and safety, I think I need to

remove this dressing gown,' Luke murmured as he slipped it from her shoulders and let it fall to the floor. 'You could trip over that sash all too easily.'

Maddy pushed it to one side with her foot. 'Your concern is touching,' she replied softly, letting her fingers slip lazily between the buttons of his shirt, causing Luke to inhale

sharply. 'In fact,' Luke continued, his voice lowering, 'just to be on the safe side I think ought to see you safely to your room.'

Maddy agreed. And this time there was no question as to where Luke would be sleeping.

Long after Luke had fallen asleep with his arms around her, Maddy lay awake smiling in the darkness, her head resting on his chest. It couldn't have been more different from the last time they'd spent the night together. That had been an exercise in ensuring they remained as physically far apart as possible, their stilted conversation a way of trying to normalise a very abnormal situation. Admittedly, this time Luke hadn't actually talked very much, but Maddy was more than ready to accept that sometimes actions spoke louder than words.

Chapter Twenty-Seven

...it is as well to have as many holds on happiness as possible.
Henry Tilney, *Northanger Abbey*

While living in Clapham, Maddy had occasionally glanced over one of the free papers commonly found at train stations or on the London underground, but it was more for something to do than a lack of reading material, and the contents rarely related to her immediate area. However, she had been pleasantly surprised to discover that a local county newspaper was a vastly different arrangement to those distributed in London.

The *Haxford and Kingsfordly Gazette*—apart from sounding like it belonged in the eighteenth century—was a cosmos of local information covering the main town of Haxford and its surrounding villages. Having popped into the offices of the paper last week to explain about the literary festival, Maddy found the editor very enthusiastic about promoting the event and she had happily supplied an article encouraging local authors who might be interested in speaking at the festival to get in touch.

From her comprehensive study of previous years' festival programmes, Maddy had spotted a depressing level of repetition in speaker names over the last ten years. The earlier programmes were more interesting, and some of the speakers listed had gone on to become recognised authors. It had struck her that Nigel's original collective of literary friends would have been the new kids on the block thirty years ago, and she was proud to think that he had helped them take their first steps towards a literary career.

With the passing of years, the festival had clearly but quietly stagnated; now Maddy would find out whether they could revive Nigel's original premise. The paper came out today so it would be exciting to see how quickly they received any responses.

The general store was already busy by the time she had walked down to the village. It was tourist season now, and the thousands that flocked to Haxford's picturesque Old Town frequently combined their trip with an exploration of the surrounding villages. With its church boasting a reredos by one of William Morris's apprentices, and the Wonky Table pub listed in the top ten places to eat in the county, Cotlington saw a regular stream of day trippers over the summer months, and the postcard carousel standing outside was already attracting interest.

Standing there with the warm sun on her face, watching a family with young children select their postcards, Maddy had a sudden urge to send one.

Ordinarily she would FaceTime her parents, and she kept in touch with friends on social media, but there was something nice about receiving a handwritten card from someone. She selected two postcards of the attractive village hall with its light brick façade and dark timber framed windows, before nipping inside to find the newspaper section.

After picking up a copy of the *Gazette*, she also added some Hobnob biscuits for Luke, doggy treats for Buster, and some freshly baked rolls for lunch. It was a shame that they didn't have a coffee shop here; having her early morning mocha from the shop at the end of her road was one London habit she really did miss, despite having Luke's coffee maker installed in the kitchen.

It was as she was leaving the shop that she spotted a familiar face. Being the end of July, the rest of the county had transitioned into T-shirts, shorts or casual beachwear, but Leonard clearly felt more at home with his white collared shirt and smart trousers—although in deference to the change in the season, the jacket had been replaced by a smart blazer.

'Hello, Maddy, I see we both came in to buy the same thing.' Leonard pointed at the paper sticking out of her bag.

'I've put in an ad this week for local authors to speak at the festival; the job of finding speakers was left to me so

I'm trying something new. I expect not everyone will agree, which is why I just went ahead and did it.'

'Some people don't like new ideas,' Leonard said sagely, 'but I admit Joyce is right, you do have to move on with the times, otherwise they move on without you.'

He sounded almost nostalgic, and Maddy wondered whether he missed teaching. She'd never been inside his house, but Sally had told her it was crammed with bulging bookcases—evidence of a lifetime's love of language.

'Let's hope we can bring in fresh local talent,' Maddy replied with her fingers firmly crossed. 'Otherwise,' she lowered her voice, 'it'll be another reading from *Gardens I Have Visited*.'

Leonard proffered a wry smile. 'Myra will certainly have something to say about that.' He glanced at his watch. 'Sorry, I need to keep an eye on the time; *PopMaster* is on in half an hour and I don't like to miss it. I have been known to score over twenty,' he added proudly.

'Your talents are clearly wasted on us,' replied Maddy, having no clue about the scoring system. 'Although they came in handy in identifying The Faultliners from my newspaper cutting.'

'Oh yes! Did you ever find out how Nigel was connected to them?'

Maddy explained briefly how she'd trawled the internet and come across Rob Pinto's memoir, which Luke had obtained for her from his American publisher. Finding that clue in Rob's book had felt like unlocking a treasure chest, only to find another locked box inside.

'Gosh,' Leonard's eyes widened in excitement. 'I'd

love to borrow the book after you've finished—that's if you don't mind, of course. It sounds right up my street; I was totally obsessed with the group as a teenager.'

Maddy couldn't quite picture this grey-haired, avuncular pensioner as a rock-obsessed youth. Instead, she said, 'There are some tantalising clues in the book that hint at an Englishman hanging out with the group, but none of the band are alive now and Darius Locke's girl-friend, Libby, is untraceable. I suppose she could be dead too for all I know.'

'I had rather a crush on her in my youth,' Leonard admitted bashfully. 'I know that after she split from Darius, she married an English session musician called Mickey Allen, and they settled in Oxfordshire. He died only five years later in a skiing accident and she never remarried. There's a big Faultliners fan club online though—I'll see if anyone has any information.'

As soon as Maddy arrived home she opened up the newspaper on the kitchen table and stared proudly at her quarter page advert. Under the heading there was a small picture of Meadowside, alongside the names of her two star speakers, Cameron Massey and Randall Jacobson. In a tribute to cousin Nigel, she had added:

Cotlington Literary Festival is proud to support local authors and if you are published, whether traditionally or independently, and are interested in speaking at the festival, please contact Maddy Shaw at the email address below.

'So you've done it, have you?' said Luke, returning to

the kitchen with an empty coffee mug. 'I'm glad it's not me that has to tell Myra Hardcastle.'

'She put me in charge of organising speakers,' replied Maddy. 'Mostly because last year's lot had either declined to talk or were only communicable via a Ouija board. And in any case, I think Nigel would have approved.' She raised her chin defiantly, daring Luke to contradict her.

He held up his palms. 'You won't hear any argument from me.'

'Really? Can I have that in writing?'

'Definitely not. Anyway, you have an email to reply to.'

'I adore your optimism, but I seriously doubt anyone has replied that quickly.' Maddy pulled her phone from her bag anyway just to double check. 'Hey! There's one here from you. What's that about?' She gave him a playful nudge. 'You're already down to talk in case you'd forgotten?'

'It's nothing to do with the festival. It's just a job offer I heard about.' Luke was clearly doing his best to sound mysterious, but Maddy detected a distinct note of gleeful anticipation.

'Really?' A frisson of excitement zipped through her, swiftly followed by the lurking suspicion that this might be a wind-up.

After several weeks of emailing editors and pitching ideas for articles, there had either been one-line negative responses or an infuriating silence, so if it *was* a genuine offer of work, Maddy would take it; she didn't care whether it was an interview with a Z-list celebrity organising a comeback, or an article about competitive duck herding.

Luke's email comprised two words: *see below*. As she scrolled, she saw an email addressed to Luke from his literary agent. She quickly skimmed over the text…

Effusive praise for the first ten chapters, a request to turn this into a series, offer of a joint meeting with his editor to discuss arrangements for the launch of the book, praise for keeping out of social media rows, and an opportunity for an interview with one of the Sunday supplements.

'Your agent is suggesting updating your press release and doing an interview for the Sunday papers. Sounds sensible to me.' She looked up from her phone. 'Unless you need someone to write the press release, I can't see what I can add though.'

'I thought you could do the interview. I know you're a competent journalist and I also know you could do with the money.'

'That's very thoughtful of you, but I suspect they'll want one of their own journalists conducting the interview.'

'Too bloody bad. I've already told them I want you to do it. I don't want to be stitched up by some journalist with a point to make.' Maddy smiled at the brief glimpse of the unpredictable Cameron Massey of old.

'That is, of course, unless you're too proud to accept a helping hand?' he added cheekily.

Maddy held out her hand. 'Au contraire, Mr Crime Writer. You've got yourself a deal.'

Chapter Twenty-Eight

Do not consider me now as an elegant female intending to plague you, but as a rational creature speaking the truth from her heart.
Elizabeth Bennet, *Pride and Prejudice*

No one was going to accuse Maddy of not doing her homework on this assignment. Not that she had ever cut corners on any job before, but she was aware that if she was going to make a go of being a freelance journalist, she needed to prepare properly. Interviewing one of the country's best known crime writers was a gift, and she was aware that she'd only got this gig because Luke had insisted.

Having looked over the various reviews, articles and occasional interview from the last year or so, there was a definite angle to many of the headlines:

Is the two-time winner of the silver spanner losing his golden touch?
Cameron Massey—boring or bored?
Debate and Debacle at Crime Writers' Forum from Massey

Even the articles that were more favourably written brought up references to past arguments, often quoting comments directly from his Twitter feed. At some point she might suggest he deleted some of those.

While Luke did have a tendency to be outspoken and combative, there was also a more compassionate side to him that readers never got to see; it seemed that in some circles, heated rows and confrontation were more news-worthy than stories of literary acclaim and a star-studded past.

Maddy had set up a small table in the library by the French windows. Ahead of the actual interview, she had taken a few photos which would accompany her article. Her favourite one was of Luke sitting at Nigel's green leather-topped desk in the library, an open notebook in front of him, with Nigel's shelves of books in the back-ground. Luke was wearing a white shirt with a small car print design and cutaway collar, teamed with navy chinos. The top two shirt buttons were left casually undone, and his relaxed smile showed him at his photogenic best and every inch a magazine heartthrob. As Alice had pointed out all those months ago, definitely swoonworthy. After the last ten days, Maddy could happily add plenty more adjectives of her own.

There was also a close-up of his bestselling novels

against the backdrop of the wood floor, with a few care-fully staged props referenced from the plot of the books. Maddy was particularly pleased with the polished silver key—an item that featured in *The Cornish Key Cutter*. It had taken her over an hour with the chunky key she'd found in the attic and an ancient jar of Duraglit to achieve that level of sparkle but it looked impressive.

Maddy took her time over the photos and then down-loaded them all to a separate folder. This afternoon was earmarked for the interview. Her old journalist's tape recorder had been left in storage with Alice back in Clapham, but her phone would do equally as well.

The guest of honour was preceded by Buster, carrying in his latest toy—an old shoe that he'd found in the field. (Attempts to persuade him to abandon the unhygienic-looking article had so far failed).

'Okay, I'm ready for the interrogation,' announced Luke, now back in well-fitting jeans and a T-shirt with a dog design on the front. 'Where d'you want me?' he asked proffering a sexy smile and striking a pose as he leaned on the edge of the desk.

'Ooh, too many choices,' replied Maddy with a grin.

They settled on the chairs by the window, although it was hard to remain professional in the face of such a distraction. What would Jane Austen make of this modern-day hero? Would she be shocked or fascinated? One thing was for sure: military uniform or not, the younger Bennet sisters would be positively hurling them-selves at him.

'If you don't mind, I'm going to record the interview?

I'm not aiming at a word-for-word transcript but it saves me writing everything down. My shorthand has gone a bit rusty over the years.'

'Fine by me. I always wondered whether those squiggly hieroglyphics were a representation of what I said or something totally different.'

'Great. So I'll ask the questions to give us general areas for discussion and then I'll type up the article as an interview.' Maddy tapped at the phone screen. 'So I'm starting recording now. Let's kick off with a few facts. Do you have a publication date yet for your next book? And what can you tell us about it?'

'The scheduled date is currently the beginning of February next year, and it's a cosy crime, which is a bit of a departure from previous books.'

They chatted for almost an hour with Maddy reading out the questions from her list. What started out as a question-and-answer format gradually morphed into a comfortable chat about all sorts of topics including Luke's inspiration for writing, his reputation for lively debates, his views on social media and the trends in crime writing, the bodies in his own garden that had nothing to do with a crime – although they both agreed it would make for a great story – and a look back at his previous books. Maddy was secretly pleased that Luke specifically mentioned *End of the Roadie* and how he hadn't realised at the time that the storyline was based on a real incident, but gave Nigel Shaw full credit for the idea.

There was also a bit of a story teaser for the new cosy crime novel. Being the first to reveal the details would do her journalistic reputation no harm at all, although Maddy nearly fell off her chair laughing when Luke told her the title. The premise sounded even more entertaining if that were humanly possible, and Maddy decided on the spot that the book was going straight to the top of her pre-order list, and would no doubt rocket up the bestseller lists too.

———————

It took her most of the evening to type up her notes; she would review everything tomorrow before sending it off to Luke's agent but she was thrilled with her article—not only because she would be paid for her efforts but also because it enabled her to show a more relatable side to her interviewee.

To top off a successful day, as she was getting ready for bed she spotted a text from Leonard saying that he had tracked down some information for her on Elizabeth Allen and would she like to give him a call. It took her a few seconds to realise that he was referring to Libby—girlfriend of Darius Locke—and now possibly the only person who knew Nigel during his time in America. She fired off a quick thank you and said she'd call him back in the morning. What on earth could he have found out? Was she still alive? Did he know where she lived? If it were possible to tell from a short text, Leonard was very excited. She wondered whether Leonard was a lark or a night bird, and whether nine o'clock in the morning was a bit too early to ring someone.

Chapter Twenty-Nine

10TH AUGUST

Every impulse of feeling should be guided by reason; and, in my opinion, exertion should always be in proportion to what is required
Mary Bennet, *Pride and Prejudice*

Maddy had heard about the concept of six degrees of separation—the idea that a person could be connected to anyone in the world via only five other people—but never in her wildest dreams did she ever believe it was actually true. It was just one of those urban myths that sounded plausible and made the world feel a little better about itself.

She had clearly not taken into account the power of dedicated fandom combined with the global reach of Facebook. After Leonard had posted his question on a Faultliners fan site, he had apparently made contact with a superfan in the US who, it turned out, knew a relative of the band's former manager, who had a contact within the financial firm who still managed royalty payments on behalf of the deceased band members, who in turn was able to contact Elizabeth Allen—the inheritor of Darius Locke's estate after his death in 2004. Ten short days later and after a few exchanges of emails, they were—amazingly—now on their way to meet her.

When Leonard had offered his services as chauffeur it didn't take Maddy more than a nanosecond to accept; she had no car and having looked at the public transport options, there was no easy way on a Sunday to get to this village that was on the far west of Oxfordshire, without a complicated combination of train, buses and taxis. She also recognised that Leonard might have reasons of his own for offering, and after all the trouble he had gone to on her behalf, he deserved a lot more than just grateful thanks.

Maddy had chosen her favourite russet print dress with a heart-shaped neckline that complemented her copper hair, and dug out a pair of heels for the occasion. Her hair—usually scraped back for convenience—had been treated to the curling wand and the ensemble had earned an admiring glance from Luke. Maddy noted Leonard had dressed for the occasion too, sporting a light-weight blazer and brown leather brogues that had been polished to a shine.

'I still can't quite believe this,' said Maddy excitedly, as they passed a road sign saying *Shrivenham, 4 miles*. 'We've been invited to take afternoon tea with a rock star's ex-girlfriend who once went to fetch a can of petrol with Nigel Shaw!' She rummaged in her bag for her lipstick.

'It's a dream come true for me,' admitted Leonard. 'I've waited fifty years for this.' He slowed the car as they entered the village.

'Oh, look at the police station!' said Maddy pointing upwards. 'There's a model of a policeman on a bicycle attached to that tree. How cute is that!' They drove on past a row of individual shops in a mixture of architectural styles. By comparison, Cotlington, with its one village store, pharmacy and pub, made this place look positively cosmopolitan. The thatched house at the end of the high street appeared to be some sort of beauty salon and there was even a gift shop with an eye-catching window display. On another day, and if they'd had more time, Maddy would have suggested a quick look around.

The satnav directed them down a side road and then along a lane that passed a row of well-presented houses. Maddy counted the house numbers. 'I think we should pull over anywhere here,' she said, rechecking the address.

Number eighteen Canons Lane was a double-fronted white house with a newly tiled roof and a blue front door. The small front garden was neatly trimmed and edged with a fragrant lavender hedge that brushed against their legs as they walked up to the front door. Little sparks of nervous excitement burst inside her and she wiped her palms against her skirt as Leonard rang the doorbell.

In all her searches online, Maddy had only seen a couple of small photos of Libby, clearly taken in the seventies judging by the maxi dresses and ponchos. She often had her arms draped possessively around Darius, although there was one picture of her posing naked and laughing as she held Darius's strategically placed guitar. Shockingly, Maddy realised this blond bombshell would be a pensioner now. Was she living a quiet village life baking cakes and going to Pilates every week, or was she still a bit of a rebel on the side? Maddy was still trying to work out exactly how old she might be when the front door opened.

Elizabeth Allen was taller than she appeared in the photos. She was dressed simply but elegantly in white calf-length trousers and a coral V-necked blouse that revealed a thick plaited gold necklace around her throat. Her blond hair was swept up in an elegant arrangement held in place by sparkling Cloisonne combs.

Leonard looked totally starstruck as they were greeted warmly and ushered into a large sitting room.

'Isn't she amazing?' whispered Leonard, his eyes sparkling, as their hostess disappeared into the kitchen. 'I wish I could take a photo, just to remember this moment.' Maddy had never heard him so animated.

She looked around while they waited. The ivory walls and light-coloured furnishings were offset by spots of strong colour; patterned cushions in rainbow colours lay scattered around the chairs and a woven scene depicting silhouetted grazing African animals decorated one wall. An exotic-looking plant dominated one corner of the room. On a low table by the door there were plenty of photos in varnished wooden frames but Maddy didn't recognise any of the people in them. Maybe Libby didn't think back to the heady days of The Faultliners anymore. The fluttering nerves kicked in again as their smiling hostess returned and placed a sturdy wooden tray decorated with letters and swirls, holding two teacups and a plate of cinnamon biscuits on the coffee table in front of them.

'My husband did all the pyrography,' she said proudly. 'Micky loved trying any sort of hobby.'

'It's impressive,' agreed Leonard. 'He clearly learned his craft well. I was hopeless at woodwork at school, usually too busy with my nose buried in a book or listening to music on my tinny radio.'

'Ah yes, your love of music. You mentioned that in your emails. It's what brought you here, isn't it?'

'And we are very, very grateful that you agreed to meet with us,' Maddy said. 'May I just ask, do you go by the name Elizabeth these days or do people still call you Libby?'

'I prefer Elizabeth or Lizzy. Libby was…' She sighed almost wistfully and just for a second her eyes clouded over. 'She was part of my past, which I'll never forget but hey, life moves on, doesn't it?' Her expression was one of acceptance but there was something else. Regret?

'But of course I understand the past is what you came here to talk about, isn't it? My time with The Faultliners.' She turned to give Leonard her full attention. 'I'll be honest with you guys, the reason I agreed to meet was because of your obvious devotion to the band, and not just because some absent member of the Shaw family suddenly wants to reconnect with their rich but conveniently dead relative.'

Maddy winced and her face flushed with a heat that had nothing to do with the steaming cup of tea in front of her. 'I'm sorry. I understand how this must look to you, but not everyone in the family despised him. Sadly I never even knew him.'

'If there's one thing I've learned in life, honey, it's that doing nothing isn't the same as speaking out about things that aren't right.'

Leonard swiftly and skilfully steered the conversation into less contentious waters and for a while, he and Elizabeth chatted about their shared love of music. It was clear the two of them had similar tastes over many different genres, and Maddy had a fascinating insight into the world of a teenage music-obsessed Leonard.

Eventually Maddy asked, 'So after living the high life in California, what made you settle over here in a quiet English village?'

'Mickey was British; his folks lived in a place called Watchfield, not far from here.' Her hands fluttered as she spoke. 'We met in Nevada—I was visiting friends and he was working—and we married a few years later. Then his mom became really sick, so he came back here to look after her and I wanted to be with him so...' She smiled and waved her hand. 'Here I am! After she passed, we just kinda stayed, so we bought this place. I still get Darius's royalty payments, which pay the bills.'

'I'm sure his mum appreciated him coming home,' said Maddy tactfully.

'She sure did. She died eight months later with Mickey and his sister at her side, and after that Mickey didn't want to go back to the States again. He did studio work for various groups, and the slower pace of life kinda suited us, you know?'

The conversation stilled and Maddy became aware of the clock on the wall ticking softly as Elizabeth's words echoed uncomfortably round inside her head:

...doing nothing isn't the same as speaking out about things that aren't right...

Maddy sighed. 'You're right, of course.'

'Sorry?'

'About what you said. Instead of accepting my grand-parents' view of the situation, other members of the Shaw family could have challenged it. I'm sorry they—we— didn't. But I do want to hear about how you met my cousin and what he was like. Over the last few months, I've met his friends and neighbours and it's clear he meant the world to them, but there's twenty-five years of the puzzle missing that only you know about.'

'So why now?'

'I live in his house. I'm surrounded by his possessions. It's an extraordinarily generous bequest and the least I can do is to find out the real story of this person whom everyone else knows better than I do.' Maddy pulled out her phone and selected a photo of Meadowside which she held up to show her. 'This is where Nigel lived for the last thirty years of his life. It's an amazing house. I'm guessing he must have come into some money at some point in order to afford that.'

Maddy had become accustomed to expressions of amazement from people when she showed them where she lived, but to her surprise Elizabeth laughed and clapped her hands. 'Hey! The boy did good. I knew he would.'

Maddy and Leonard exchanged glances.

'So, where do you want to start? What do you know?'

Maddy pulled a face. 'Not very much so far. Only the story mentioned in Rob's memoir about how you and an English guy were once despatched to fetch help for the van.'

A broad smile stretched across Elizabeth's face and lit up her eyes. 'Oh my! I remember Rocket—that useless van! We had a love-hate relationship with that thing. Nigel sweet-talked the mechanic into coming out to repair it. He had such a lovely posh voice that he used to put on for those occasions. I reckon they thought he was British royalty on the run.' She laughed. 'We always got him to do the talking whenever we needed favours.

'It was Chuck that got to know him first though. Chuck collected people, and he adored this eccentric English guy who was miles from home, with no money, no job. Found him a dirt-cheap room-share, and in exchange, Nigel did jobs for the band. Chuck paid him when he could. When he couldn't, the band gave him gifts like books and stuff instead.'

Maddy recalled the books and other random objects in the box simply labelled F. 'Did he ever talk much about home?'

Elizabeth shook her head. 'Only once. It was when

Nigel couldn't afford the rent and he moved in with us for a bit. Slept on the sofa. Darius asked why he didn't want to go home to his folks. Nigel just shook his head and said in that cute British way, "That boat has sailed". Chuck and the others became'—she shrugged as if she couldn't find any other suitable word—'his surrogate family.'

'So that's how he came to be standing in the back of the photo taken at the inquest of Mason Garcia, the guy who died after the incident at the diner?'

Elizabeth shuddered. 'That should never have happened. Chuck was really cut up about it. Everyone had been off their heads that day. Drinking. Shouting. All because of a stupid song.'

'A very famous one though,' added Leonard.

Elizabeth nodded. 'And one that's earned some folks a lot of money.' She stood up. 'Let me fix you another drink and then I'll tell you something that I think you're gonna want to hear.'

Chapter Thirty

Angry people are not always wise.
Narrator, *Pride and Prejudice*

The journey back was quiet, each lost in their own thoughts, savouring their memories of a frankly astonishing afternoon. She couldn't wait to tell Luke: given that he had known Nigel longer than she had, she was sure he'd be as excited as they were. In fact, there was no doubt the whole village would be agog to hear about it. She would have to be careful about who she told first though and in what order; village sensibilities were easily offended when big news was the currency of the day.

Unless… Maddy turned to face her driver. 'Leonard, can I ask you a huge favour?'

'Of course. Ask away. Unless it's Tuesday. I said I'd take Joyce to the doctors that morning.'

'Can we keep what we found out to ourselves, just for a little while? I don't mean the rock star stuff, just the…'

'Yes of course. You need time to think about it all—it must have come as rather a surprise.'

Leonard dropped her off at the bottom of Springfield Lane. Maddy wanted to walk the last stretch as the day was still warm, and she relished the chance to stretch her legs after sitting in a stuffy car. Every day now it felt as though the temperatures nudged a little higher, and even Luke had switched into shorts over the last few days, which Maddy found a huge, but far from unpleasant, distraction.

The first thing Maddy noticed as she reached the bend in the driveway that afforded the first view of the house, was that Luke was standing with half his body inside the car with his bum sticking in the air. She smiled as she allowed herself a quick ogle before announcing her presence.

She waved as she shouted, 'Hello! I'm back!'

Luke straightened up and headed back into the house without acknowledging her presence. Clearly he hadn't heard her. Several seconds later he re-emerged with a large cardboard box in his arms, which he deposited on the back seat. What was going on? Maddy jogged the last few metres.

'Luke? What's with all the box moving?'

Luke ignored her and walked back into the house. Maddy followed him, noticing as she entered the hallway that several more bags and boxes sat in the middle of the parquet floor. Luke picked up a couple of bags but Maddy stood like a roadblock in his path, confusion swirling inside her. The earlier excitement of her startling news was replaced by a gnawing anxiety that something had happened of which she was currently unaware. Had there been a death in his family?

'Luke? Can you tell me what's going on? What's with all the boxes?'

'I think it's time I found somewhere else, don't you?'

'What?' Maddy reeled from the verbal shockwave. 'No… why? I don't understand.' Nausea rose in her throat and she raked her hand through her hair to push it off her face. 'I thought we were—'

'And right there, you put your interfering finger on the nub of the problem.' Luke threw down the box he was carrying. 'I trusted you. I told you things that I've never told anyone else. I *assumed*'—he emphasised the word in a highly sarcastic tone—'that they were private conversations. Clearly that wasn't how you saw it.'

'Luke, I still have no idea what you're on about.' Maddy's panicked voice sounded almost shrill and she made a concerted effort to bring it down an octave. 'Can't we just sit down and talk about this?'

'So that you get more tittle tattle for another interview? I think not.'

'What do you mean? I haven't got any other interviews.'

'Given what you wrote last time around, I think that's just as well, don't you?'

'Oh! Is it published in today's supplements then?'

Luke picked up the box again, but Maddy didn't step

aside. 'Didn't you like it?' she asked in a quiet voice as the anxiety stepped up a gear. She thought she'd written a fair piece. The brief was to promote the books and the author and that was exactly what she'd done. She had included some teasers for the new book, which sounded both intriguing and hilarious, and plenty of praise for previous ones, while avoiding the usual journalistic swipes at the temperamental author stereotype that he did nothing to dispel.

The man she had come to know over the last few months had little in common with the man she'd met back in February, and she wanted the world to see him as she did: a caring, personable man whose only crime was to value his privacy, unlike today's wannabe celebrities who craved the complete opposite.

'I didn't ask for copy approval because I knew... I thought you'd be fair. Clearly I was wrong.' Luke took a step closer and now Maddy could clearly see the anger sparking in his eyes. 'Please step aside so I can finish this and then get out of your way.'

Tears prickled the back of Maddy's eyes as she reluctantly stood aside. Unlike nearly every other interview she had read online, she hadn't written anything awful about him. If anything she had gone out of her way to show the complete opposite. No mention of storming out of interviews, snappy answers to questions, blazing rows on social media. She'd simply wanted to right a wrong—let people know that Luke wasn't always the villain of the piece, and that his broken engagement wasn't his fault.

She turned and grasped his arm as Luke tried to get

back into the hallway. 'Luke, can't we just talk about this? Please? If I've offended you, I am truly sorry. That was never the intention.' She blinked to prevent any wayward tears appearing. 'You are a decent, kind, caring person and I wanted people to know the real you.'

'So you decided to do that by trying to drum up sympathy?'

'No! It wasn't done for sympathy, it was telling the truth.'

Luke brushed her hand away. 'Did you never consider that by allowing Clara to blame me, I felt just a little less guilty about causing the breakup?'

'But it wasn't your fault!'

'Maybe you thought that by making people feel sorry for me, they'd rush out and buy my books, is that it?'

'Not at all. Look if that's what this'—Maddy waved her arm across the diminishing pile in the hall—'is all about, don't you think you might be over-reacting just a little bit?'

'Thanks for your professional opinion. Now please step out of the way—this is actually quite heavy.'

How had this gone so wrong? He must know she would never deliberately want to hurt or humiliate him. Quite the opposite. Maddy turned aside so that he wouldn't see her dash the tears from her cheeks. Her amazing afternoon had done a complete about-turn.

She'd actually been really proud of her article—the first she'd done since moving to Meadowside. She'd hoped that it might be the first of many, but right now that seemed unlikely if everyone else's reaction was the same as Luke's.

She sat on the bottom of the stairs, waves of misery washing over her, as she watched Luke load the remaining boxes into the car. He then returned and deposited a key on the table in the hall. 'I won't be needing this any longer.' He did that amazing fingers-in-mouth whistling thing. 'Buster! Come here!'

Maddy hadn't seen or heard any sound from Buster since she'd returned, but now he padded into the hall from the direction of the library. His ears, normally alert and standing to attention, were flattened back against his head, and his tail hung limply between his legs. He clearly knew something was happening. Ignoring his master, Buster trotted over to Maddy and stuck his nose in her hands, then looked up at her with large soulful eyes and whined softly.

Another wave of emotion crashed over her as Maddy pinched her lips together and allowed her hands to roam over his soft coat and stroke his velvet ears, but it didn't soothe the jumble of painful thoughts spinning around inside. Luke slapped his thigh but Buster resolutely ignored him. Instead he whined again, making a pitiful anxious sound, then shuffled closer to Maddy and pressed his body against her knees.

'I know,' she whispered as she bent over to hug him. 'I don't understand either.' Maddy looked up at Luke. 'You don't have to do this. Help me to understand. I've said I'm sorry—please stay.'

Luke looked at her steadily. 'I think I've talked quite enough.'

Maddy got to her feet and reached for Luke's hand but he held it stiffly at his side. 'But can't you at least tell me where you're going?' Maddy hated the desperation in her voice. 'And what about the literary festival? It's only four weeks away. We're selling the programmes. You're doing the keynote speech.' The thought of him leaving now made her feel physically sick. Maddy pressed her hand against her chest as her insides constricted sending a shard of pain through her.

'I honour my commitments,' he replied brusquely.

Luke walked over, bodily scooped up Buster and marched out. The last thing Maddy heard was a plaintive whine, a slam of a car door and the harsh scrunch of tyres on gravel.

Maddy sank down onto the stairs, her head resting uncomfortably against the carved wooden spindles as she let the tears fall.

———

Maddy wasn't sure how long she'd sat there waiting. Or why. After all, it seemed unlikely that Luke would return. However, logic didn't remove the need to talk to him, explain, apologise. She would never have intentionally offended him or embarrassed him—she had only added a few personal asides because she wanted people to see the real person behind the social media tempest. *Maybe he didn't want to show that side of himself, Maddy?* And now, in her enthusiasm to show the world his better side, she had driven him away. Should she text him? Ask where he is?

The house suddenly felt empty. At this time of the day Luke would have finished writing and would be making coffee in the kitchen, or taking a beer out onto the terrace to soak up the late afternoon sun. Buster would be cavorting around with his latest favourite toy, or begging for a tug of war with the doggy rope.

Maddy rubbed her forehead, as a dull, heavy ache settled over her. The truth was she'd never come across any man like Luke Hamilton. Most men she'd met were either desperate to show off talents they didn't have, or were nerdily knowledgeable about non-riveting subjects. Luke was clever but didn't flaunt it. Infuriatingly opinionated at times, and loved a debate. A massively competitive board game player who hated losing—probably a by-product of having two older brothers. Yet underneath the clever, opinionated, competitive facade she had gradually uncovered a wonderful, funny and caring man that people never got to see. Like the Nigel Shaw family legend, sometimes folks saw only what was in front of them and didn't try to look beyond.

'I'm sorry, Luke,' she said as she brushed away more tears. 'I know that your good opinion once lost, is lost forever, but I love you, and if I was wrong, please know I was doing what I believed to be right.'

It seemed ironic that she'd spent the last few years helping other people understand and resolve the problems in their own relationships, but had made such a mess of her own. She wished she had a 'Dear Jane,' to write to for advice, although Maddy wasn't sure even Jane Austen had an answer for this. Right now though, she'd settle for a sympathetic and familiar voice; she retrieved her phone from her bag, still sitting in the hall, and called Alice's number.

Chapter Thirty-One

. . . though where so many hours have been spent in convincing myself that I am right, is there not some reason to fear I may be wrong?
Colonel Brandon, *Sense & Sensibility*

Maddy kept Luke's room aired and dusted but after a week there was still no word despite the couple of texts she had sent. In contrast, Alice had been a tower of strength and was contacting her daily with encouragement, comfort and promises of seeing her very soon. Maddy found herself shutting the library door even though there was no one working in there; it was just part of her daily routine that she was loath to let go of. She discovered Buster's prized find—the old shoe he came across in the field—under the dining room table where he'd presumably placed it for safekeeping. Maddy now shut the door to that room too.

Aside from the promise of payment, the only good thing that had come out of her interview was the response from Luke's agent, who had emailed to say he was delighted to read positive comments about his client for once, and that there had been a noticeable increase in his social media following, and his fans were busily discussing both the article and his books online, which would hopefully translate into sales. Maddy had already decided that even if Luke didn't turn up for the literary festival his books would still be available, and two days ago she had placed an order for a large stock of all eight books and added it to her credit card debt as a silent apology.

The literary festival was now only just over two weeks away. With Cameron Massey and Randall Jacobson topping the speaker list, ticket sales were buoyant, and following responses to her advertisement in the *Haxford and Kingsfordly Gazette*, she had selected another four local authors to do a reading or talk about their books, which covered a variety of genres.

Leonard had confirmed that entries for the haiku competition were also flooding in, although some people hadn't quite grasped the concept of haiku and he'd received several limericks, a couple of page-length poems, and one recipe for spiced cranberry bread pudding. Presumably somewhere in the country, the judges of a baking competition were looking similarly puzzled.

Joyce's ankle had been pronounced fully healed, and both she and Sally were busy designing posters advertising the literary festival as well as laminating large fluorescent yellow arrows to attach to the fence posts on Springfield Lane. Jem was busy deadheading the flower beds and pruning back any shrubbery that might impede the erection of the marquee the following week. Even the August edition of *Cotlington Chat* had very little gossip and was largely given over to the literary festival, with only a small write-up of the litter pick along Church Lane.

Maddy's name was already added to the speaker list; her role was to open the festival, as Nigel had done last year, introduce the speakers and say something appropriate at the end. This was her chance to tell everyone what she'd found out from Libby and to right a wrong. It would also give the villagers something new to talk about. She found it difficult not to tell anyone though, and the one person she could have relied upon to keep the secret was now uncontactable, or more accurately, refusing to respond to messages, even though he was never far from her thoughts.

It wasn't long before Jem and others started to comment on Luke's absence; the Cotlington grapevine had always been far more efficient than its – rather unreliable – broadband signal.

He might have gone to visit a friend.

Just getting away for a few days.

A writing sabbatical.

It was amazing how easy it was to hint at a fictional reason to explain Luke's absence—not that she was obliged to supply an explanation—but once she'd started, it seemed simpler to keep it up. However, it wasn't long before the editor of *Cotlington Chat* came looking for more detailed information than that freely available in the village.

'Myra, what an unexpected pleasure.'

Maddy wondered why after all these months she was still doing that British thing of pretending it was such a delight to see someone who was actually rather interfering and had basically invited themselves round.

'Can I offer you a cup of tea? Coffee? Something stronger?'

Without waiting for a response, Maddy retrieved the half open bottle of wine from the fridge and poured herself a large glass.

'Coffee for me, if you don't mind.'

Maddy reached into one of the cupboards for the box of coffee pods before realising that the coffee maker no longer occupied the corner of the worktop. Another conspicuous absence. 'Sorry, I've only got instant, is that okay?'

For a few seconds, she busied herself making coffee and opening a packet of digestives to prolong the point at which she would have to sit down and explain to Myra why her lodger and the literary festival's keynote speaker had upped sticks with only an 'I honour my commitments' for reassurance.

They took their drinks through to the sitting room. Despite the yellow and orange décor, the room was bright and comfortable and Maddy didn't mind it as much as she used to.

'I'll get straight to the point, Maddy,' said Myra in her

usual brisk fashion. 'Jem tells me that Luke is no longer living here.'

The mention of his name stabbed at her insides, and Maddy's grip tightened on her glass. 'That's correct.'

'And you have no date for his return?'

'No,' said Maddy, feeling like she was in the witness stand being cross-examined by a particularly keen prosecuting barrister.

'The builders are still working on his house, so where's he gone?'

Maddy took a large gulp of wine. 'No idea.'

'But he's still returning to speak at the literary festival, isn't he.' It was more a confirmatory statement than a question.

'Maybe. I hope so. I really have no idea, sorry.' Maddy rubbed her forehead.

'This is ridiculous. He's left you without any sort of explanation whatsoever!'

It wasn't clear whether her indignation resulted from a failed attempt at neighbourly support, or the fact that Luke had had the temerity to leave after she'd gone to the trouble of organising lodgings for him.

'It's not his fault,' Maddy blurted out.

'Of course it is!'

Maddy kneaded her fingers together. The combination of not sleeping well and worrying about having half the village in her back garden in a few weeks' time was exhausting, and her stamina was severely depleted.

'It's my fault. I tried to help and I made things worse. I thought the world deserved to know that he's not the mean, snarky, fiancée-dumping man that he's made out to be. He's not a saint—I know that—but he was virtually coerced into accepting the proposal. He's never tried to defend himself and he let that woman throw all the blame on him. It's no wonder he hates all that Valentine's Day stuff. I didn't put it in the article, but she got his publishing deal pulled too.'

'I read your interview. Very well written by the way. Balanced, not overly syrupy.'

'Oh. Thank you.' Well, that was unexpected. And *not overly syrupy* counted as a high praise coming from Myra.

'And of course you're entitled to feel hurt,' Myra continued. 'You've been let down by someone you trusted. I know what that feels like.'

Her words, although well intentioned, ripped open up a wound that had barely started to heal, and Maddy covered her face with her hands as tears plopped onto her lap.

'Oh, you poor girl.' Myra rose from her seat and positioned herself next to Maddy on the sofa, putting a comforting arm around her shoulders. 'This isn't about the money, is it?'

Maddy shook her head.

'So, the next question is, what are you going to do about it?'

'There's nothing I can do,' sniffed Maddy. 'He gave the impression that he'll come and do his talk but then…' She wiped her face with her fingers and tried to sound as though she wasn't really falling apart inside. 'Then he'll go I suppose.'

'Only if you let him. Have you told him how you feel? That's an important thing to communicate in any relationship.'

Maddy smiled despite the tears. It was the same advice that she frequently gave her Dear Jane readers. 'I think it's a bit late for that now. Luke doesn't do second chances.'

Myra made a tsk sort of noise. 'That's because some people think it's an admission of weakness to change their mind. Once they've decided something'—she clapped her hands together—'that's it, it can never be changed.' She placed one hand over Maddy's and squeezed it gently. 'Please don't let your chance of happiness slip away. Life's too short.'

It felt strange to be on the receiving end of relationship advice and even stranger hearing it from Myra Hardcastle. Maddy was grateful for her support though; her own mother always floundered at the wrong end of the sympathy–advice ratio.

Myra pulled a packet of tissues from her handbag and passed them to Maddy. 'You may find it hard to believe, but I too was once young and madly in love.'

Maddy extracted a tissue. 'It's good to know that some relationships last,' she mumbled in between noisily blowing her nose.

Even though Joyce regarded the rarely seen Mr H as the most boring person in the village, it was still nice to know there'd been romance, stars and passion at the start. Maddy stared at the overly patterned rug on the floor as she tried and failed to picture Myra as young and carefree. Maybe that was the arrogance of the younger gener-ation to assume they have the monopoly on youthful romance.

Myra's voice broke into Maddy's thoughts. 'I think it's fair to say both Stephen and I went into this marriage with our eyes open. He knew I was in love with someone else,' she added matter-of-factly.

Maddy's head jerked up. What? Was this common knowledge? Probably not, otherwise Joyce would surely have mentioned that nugget of news? Maddy's curiosity temporarily overrode other emotions. Had this been an impossible relationship? Maybe the man had been married? Maybe, like Luke, this man hadn't wanted commitment. Or maybe she was jilted at the altar. Maddy shuddered. That would be awful.

'That's really sad. It must have been so difficult for you. Did this man know that you loved him?'

'He did. And what you really want to ask is why on earth did I marry someone else.' She sighed. 'It all happened so quickly. For me it really was instant: love at first sight. Stars and fireworks. He was rich, charming and entertaining. By comparison, my on/off boyfriend at the time suddenly seemed very boring and ordinary, so when he got sent overseas for a two-month secondment I thought the universe was giving me permission to have some fun. I didn't care that my parents disapproved, in fact it added to the excitement. They didn't like the fact that we didn't know his parents, that he was fifteen years older than me—as if any of that mattered. We had a glorious summer together full of poetry, picnics and passionate kisses. Neither of us talked of the past, or had expectations for the future, we just lived in the moment.'

'It sounds idyllic.'

'It was.' She clasped her hands together. 'It never went any further than that though—he was oddly traditional in that respect, even though I wasn't a complete novice in that department as Stephen and I had slept together a couple of times, but I was happy to wait. I thought we had all the time in the world, you see. I planned to end the relationship with Stephen—I didn't want to hurt him, but he could never have made me feel the same, not in a hundred years.'

'I'm guessing something happened?' asked Maddy delicately.

'I discovered rather belatedly that I was pregnant. Maybe I had just ignored any inconvenient facts. Anyway it reached a point where I had to make some choices.'

Maddy's mouth dropped open. This was like one of her Dear Jane letters. Except that this wasn't some confused young girl; this was Myra! Somewhere at the back of her mind, Joyce's words came back to her:

…*she used to be such a lively young woman and then just like that, she's married, and popped out a sproglet.*

'Did you tell your parents?'

'I had to; I lived at home. They were furious. As soon as Stephen returned from Europe, they arranged every-thing.' She heaved a sigh. 'Including the wedding.'

'But what about this other man? The one you loved?'

'As soon as the "p" word was uttered, he backed off. I would have married him in a heartbeat, but he knew the baby wasn't his and he thought he was doing the right thing. Reinforced no doubt by the strident views of my father whose moral code was stuck in the Victorian era as far as sex before marriage was concerned.'

'And was it the right thing?'

'Of course not!' said Myra, sounding more like the person Maddy thought she knew. 'But he felt he was being honourable; that it was best for me and the baby. He never changed his mind. I should have spoken up, done something. Instead, I went along with everything. I wept on the morning of my wedding and they were not tears of joy.' She turned to face Maddy with a look of fierce determination. 'I'm not telling you this for sympathy, but because I don't want you to make the same mistake I did and just let someone you love walk away for the wrong reason.'

For a several minutes they both sat in silence, each lost in their own thoughts. Maddy wasn't sure Luke ever wanted to speak to her again but shouldn't she at least make more of an effort? Was it ever too late for love? Was it too late for Myra?

'Myra, don't you ever wonder what happened to the man you loved? I know it was many years ago but…'

Myra took her hand as she smiled, but her eyes spoke of weary sorrow. 'I didn't need to wonder. He carried on living in this house till the day he died. And I think a little bit of me died that day too.'

Chapter Thirty-Two

If I could but know his heart, everything would become easy.
Marianne Dashwood, *Sense and Sensibility*

Long after Myra had departed with an unexpected and spontaneous hug, Maddy was still turning over everything she had heard earlier that afternoon. Just when she thought she'd found out all there was to know about her mysterious cousin, another incredible part of the puzzle had come to light, although it went without saying that this piece was never going to be for public consumption.

Who'd have believed it? Nigel Shaw was Myra's secret lover, and like Cotlington's own version of *Romeo and Juliet*, they had been forced apart by circumstance and family pressure. Once Myra was married, there would have been no going back and yet, in spite Nigel's decision to step back and let Myra make a marriage of convenience, he must still have loved her. Why else would he have made that clause in his will leaving everything to Myra if Maddy didn't stay for the stipulated twelve-month period?

Suddenly a lot of little things made sense. The flowers on the grave, paying for the electrical work that was over and above what was actually needed, and the reverence with which she wanted to continue the literary festival exactly as Nigel had set it up. Because without doubt, that was his love letter to her. The things that he could not express directly he had written into his flowery poems and Myra had understood.

A further, uncomfortable thought struck her as she was getting ready for bed later that evening. If Myra and Nigel had married, this house would have been Jem's inheritance. Would still be, if Maddy left before the 14th March. But if Maddy saw out the year and sold up as originally planned, Meadowside would probably be turned into flats, or possibly even pulled down to make way for a larger housing development. No one these days wanted a property with this much land unless they had significant funds for its upkeep. She certainly didn't. And what happened to the housekeeping budget after the year was up? It was about time she had another chat with the solicitor Mr Chapman, and she scribbled a note to herself to make an appointment for the week after the literary festival.

She wished she had Luke to talk to about all this. He might have been scathing about matters of the heart but as far as business and finance was concerned, he was truthful and knowledgeable and could be totally relied upon for his discretion. Now there was no glow of light from the room at the end of the landing, no canine footsteps signalling the last patrol before settling down for the night. Where had he gone? For the first time Maddy felt very alone, and she lay awake in the dark for another hour before finally succumbing to sleep.

In the days leading up to the festival, Maddy had little time for regrets as there was a constant buzz of activity centred around Meadowside. Every day at least one or more of the committee could be found in the house either organising, planning or seeking her opinion on something. There were also several invoices requiring payment—the big one being the one for the hire of the marquee, tables and chairs. The money Maddy had received in rent from Luke had mostly been spent on essentials, but the payment from Randall Jacobson's company had finally arrived in the nick of time, although there had been three deductions from the agreed sum of which only one made sense. She was too busy to argue about it.

Yesterday, while the main marquee was being put up on the lawn, Jem and Leonard had set up a small gazebo in the rose garden for book sales, and the next job on Maddy's long to-do list attached to the clipboard tucked under her arm was to arrange the tables. More of Sally's laminated arrows and signs pointed the way through the trellised arch but you could equally as well follow your nose, as the glorious scent of summer roses hung in the air like warm perfume.

She set up the wooden tables in a horseshoe shape with one large table in the middle reserved for Luke's books. The hefty box had been delivered from his publisher last week and Maddy had unpacked it reverently, looking over the familiar titles and wishing, not for the last time, that he was here to share this with her.

There had been a surprisingly enthusiastic response to Maddy's advertisement in the local paper, and not only did they now have a full complement of speakers, but also many local authors who were happy to come along and sell signed copies of their books.

Maddy had just placed the last of the name labels around the table when she spied Myra marching in her direction. 'Sorry I'm a bit late, I couldn't get an earlier appointment, and then the stylist did far too much chatting.'

'Well, she did a great job – the blond highlights suit you.'

Spots of pink appeared on Myra's cheeks and she appeared momentarily flustered. 'Really? Thank you, it was Sally's idea.'

'So what do you think?' asked Maddy pointing at the tables. 'Do we have enough space for everyone?'

'How many are you expecting?'

'Randall Jacobson, obviously, I'm putting him over there.' Maddy pointed to one end of the tables, and as far away from Luke's display as possible. 'Plus another twelve local authors covering a wide range of genres.' She counted on her fingers. 'We have writers of romance, crime, thrillers, short stories, science fiction, historical—both fictional and actual—plus a biography of the fifth Earl of Haxford.'

Myra nodded approvingly. 'I'll be first to admit that I'm not a great one for change, but you've shown all of us how it's possible to adopt new ideas without throwing out the old ones.' She gestured at the tables waiting for tomorrow's booksellers. 'This is all down to your hard work.'

Maddy made a dismissive noise.

'I beg to differ. It pains me to say it, but Joyce was right—last year the book stall was a meagre selection of tired old books that everyone had either already purchased the year before or didn't want in the first place.' Before Maddy could respond, Myra softened her voice as she asked, 'I presume you haven't heard anything yet from Luke?'

At the mention of his name, the near-permanent leaden feeling in the pit of stomach intensified. Maddy shook her head.

'Never mind. There's still plenty of time. We're living in the digital age now; it's amazing what can happen in twenty-four hours.'

Since when was Myra prone to fits of cheery optimism? Luke didn't do surprises or second chances, no matter how often Maddy might wish it. As Jane Austen had observed, to wish was to hope, and to hope was to expect. No, that path would only lead to disappointment.

After days of tears and self-recrimination, feeling that she had driven him away, Maddy had begun to feel a little resentful of Luke's knee-jerk reaction and continued silence. His agent had been thrilled with the interview and so were a lot of other people, including his publisher. Even some of those people who had formerly been very critical of him were now swayed by the groundswell of public opinion, and Maddy had been surprised to see how even the merest suggestion of a coerced proposal had led to heated discussions on social media about entrapment, with several contributors protesting volubly on the absent author's behalf.

'So what's next on the list?' Myra asked, nodding at Maddy's clipboard and dragging her attention back to more urgent matters.

'You and Jem are making sure everything is organised in the hospitality tent, and I'm heading indoors to get the guest room ready for my friend Alice who's arriving later today. We over-ordered on the flyers so I suggested Joyce and Sally might like to do a last-minute leaflet drop around Haxford. Although,' she added with a wry smile, 'they were disappointed to discover they would be travelling in the back of Leonard's car. I don't know why, but the two of them were somehow expecting a trip in a low-flying aircraft.'

A look of horror flashed across Myra's features. 'Oh good lord, can you imagine that!'

Maddy chuckled. 'I can see the headlines now: Haxford's pedestrian area strafed by over-enthusiastic pensioner.'

'Definitely not the sort of publicity we are after,' agreed Myra. 'Although you have to hand it to Joyce, since you got her started on social media, she's opened up a whole new world of opportunities for herself—apparently she's now following a huge number of people including dozens of celebrities and famous authors.'

'I'm pleased for her.'

'She's also planning some live tweets from the festival tomorrow.'

'Welcome to the digital age indeed,' marvelled Maddy.

'It's not the only change around here—I don't mind admitting you've injected new blood into this festival and whatever happens tomorrow, I just want to say that Nigel would have been very proud of you and what you've achieved.'

An unexpected swell of emotion rose within her as tears formed in the corner of her eyes, and Maddy wished more than ever that she had met this man, who was part of her family and who had entrusted her with continuing his vision.

Maddy smiled as she patted away the tears with her fingers. 'Thank you, Myra. I think tomorrow Nigel might have one last surprise for you too.'

Chapter Thirty-Three

*I have blamed you, and lectured you, and you have borne it as no
other woman in England would have borne it.*
George Knightley, *Emma*

'Good morning, and welcome to Meadowside.'
'Thank you, it's lovely to see so many people here.'

'You're welcome—a programme of events is on sale just over there.'

Maddy was determined that her personal disappointments would not put a damper on the day, and now Alice was here, her confidence had received a much-needed boost. They had talked non-stop from the moment she had arrived yesterday, and Maddy had given her the full guided tour after dinner. This morning Alice was keen to help out, and was currently assisting Maddy with the meet and greet.

Over the last hour, with a determined – if slightly forced – cheeriness, Maddy had been greeting not only the residents of Cotlington but people from all over the county and beyond, as well as journalists and bloggers. It was becoming clear from responses that Joyce's efforts on Twitter had not been solely directed to celebrity-watching, and many had been drawn here by her two celebrity speakers.

Sally and Joyce, resembling a pair of highlighter pens, being dressed in vibrant pink and yellow respectively, were currently busy directing cars to designated parking areas. As the committee's appointed photographer, Leonard was busy fulfilling his brief to capture the day in pictures while overseeing book sales in the rose garden.

In spite of her resolve to stay emotionally detached from the events of the past few weeks, with each new influx of guests Maddy's eyes scanned the crowd for that familiar face, that pair of piercing dark eyes, even though they would no longer look fondly at her.

Randall Jacobson had already arrived with much fanfare and was busily being feted by a coterie of admirers led by her mother. In the interests of not becoming the unwitting subject of an arranged marriage, Maddy decided he might need rescuing.

'Maddy, darling, how lovely to see you again!' There was a definite look of relief on Randall's face, one of amusement on Alice's and rapturous expectation writ large over her mother's. 'I got your message; I'll be more than happy to be your first speaker.'

Maddy had spent most of the previous evening considering various options should Luke not appear, but the only one that made any sense was to let Randall make the keynote speech instead of Luke, thus keeping everyone's timeslots unaltered until after lunch when she would fill Randall's original slot. Her own speaker notes and revised running order were scribbled down in her copy of the festival programme, which she was pleased to see was selling well.

Randall beamed his toothpaste smile and slipped his arm around her waist in a casual but unwelcome gesture. 'Such a shame that Cameron Massey appears to have been delayed.' The first three words were drawn out—presumably for effect—but Maddy didn't detect the slightest hint of regret in his voice. Then again that was hardly surprising.

What was, was a familiar voice behind her that replied in a distinctly frosty tone, 'I was a little delayed. The traffic this morning was appalling.'

Maddy spun round, at the same time extricating herself from Randall's embrace. Where had he come from? Clearly not anywhere local, as rush hour in Cotlington was classed as anything more than four cars and a milk float. After weeks of silence, she desperately needed to talk to him. Preferably in private. 'Luke! Can I get you a coffee or something before we start?'

His glance slid over to Randall still standing next to

her. 'I won't disturb you; I can see you're already occupied.'

'No, I'm—' She watched, dismayed, as Luke walked away, and tried not to scowl at Randall's triumphant expression.

'Let him go, Maddy darling,' said Randall in an overly loud voice. 'That man always causes trouble.'

Luke whirled round and marched back, his face straining with a look of barely controlled rage. 'Oh yeah? And what sort of trouble would that be?'

'Well, since you seem determined to air your dirty laundry, let's start with how badly you treated my poor friend Clara.'

So that's what it was all about—no wonder they disliked each other! Luke glared at his opponent, his eyes narrowed to hard flints, and his arm tensed as his hand curled into a tight fist. Several people had now stopped to watch the altercation, and were busy pulling out their phones. Oh God, that was all she needed—the reputation of the Cotlington Literary Festival trashed over an authorial hand-bags-at-dawn on the lawn, featuring her two star celebrities.

'So what happened to poor Clara?' asked her mother.

'Do you want to tell her or should I?' asked Randall, with a smile that didn't reach his eyes.

Maddy glanced anxiously at the crowd gathering around them and then at Luke. Their eyes met for a second, sending a wave of longing through her, before Luke's gaze returned to fix his opponent with an icy stare. He took a long, measured intake of breath that swelled his chest. 'Randall, I don't care what you think or what fictional pathos you want to peddle; the people who matter already know the truth.'

With that Luke strode off towards the marquee, and Randall muttered an excuse about checking on book sales.

'Was it something I said?' asked her mother with a puzzled expression.

'Mrs Shaw, I think I spotted your husband in the hospitality tent. How about we go and get ourselves a cup of tea?' Alice suggested tactfully. Maddy threw her a grateful glance; she would satisfy her mother's curiosity later. For now, she needed to find Myra. Her calm, no-nonsense approach and years of experience were exactly what Maddy needed for the next thirty-five minutes.

'Good morning and welcome!' Maddy spread her arms feeling like one of those television evangelists as she smiled at her seated audience.

The previous day, as they'd lined up the chairs in rows allowing spaces for access and wheelchair attendees, she'd wondered whether they'd been ridiculously over-confident about numbers, but for the last hour, Jem had been an absolute gem, rearranging chairs and wedging in more seating at the back. The front row was reserved for committee members plus guest speakers—the majority of whom were local writers, and were now sitting nervously clutching their books and casting admiring glances at the keynote speaker in their midst.

Maddy did the same as she continued her welcome address and found it hard to drag her gaze away. 'My name is Madeleine Shaw and I am proud to be the chair of what has become a long-held and much-loved tradition in this village—the Cotlington Literary Festival. We have a wonderful diverse programme of events for you today'—she waved her copy of the programme in the air —'and with the exception of the Mystery Channel's celebrity ghost hunter'—she clocked the look of disdain that flickered across Luke's face—'all our speakers are local authors.

'You will find the hospitality tent has a range of refreshments available, and for those brave enough, I've been told there's some home brew on offer too. All of today's speakers will be selling signed copies of their books in the rose garden gazebo, so do go and have a chat with them during the day.' She was thankful that Randall was already ensconced there and out of Luke's way.

'So, without further ado, please let me introduce our keynote speaker and everyone's favourite crime writer, Cameron Massey, who frequently tops the bestseller lists and is two times winner of the coveted Silver Spanner Award. After his talk, there will be an opportunity for questions, and I have it on good authority that we may also be treated to an excerpt from one of his books.'

Maddy stepped away from the microphone and slipped into the seat she had reserved for herself at the side of the marquee. Her heart thumped as adrenaline whooshed through her, and she fanned her face with the programme in her hand. Just seeing him again brought back a flood of conflicting emotions, chiefly regret. If only she hadn't tried too hard: she wasn't an agony aunt trying to heal wounds; she was a journalist and should have stuck to the script.

Accompanied by an enthusiastic bout of clapping, Luke stepped forward, nodded at Maddy and turned to face his audience. 'Thank you for inviting me here today. I know we have a lot of new and aspiring authors here, so first of all I'd like to tell you a bit about my journey to publication.'

She had to hand it to him, he was a brilliant speaker. This mercurial man who could be snarky and sour one minute, charming and entertaining the next, clearly knew how to hold the attention of an audience, who were now hanging on his every word. From time to time, Joyce held up her phone and took a picture, presumably tweeting live to her followers. Maddy hadn't had much time to look at social media in the last couple of days, but tonight she'd catch up with everything. At least Luke would get plenty of publicity out of this, and she hoped his books sales would do well. She'd bet good money that Randall would be keeping tabs on their respective book piles!

'...The unhappy truth is that many people start submitting their novel before they have honed their craft, and I was certainly no exception...'

Even after his abrupt departure and harsh, hurtful words, she couldn't find it within herself to stay angry with him. She sighed inwardly. Was she destined to end up like Myra, settling for second best, always pining for the one that got away?

'...write about what interests you, not what you think the current trend or fashion might be. Then get into the minds of your characters and make it real...'

Luke had his idiosyncrasies, his sometimes abrasive responses, but that wasn't the whole person, though he clearly didn't care if the rest of the world never got to find that out. Maddy let her mind drift through all their encounters and conversations: that initial Valentine's Day clash of temperaments, the surprise meeting in the fields, their Entente Cordiale dinner at Le Caprice, the unexpected ending to the ghost hunting evening, that mistaken proposal, their sofa side vigil for Buster and his joyous return. As she had gradually peeled back the layers, she'd uncovered the reasons behind so much of his actions, and come to know and love the real Luke Hamilton.

'...and I'm going to finish with something I wrote very recently.' Luke was clearly winding up his talk but then what? She was desperate to ensure that he didn't slip away before they had a chance to talk.

'As you know, my books have all been crime novels. However, a while ago I was challenged to try my hand at a totally different genre, and one that I freely admit I have scoffed at and berated in the past—romance.'

Maddy stared at him. He said he'd been challenged—was *she* the person he was referring to?

'It's fair to say I found even a short story far more difficult than I was expecting, and it's very unlikely to get published, but I admit it has been an interesting exercise in all sorts of ways.' There was a polite ripple of laughter in the audience and Luke cleared his throat before he started speaking again. 'So ladies and gents, for the first and definitely last time, this is an excerpt from a romance that I've been trying out.'

Maddy experienced a flutter of anxiety. Despite her teasing, she hadn't seriously expected him to try, and now she wasn't sure she wanted to hear what he'd written. What if it was awful? What if people laughed? Maddy had heard of spoof awards for awful romance writing. She couldn't bear it if Luke ended up being humiliated because of something she'd said. With nerve endings jangling she watched, transfixed, as he removed a piece of folded paper from his inside jacket pocket.

An expectant silence fell inside the marquee that lasted for several seconds, broken only by a loud bark of a laugh from Luke. 'And if you think I'm reading this aloud, think again my friends.'

Luke ignored the collective gasp and nervous laughter from the audience. 'However, I am prepared to hold my hands up and say that writing romance is not as simple as it might at first appear. Furthermore, I've given some thought as to why that might be.'

This wasn't what Maddy had expected at all, and the audience clearly felt the same if the buzz of anticipation was anything to go by.

'Writing a crime novel—or any novel come to that—requires the author to create an interesting premise, maybe a puzzle, sometimes a whodunnit. Making sure you have a good cast of characters, and an interesting journey on which to take your readers. I can do all of that very easily, so why did I find it so difficult to construct a romance?

'The answer, I think, lies in the added requirement of the characters' emotional journey. I've seen some awful examples of what people think is real-life romance, and it isn't all flowers and big gestures. Nor does it have to be public declarations, surprise parties or expensive gifts.

'I started this exercise in the belief that romance books were purely about the froth, the fizz and the fireworks, and that was probably why I found it so hard to write a conclusion to this never-to-be-published story.' Luke paused, folded up his paper and tucked it away.

'In fact, it's often in the quiet moments that we see someone's true character and feelings. In real life, relationships are rarely perfect, but they are a better example for your fictional characters. Life isn't one long series of happy ever afters, so what happens when life trips you up? When people feel wronged, how do they react? Do they run away from difficulties, or do they stay and work through the problem? What motivates them to act the way that they do?

'It is clear to me now that the best relationships— whether fictional or real—encompass compassion as well as passion.' He looked across at Maddy as his tone softened. 'And loving someone is as much about saying, "Sorry I hurt you," as it is "I love you."'

For a few seconds he held her gaze and his lips formed the briefest of smiles. Maddy's eyes prickled with unshed tears as she wrestled to control the maelstrom of emotions spinning inside her.

Luke turned back to his audience. 'I know I'll always be a crime writer, but perhaps one who now has a bit more respect for those who can pull off the perfect love story.'

Maddy was first to her feet, beaming from ear to ear, bouncing on the balls of her feet until she was almost leaping in the air, and applauding until her palms were stinging. Whatever happened now, the festival was going to be a success, and the message from Luke—because that was surely an olive branch—was received and understood. She beamed at her parents, applauding enthusiastically along with the rest of the audience. Joyce waved at her and gave her a thumbs up, and she glanced over at Myra and saw the same excitement radiating from her. However, Myra's expression rapidly turned to wide-eyed concern as she pointed discreetly.

'What?' Maddy mouthed. Confused, she looked around in time to see Luke slipping out of the marquee, his task completed. No, no, no! Why would he leave now after what she'd just heard? The feeling of euphoria instantly evaporated, replaced by confusion and a desperate urge to run after him, but the next speaker was already on their feet and making their way to the front, smiling nervously. There was no point in running after him. The message from Luke now seemed loud and clear: sorry and goodbye.

Maddy forced a reciprocal smile on her face, but her voice sounded devoid of its earlier cheer as she made her introductions for the next speaker. She slipped back into her seat, pinching her lips and keeping her eyes cast downward. She was barely hearing the talk, her mind totally submerged in her own private misery, her effort diverted into not letting tears spill down her cheeks. She therefore jumped as a firm hand gripped her shoulder. 'Why are you just sitting here? Go after him!' Myra whispered hoarsely. She tugged the programme from Maddy's hands and gave her a shove. 'I can look after all this.'

Maddy wondered why she wanted to embarrass herself chasing after someone who didn't want to stay. The need to speak to Luke was too strong though, and disobeying Myra was rarely a good idea.

The cool fresh air was a welcome relief from the stuffy cocoon inside the marquee. Feeling energised, Maddy raced across the lawn and round to the front of the house where the cars were parked on the gravelled driveway. She couldn't see him but Maddy called out anyway. 'Luke! Are you here?'

A large grassy area at the front of the property had also been designated for parking and Maddy ran between the cars, looking for a familiar red hatchback. Right at the end of the penultimate row she spotted it, parked in the shade of the overhanging beech trees; the windows were all left open a couple of inches and the windscreen was covered with a sunshade. He was still here then, but where? Maddy ran back towards the gardens, checking the house and the hospitality tent along the way. There were a couple of visitors wandering the grounds, taking in the late summer sunshine, and a small crowd in the rose garden gazebo were perusing the bunting-festooned book stall.

'Has anyone seen Cameron Massey?' There was a general shaking of heads. Her shoes were a hindrance on the springy grass and she kicked them off and carried them as she ran through the formal planted area and on to the wildflower garden at the edge of the property. She cupped her hands around her mouth as she called out, 'Cameron! Luke!' The only responses were the amplified voice from the marquee, a burst of laughter from somewhere, the slam of a car door and the distant bark of a dog. Another reminder of another loss.

Maddy sighed despondently. She had duties to perform and ought to be back in the marquee. The second bark seemed louder though and she spun round, trying to identify the source. There was no dog in the grounds, but the wooden gate wasn't bolted. She stared across the fields, not daring to believe what she was seeing, then let out a jubilant shriek as Buster galloped towards her, ears flapping and tail wagging furiously.

'Buster!' She dropped to her knees in the long grass and Buster ran into her open arms, licking her hands and face, clearly overjoyed at this reunion. The feeling was mutual and Maddy hugged his wriggling body. 'I have missed you so much, you darling dog—where've you been!'

'He's missed you too,' said a familiar voice. Maddy looked up to see Luke approaching with Buster's lead in his hand, smiling down at her. 'He needed a walk. That's why I hurried off.'

'You mean… You weren't leaving then?'

'Of course not. That is'—his eyes suddenly clouded with uncertainty—'unless you'd prefer me to?'

'No! No, I wouldn't.'

Something between a choke and a sob caught in her throat and she took several sharp intakes of breath to calm herself. Luke's hand was warm and comforting as he helped her to her feet; she kept tight hold of it, not wanting to let him slip away again. They both spoke at the same time.

'Maddy, I owe you an—'

'Luke, I'm so sorry—'

They paused. Luke squeezed her hand. 'You first.' He pulled Maddy gently towards him and slipped his arms around her. 'No, I've changed my mind—me first.' He kissed her gently, then a long lingering kiss that made Maddy's insides flip over and her knees sag. It was as if the world had pressed pause for a few seconds, and they stood melded together, as the grass and wildflowers brushed lazily against her bare legs.

The well of tears that she had tried to hold back flooded down her face as she tightened her grip. 'I never meant to offend you. Or embarrass you. I only wanted to—'

Luke placed his finger on her lips and kissed away her tears. 'I know. It was my stubborn pride that wouldn't allow me to admit that. I felt guilty about what happened all those years ago, even though it wasn't entirely my fault.'

'None of it was your fault,' Maddy protested.

Luke smiled. 'I admire your loyalty but people have to take responsibility for their actions. I should have made it clearer to Clara at the outset what I wanted. Or didn't. Lessons for the future.'

They strolled back in the direction of the marquee, their arms wrapped around each other. The million questions could wait, but there was one thing Maddy was dying to ask.

'Luke, can I ask … what changed your mind?'

Luke smiled. 'I suspect you already know the answer to that, Ms Austen.'

Did she? Right now, her mind was in turmoil.

'I speak what appears to me the general opinion; and where an opinion is general, it is usually correct.'

'You're quoting Jane Austen at me!' Maddy laughed. 'Are you feeling okay?'

'I did have to look that up,' Luke admitted. '*Mansfield Park*—are you impressed?'

'Yes, but I have not the pleasure of understanding you, sir. Pray explain.'

Luke smiled. 'Haven't you seen the comments on social media?'

'Not in the last week. I've been way too busy for all that.'

'I admit I was stunned to see how many hundreds of readers agreed with you. It made me realise that maybe I'd kept everything about that part of my life locked away because I was ashamed and angry. Even though you didn't mention her by name, it would appear there are plenty of people who have a low opinion about what

Clara did. There's been something of a vehement discussion about it in the past few days, particularly on Twitter. Someone called PostmistressJ has been highly vociferous on the matter.'

'How interesting,' said Maddy, trying to disguise her amused smile. 'I must try and catch up.'

'But first you have a festival that needs your attention.' Luke gave her a gentle shove.

Maddy grabbed hold of his arm. 'Only if you promise not to leave. And maybe Buster would prefer to wait in the house.'

Luke pulled her to him again. 'I promise,' he murmured softly, before kissing her again. 'I'll be sitting in the front row where you can keep an eye on me.'

Chapter Thirty-Four

Think only of the past as its remembrance gives you pleasure
Elizabeth Bennet, *Pride and Prejudice*

Maddy had scheduled her talk last. It gave the other speakers time to relax, nip over to the rose garden gazebo to check on sales, or slip away early. She didn't mind if her audience was diminished; the people she wanted to hear her story were all here. She stood at the front letting her gaze sweep across the front rows taking in her parents almost bursting with proud, happy faces; Alice, who was wearing her companion Jane Austen T-shirt and waving discreetly from her seat; Luke smiling confidently; Libby, sitting next to Leonard and looking effortlessly chic; and the rest of her fellow committee members, all of whom she had come to know and love as both friends and neighbours.

'Many of you may have been surprised to read that my talk this afternoon is entitled Prejudice and Pride.' Maddy smiled at her private joke. She had already had this alleged typing error pointed out to her by several people, including the printers of the programme. 'I hope by the end you might understand why I decided not to plagiarise Jane Austen's more famous title.'

She waited for the polite laughter to subside before continuing. 'So let me tell you a little about myself and my family connection to the founder of this literary festival.'

Maddy briefly explained how she had inherited the house from Nigel, how no one had had any idea he was living in the country and the circumstances that had led to him leaving the country, penniless and in disgrace.

'By the time I was a teenager, the Shaw family's opinion of Nigel was well established and totally unanimous: Nigel Shaw was persona non grata. Although we didn't know it at the time, Nigel returned to the UK twenty-five years after he'd left, settling here at Meadowside. I've been told that he rarely spoke about his time in America, but after finding tantalising clues to his past, I suddenly wanted to find out more. I freely admit I became a bit obsessed with my quest—'

'Just a bit!' quipped Luke, which prompted another round of laughter from the audience.

'—but I couldn't have done it without help.' Maddy pointed as she spoke. 'Leonard's vast knowledge of rock music. Dad's facial recognition skills. The unwavering support of my former lodger. And most of all, the personal recollections of Elizabeth Allen, who has filled in so many of the missing pieces of this puzzle.

'So let me take you back to the swinging sixties and the arrival of the young Nigel Shaw in California in 1967. He'd been living hand to mouth, bumming around, doing odd jobs for people, when in 1969 he had a chance meeting with Chuck Hardimann, a singer with a struggling, relatively unknown rock group calling themselves The Faultliners. Chuck took the young Brit under his wing, helped him settle, found him a room and gave him work when he could.

'Over the next couple of years the band's popularity spread and their friendship deepened. Nigel often went with them on tour acting as a roadie. He was surprisingly practical, good at fixing things and rarely complained, unlike some of the others, so he was popular with the band. When they couldn't afford to pay him, Chuck gave him personal items as gifts, mostly in the form of books, which Nigel loved even though'—she smiled apologetically—'they had been rather vandalised.'

Maddy reached into the box beside her and pulled out an example. 'You probably can't see this but the pages are full of annotations, random rhymes, lines of verse.' She flicked through a few of the pages for her audience. 'Apparently Chuck often wrote down things he needed to remember on whatever came to hand, be it cigarette packets, paper napkins, or paperback books.

'Over time, The Faultliners became headliners and tensions became inevitable. One such altercation in 1971 reached the papers when one of their roadies died trying to intervene in a fight between band members, over lyrics to what became the band's biggest hit: "Rock Hard Road".' She replaced the book carefully and picked up the faded newspaper article. 'This cutting was where my quest started. After the death of the roadie, the band agreed to shelve their differences, record the song with the lyrics compiled by lead guitarist Darius Locke, and move on. Sadly though, the argument had caused a fracture that only deepened over time, and over the following years there were changes in the line-up. In 1974, lead singer Chuck Hardimann also left, and shortly afterwards Nigel moved on too.'

Maddy paused for a moment. 'And that could have been the end of the story, were it not for the untimely death of Chuck Hardimann in 1990 from a drug overdose. When he heard of his death, Nigel felt he'd somehow abandoned the friend who above everyone else, had given him so much support in the early days. Maybe it was an attempt at reconnection, or just to assuage his feelings of remorse, but he started re-reading all the books of poetry and American history that Chuck had given to him, and that was when the thunderbolt moment occurred, because there—in between the pages of a dog-eared poetry book and lost for nearly two decades—were the original lyrics to "Rock Hard Road", scribbled down by Chuck in his distinctive spidery script.

'The myths surrounding the lost lyrics had all but been consigned to the annals of music history, but Nigel now realised that with the authentication of Chuck's handwriting, he was sitting on a potential goldmine. He could sell this book at auction and become famous as the man who discovered the lost lyrics to one of rock music's enduring songs.

'And maybe a greedy man might have done just that, but Nigel wasn't greedy. Far from it — in fact he was the complete opposite,' Maddy said triumphantly. 'Applying the Shaw family morals of right and wrong, which had been used to batter his reputation for so many years, he took what was for him the most logical decision. He offered the book for sale to Darius Locke—the person who was credited with the revised lyrics. Nigel guessed correctly that Darius didn't want to risk the damage to his reputation should the book be sold on the open market, after having pocketed years of royalties which by rights, should have been shared with the band.

'We don't know exactly what amount Nigel received— Darius's then girlfriend was excluded from that conversation—but it clearly enabled Nigel to move back to the UK shortly afterwards and purchase Meadowside. Here in Cotlington, he revived his love of poetry and was content to share his good fortune with the people of Cotlington who welcomed him with open arms.

'Ladies and gentlemen, members of the Shaw family, it always struck me as strange that the name Nigel Shaw was so beloved in this village but so disparaged within his own family. It was this prejudiced view, created by an earlier generation but upheld by subsequent ones that I wish to dismantle today. I for one am hugely proud and honoured that Nigel entrusted his legacy to me, and long may the Cotlington Literary festival continue at Meadowside.'

A loud cheer erupted from the front row as the applause rang out. Luke was first on his feet doing his amazing fingers-in-mouth whistling thing and punching the air, but everyone else swiftly followed.

Maddy felt almost drunk with elation. It took the best part of a minute before the clapping stopped, and the audience began to file out clutching their programmes, the air filled with excited chatter. Her parents rushed forward to hug her. 'We're so proud of you, love, we could burst,' said her dad.

'You've put the Cotlington Literary Festival firmly on the map,' said Alice with a huge grin. 'Your mum and I are off to sample some celebratory homemade gin now!'

The committee dispersed to their allotted areas: Leonard to the book stall in the rose garden gazebo, Sally and Joyce to the car parks, Myra and Jem to the hospitality tent, until there was just Maddy and Luke remaining.

'So … was it as good as you expected?' asked Luke.

Maddy let out a sigh of relief. 'No … it was better! I just hope tomorrow isn't going to feel like a massive anticlimax.'

Luke's arms slipped gently round her waist. 'Not if I can help it,' he murmured, his eyes twinkling mischievously. 'That is assuming you don't mind me hanging around?'

Maddy smiled. Her dad wasn't the only one who felt

like their heart was bursting, and she joyously threw her arms around Luke's neck. 'Nobody minds having what is too good for them.' As if to prove her point, she kissed him. 'That's *Mansfield Park* too.'

Epilogue

14TH FEBRUARY

It's such a happiness when good people get together.
Miss Bates, *Emma*

I t was a truth universally acknowledged by the residents of Cotlington village that a single person in possession of a large house must be in want of a purpose. As a resident herself, Maddy wholeheartedly agreed.

Maddy's objective of making Meadowside her permanent residence after her year was up on 14th March was helped in no small measure by the sure and certain knowledge that her cousin Nigel would have approved of all the changes she had made in the last six months.

Unlike the first few weeks when she'd had way too much time on her hands, nowadays she was too busy to reminisce. However, as she sat waiting to be summoned, it felt significant to think back to a year ago, almost to the hour, when she and Luke had met in this pale-green waiting room with its drab grey sofas and nearly dead spider plant that was still clinging to life. What a difference a year had made! Today though, it was her and not him tapping away on her phone, catching up with emails.

'Oh good grief, look at this, Luke! You're not going to believe it.'

Maddy passed over her phone and watched as expressions of curiosity, amazement and finally a wry amusement flashed across his face. '*UpClose* magazine want to offer you the position of senior editor, and with a pay rise? Do you think this has anything to do with the fact that you heard last week on the Briony hotline that two of their editors resigned?'

Maddy laughed. 'Very possibly.'

'So what will you do? It's not too late … yet. We don't go on air for another couple of minutes?' He gave her a look that was meant to be teasing but Maddy saw the brief flutter of uncertainty in his eyes too.

'Oh no, it's way too late for all that. I'm not some journalist of last resort.'

Luke's arm snaked around her shoulder as he pulled her closer and lowered his mouth to her ear. 'I'm very pleased to hear it,' he whispered before kissing her softly on her neck. Maddy's skin tingled as his warm lips caressed her neck, and she marvelled—not for the first time—at how the man who last year she'd have happily labelled the least romantic of her acquaintance had in the last six months become her own personal Mr Darcy.

She turned her head to gaze at her handsome hero

and trailed a finger along his stubbly cheek. 'And anyway,' she added cheekily, 'we all know Buster prefers the peace and quiet.'

Before Luke could respond, they were shown into the studio where they were greeted warmly by Angie Turner sitting on the other side of a glass screen. Today, Maddy and Luke were on the same side, literally and metaphorically, and linked hands as they were introduced on air.

'...and today in the studio—back by popular demand —we have bestselling author Cameron Massey together with journalist and former agony aunt Maddy Shaw. Last year, my two guests made an in-depth and passionate defence of their favourite writing genres, and I think it's fair to say that sparks flew.'

Maddy and Luke both laughed.

'But since then, it appears there's been something of a shift on both sides. So how has that come about?'

'We've both got better at seeing different points of view,' said Maddy. 'And as Jane Austen wrote, it is particularly incumbent on those who never change their opinion, to be secure of judging properly at first.'

'And I think I've conclusively proved that it's harder to write a romance than I might have thought,' said Luke, holding up his palms in a gesture of surrender.

Maddy smiled. 'I think you underestimate your abilities. Your "reading" had quite an effect!'

'Which brings us nicely on to the Cotlington Literary Festival,' said Angie. 'I believe it came as a bit of a surprise when you found you had inherited this role.'

'It certainly did.' Maddy gave listeners a recap of

events, starting with the phone call from her dad last Valentine's Day, the amazing inheritance, the unexpected committee role, and then—in spite of her doubts and worries—a hugely successful literary festival headlined by two celebrities.

'And I believe there have been further successes on the back of this?'

'Indeed,' confirmed Luke. 'One of the unpublished authors who did a reading at the festival has since been offered a two-book contract with a major publisher, and we couldn't be more delighted.'

'So what's next for you two? You're already punching above your weight as far as the festival is concerned, but I believe there is more to come?'

Maddy looked at Luke, uncertain as to whether he wanted to respond, but he merely smiled and gave her his best go-for-it look.

'Absolutely. There is a saying in our village: Cotlington finds a purpose for everyone. I saw what an amazing opportunity the literary festival was for fledgling writers, not just to provide a venue for networking but to talk to those who had already hit the heights of the bestseller lists.' She grinned at Luke who was busy huffing on his clenched knuckles and polishing up imaginary medals with a silly look on his face. 'I realised we could provide writers at all stages of their career with a fabulous opportunity. But … as with all such projects they needed money.'

'Maddy had the property; I had the income; so we've pooled our resources,' continued Luke. 'My house restoration project had ground to a halt, and the garden was full of archaeological problems, so I am now very happily and permanently based at Meadowside.'

Maddy squeezed his hand. 'Although the house was really too big for just the two of us—'

'—even with a mad dog.'

'So...' Maddy paused for dramatic effect, 'we are delighted to announce that the Meadowside Writing Retreat is now formally open and taking bookings!' She still couldn't stop herself grinning as she uttered the words.

'We will be offering a combination of short-stay or week-long retreats, and we're hoping to attract guest speakers as well as providing in-house tutoring from probably the best crime writer in the country.'

'Probably?' queried Luke mischievously, and furrowing his eyebrows in mock reproof.

Maddy blew him a kiss. 'We can't let you get too big-headed after all the adulation over your new book,' she joked.

'Which I believe has been at the top of the bestseller lists for the last two weeks,' added Angie. 'You must be delighted. So what prompted you to take your writing in a new direction?'

'There's still a crime committed. There's still a detective. It's not too much of a radical change, but you know, sometimes life just surprises you. You get up one morning, someone says something and just like that it sparks an idea that doesn't want to let go.'

Angie nodded. 'Well, I don't know about anyone else,

but I absolutely inhaled this book from start to finish and almost choked myself laughing. So will there be more work for nearly retired Detective Inspector Friend?'

'Oh undoubtedly.'

'But still no romance or matrimony?'

'Not for the detective,' Luke replied with a wink.

'Well, I am delighted to share your exciting news with our listeners and wish you both every success with your new venture.' Angie gestured to Maddy. 'Maybe our former agony aunt has one last piece of advice for our listeners?'

Maddy smiled knowingly. 'I think Jane Austen says it best. Know your own happiness. You want nothing but patience—or give it a more fascinating name, call it hope.'

The End

Nearly……

Afterword

Death of a Ghost Hunter
by
Cameron Massey

According to Catherine Burgess, in a quiet country village you have to make your own entertainment, and she enjoys organising local events where her neighbours and friends can share their love of puzzles, ghost stories and whodunnits.

But when Catherine's guest speaker is found dead behind the curtains of her home at Northanger Hall, the friends are pitched into their very own mystery. Local resident Detective Inspector Jason Friend quickly becomes involved, but increasingly finds his investigation hampered by the enthusiasm of the amateur sleuths. And not all of them are telling the truth...

Afterword

'I want to give this six stars – an absolute joy.'

'A clever plot and laugh out loud hilarious.'

'Massey is back and better than ever!'

Acknowledgments

Thank you for choosing to read my book – it's an amazing experience to be able to share with the world something that started as an idea, then sat as a document on my laptop for so many months, and which has occupied so much of my time. Of course this transition from idea to book doesn't happen all by itself, and I have plenty of people to thank for their help along the way.

First in the thank you line up is my wonderful editor Charlotte Ledger, who has given me so much encouragement as well as lots of useful feedback and helpful suggestions. I know there is a whole team at One More Chapter working hard behind the scenes so my thanks to all of you. Also to Hana Rowland and the eagle-eyed Dushi Horti for their editorial input, and Federica Leonardis for proofreading.

When my editor suggested adding a Jane Austen quote at the start of each chapter, I had huge fun researching quotes online. However, it was a shock to discover quite how many quotes on the internet are attributed to Ms Austen but are not actually words taken from her books. Many of the quotes were from the various screenplays and film adaptations, but bizarrely some had no Austen connection whatsoever. For signposting this issue, I have to thank author and journalist Deborah Yaffe, whose blog first alerted me to the misquoting online. I've tried to cross-check all my quotes, but clearly any inaccuracies are down to me.

Huge thanks are also due to my friend Nuala Giblin who was not only happy to share her extensive knowledge of life as a journalist but also dashed over on more than one occasion to rescue me when I'd written myself into a corner and needed a listening ear or someone to brainstorm ideas with – I am eternally grateful.

Writing is rather a solitary occupation, so I owe a big thank you to my wonderful friends and family who have cheered from the sidelines and kept me going. You know who you are and it means the world.

As always, my writing buddies have been wonderful, but special mention must go to fellow members of the Romantic Novelists' Association, Alison Sherlock, Jennifer Bibby and Jenny Worstall for their ceaseless encouragement and support – it is hugely appreciated.

I also want to thank all the book bloggers who joined the blog tour for my previous novel, *Love You From A-Z*, and Rachel Gilbey for organising the tour and making it such an amazing experience – it was a pleasure working with you.

Last but not least, thank you to my wonderful husband who, as always, keeps everything going in the house and garden while I tap away at the keyboard. You are my hero.

ONE MORE CHAPTER

YOUR NUMBER ONE STOP

FOR PAGETURNING BOOKS

The author and One More Chapter would like to thank everyone
who contributed to the publication of this story...

Analytics
Emma Harvey
Maria Osa

Audio
Fionnuala Barrett
Ciara Briggs

Contracts
Georgina Hoffman
Florence Shepherd

Design
Lucy Bennett
Fiona Greenway
Holly Macdonald
Liane Payne
Dean Russell

Digital Sales
Laura Daley
Michael Davies
Georgina Ugen

Editorial
Dushi Horti
Arsalan Isa
Charlotte Ledger
Federica Leonardis
Jennie Rothwell
Kimberley Young

International Sales
Bethan Moore

Marketing & Publicity
Chloe Cummings
Emma Petfield

Operations
Melissa Okusanya
Hannah Stamp

Production
Emily Chan
Denis Manson
Francesca Tuzzeo

Rights
Lana Beckwith
Rachel McCarron
Agnes Rigou
Hany Sheikh
Mohamed
Zoe Shine
Aisling Smyth

**The HarperCollins
Distribution Team**

**The HarperCollins
Finance & Royalties
Team**

**The HarperCollins
Legal Team**

**The HarperCollins
Technology Team**

Trade Marketing
Ben Hurd

UK Sales
Yazmeen Akhtar
Laura Carpenter
Isabel Coburn
Jay Cochrane
Alice Gomer
Gemma Rayner
Erin White
Harriet Williams
Leah Woods

**And every other
essential link in the
chain from delivery
drivers to booksellers
to librarians and
beyond!**

YOUR NUMBER ONE STOP

ONE MORE CHAPTER

FOR PAGETURNING BOOKS

One More Chapter is an
award-winning global
division of HarperCollins.

Sign up to our newsletter to get our
latest eBook deals and stay up to date
with our weekly Book Club!
<u>Subscribe here.</u>

Meet the team at
<u>www.onemorechapter.com</u>

Follow us!
@<u>OneMoreChapter_</u>
@<u>OneMoreChapter</u>
@<u>onemorechapterhc</u>

Do you write unputdownable fiction?
We love to hear from new voices.
Find out how to submit your novel at
<u>www.onemorechapter.com/submissions</u>